That Moment

Tyce laughed, an easy, unselfconscious sound that filled Delaney with unexpected pleasure. It was in that moment when his face lit with laughter, that she knew this man was different from any other man she'd ever known before. Not a three-piece-suit, Wall Street sophisticate, but rugged and free . . .

Hell, he didn't even know her name. Yankee girl didn't even have enough manners to introduce herself. She was easy on the eyes, though. Dark, sassy hair that framed her face with a shining halo of waves and curls and Beautiful, deep brown eyes.

Forget it! He could have tolerated the Yankee in her, but . . .

ROSES
FOR
CHLOE

ELAINE GRANT

JOVE BOOKS, NEW YORK

HAUNTING HEARTS is a registered trademark of Berkley Publishing Corporation.

ROSES FOR CHLOE

A Jove Book / published by arrangement with the author

PRINTING HISTORY
Jove edition / December 1998

The Penguin Putnam Inc. World Wide Web site address is http://www.penguinputnam.com

ISBN: 0-515-12439-7

A JOVE BOOK®
Jove Books are published by The Berkley Publishing Group, a member of Penguin Putnam Inc., 375 Hudson Street, New York, New York 10014.
JOVE and the "J" design are trademarks belonging to Jove Publications, Inc.

PRINTED IN THE UNITED STATES OF AMERICA

10   9   8   7   6   5   4   3   2   1

To all who believe in
dreams come true.

And to my husband, Tony, and my son, Justin,
who gave me the time and space
to follow my own dream.

Chapter One

CAROLINE PLANTATION
NEW BIENVILLE, LOUISIANA

"Traitor!"

Tyce Brandon raised his beer bottle to the empty ballroom in a mock toast before downing the last bitter swallow. "Here's to you, Miss Donet!"

He stood in the white ballroom at Caroline plantation: the envy of its time a century ago. Twisting the top off another bottle of beer, Tyce studied his handiwork with glum satisfaction. Months of backbreaking labor were going to be wasted. Miss Donet Bienville had desperately wanted this magnificent room restored before she died, and it had been done to perfection, thanks to him.

Tyce sat with his back propped against one of four

1

massive columns that split the room into two symmetrical areas, each section a mirror image of the other.
Sweeping arches encrusted with detailed frieze-work
roses and twining vines spanned the columns at ceiling
height. Everything was white, from the twin marble
mantles, hand carved in Italy, to the gleaming wooden
floor. The floor had been lacquered as slick as a mirror
according to Miss Donet's wishes. To reflect the colors
of the ladies' brilliant ball gowns, she told Tyce when
they were discussing his plans to restore the old plantation to its original glory.

Today, alone in the silent mansion, he had no trouble
imagining the splendor of the balls held more than a
century ago when the plantation was in its prime: the
myriad swirls of dazzling color reflecting off the floor
in the pale light of the candles and blazing fires in the
fireplaces; the rustle of silks and satins punctuated by
the staccato tapping of the dancers' heels on wood; a
living painting, with the muted colors of the dancers ever
blending and separating to the flow of the music. Each
of the eight tall, double-hung windows set into the gently
curving walls could be raised high so that the dancers
could glide out onto the semicircular veranda and back
into the room.

For the occasion of the room's unveiling, Miss Donet
and Tyce were the only ones there to fling open the
double doors and step into another world. She had worn
an ankle-length dress of creamy lace, high-collared and
long-sleeved in the Victorian style of her youth, with a
ruby necklace at her throat. Ruby and gold earrings
caught the light of the chandeliers. She had twisted her
pearly hair at the back of her neck and held it in place
with crimson-jeweled hairpins. The rubies were fake, of
course, Miss Donet told him; not the fabulous jewels

supposedly hidden someplace at Caroline years ago by
Chloe Bienville to spite her overbearing father.

Miss Donet had looked longingly around the room.
Tyce suspected she was hearing the music of a time long
past and imagining herself gliding across the floor in the
arms of the love she had not been allowed to keep.
Knowing her as he did, Tyce was certain that she would
never impose her wishes on him. Ladies from her time
simply did not ask such a thing of a gentleman. So he
gave her his most gallant bow and held out his hand.

"Would you share a dance with me, Miss Donet?"

The pleasure that lit her face made her young again.
Lines etched by age faded as she made a graceful curtsey
and laid her hand gently upon his arm. In the waning
twilight they waltzed around the room, the lovely old
lady in lace and the young man in jeans and T-shirt.

It had been a good evening, that one. Miss Donet
talked of it often afterward. Three months later, she was
dead. Tyce was glad he had finished the room in time.
But now it might all be for nothing.

God, he loved this house! Its history and lore. Its architecture and innovations, so far ahead of the times
when the house was built in 1854. Caroline had been a
part of him from his earliest memories. He probably
knew everything about her construction and history, leg-
ends and tales learned at his father's and grandfather's
knees—stories that had instilled in him a passion to
reclaim the now-dilapidated mansion and restore it to its
original grandeur.

Three generations of Brandon men had fought their
own personal demons to regain control of this house,
but none had succeeded. The plantation had haunted
them like a lost love, sapping their lifeblood from them
over time, leaving each one unfulfilled as he failed in

his quest. And as each Brandon heir breathed his last, he passed the legacy on to his son: *Regain our stolen heritage.* That mission was etched in Tyce's mind as deeply as it had been in his father's and his grandfather's. He was determined to be the one who made the Brandon name whole again, if it took his very soul to do it. He was not going to his judgment knowing that he had failed like the rest, that he had left Caroline at the mercy of the Bienvilles for another generation.

A month ago, Tyce had held her within his hands, this forbidden love of his, had almost had her for his own. Then Miss Donet had double-crossed him and died, jerking the rug of victory from underneath him, leaving him sprawling in the aftermath, with only cold, empty promises filling the place in his heart where Caroline should have been. But if Miss Donet had expected him to give up without a fight, after she had teased him with that new will she had written but obviously never sent to her lawyer, she was sadly mistaken. He would do whatever it took to regain Caroline.

Tyce shuddered as a frigid draft stirred the lace curtains, even though the windows were boarded up on the outside. The cloying scent of roses filled the air. He glanced around in surprise, then pushed himself quickly to his feet. A tall, slender woman stood in the doorway, with her hands planted squarely on her hips, and although there was something oddly familiar about her face, Tyce was certain he had never seen her before.

He was rarely at a loss for words in any situation, but there was something disconcerting about the sudden appearance of this stranger. Where had she come from at this hour of the night? How had she found her way into a deserted ballroom in a dilapidated plantation house in the middle of nowhere?

"Can I help you?" Tyce asked when he gained command of his voice again. "Are you lost? Who are you?"

"No, I'm certainly not lost. And you, of all people, ought to know who I am." The woman's voice was clear and lyrical in its tone and timbre. Her words seemed to float in the air for a brief second, then dissipate.

"Well, I don't. And I might point out that if you're not lost, then you're trespassing."

At that, the woman threw back her head and laughed, the sound tinkling around the room like the faraway notes of a song. Her speech had an old-fashioned Southern inflection that reminded Tyce of Miss Donet. Tyce racked his brain to figure out who this intruder might be. There were no loony Bienvilles secreted away in the attic. He was certain of that because he had searched every inch of the house for Miss Donet's last will, the one he knew she had written but which now could not be located.

For a moment, he considered the possibility that the woman might be the new owner, for she was expected from New York any day. However, this was no New York City girl, unless she was playing a bad joke. He had understood that the new owner was young, but it was difficult to determine this stranger's age. One moment her face seemed ancient; the next moment, Tyce would have sworn she was no more than a girl. He shook his head to clear it of the beer and to make his eyes stop playing tricks.

She had a face like none he had ever seen before, with milky, almost translucent skin. Timeless, ageless eyes gave off a luminous glow that seemed to emanate from within her. But her manner of dress disturbed him. Made of scarlet satin, in the full hoop-skirted style of the Civil War era, the ball gown she wore was magnificent, cinching the tiny waist and displaying a generous curve of bosom, sensuous even for modern times.

Where the hell would she get a dress like that? Mardi Gras? She looked like a drunken reveler who had lost her way from a ball. Mentally, Tyce shook his head at the ludicrous thought. She obviously wasn't drunk, whatever her state of mind might be, and Mardi Gras was long past this year.

"Trespassing? Of all the nonsense, sir," she declared, gliding gracefully across the floor, the stiff material of her skirts moving gently, but oddly without the soft rustling sound he expected. Around her slender throat was a necklace, thickly encrusted with rubies and glittering diamonds. Her ears sparkled with matching ruby earrings.

Tyce frowned with sudden possessiveness. Those were Miss Donet's pieces of jewelry, the ones she had worn that night in the ballroom when they waltzed. Not only was this woman insane or deluded, but she was a thief as well.

"If you will give the matter proper thought, sir, you will realize that I belong here, just as you do." She turned to face him.

"Where did you get that jewelry?" Tyce took a step toward her. She seemed to drift away for a second, then held her ground.

"This?" She toyed with the necklace.

Tyce blinked his eyes in disbelief. Did he actually see the curtains move behind her—*through* her? "Jesus, I've had too much to drink," he muttered, attempting to convince himself that the woman was just an alcohol-induced hallucination. The problem was that he wasn't drunk; he only wished he were.

"They're mine. Zach gave them to me."

"Zach?" Tyce's mouth formed the words, but no sound came out. His eyebrows shot up. "Zach Brandon?" he managed to croak.

"Yes, of course, who else?" The woman's lovely face grew melancholy as she gazed around the magnificent ballroom. *"You did an excellent job in this room. It has been a pleasure observing as you brought it back to its glory. The frieze-work around the ceiling is slightly different, but quite acceptable. In my day, the flowers were magnolias, but I do so love roses, so your design suits me much better. It must be difficult to get such labor done these days."*

Watching him? When had she been watching him? There had been no one around when he worked, except Miss Donet now and then. Tyce listened attentively. Maybe she would say something to give away her true identity. Then he could call her keepers and have her sent back where she belonged.

Of course, he knew the legend of Caroline and her ghost—probably better than anybody. He had been raised on the stories of Zach Brandon and Chloe Bienville. According to the old tales, Zach had never returned from the War Between the States, and Chloe had pined away until her death, waiting for him, always dressed in red. He also knew that just before she died, Miss Donet had begun to believe that Chloe truly haunted the plantation house, but Tyce was not superstitious and Miss Donet was an old woman with bad eyesight.

Everybody in the area knew the old tales as well as he did. If this woman was playing a trick on him, trying to scare him away or make him look crazy, he wanted to know who put her up to it—and he wanted Miss Donet's jewelry back.

"My rubies bother you," she said, looking him full

in the face with glowing eyes. *"Ah, because you believe they are Donet's."*

Tyce involuntarily took a step backward. How could she know what he was thinking?

"Don't worry, dear, these are mine and, of course, yours in a manner. The true Brandon rubies. I had Luc commission a pair like them for my darling niece, Donet, on her eighteenth birthday. Glass. Hers were a glass copy, because by then we could not afford the genuine thing. And of course, I never would tell Luc where my rubies were hidden." She lowered her lashes coyly. *"But I might tell you, if you please me."*

The age-old story of Chloe's hidden rubies was as popular a fairy tale in the Brandon family as *Cinderella* was in other homes: how Chloe had hidden the priceless ruby jewelry given to her by Zach as an engagement gift; how the Bienville men for years had tried to pry the location of the jewels from her; how the demented woman had tormented them with one wild-goose chase after another until she finally died, taking all hope of finding the gems to the grave with her.

Tyce gave her a wry look. "Yeah? And what do I have to do? Move heaven and hell?"

"Young man, do not use blasphemous language before me. And must you be so melodramatic? Were you not taught proper deportment by your mama? The jewels—and Caroline, for that matter—belong to the Brandons and the Bienvilles together. That is the way it was intended but never happened. It must be made right."

The woman looked at Tyce with such deep sadness in her eyes that even he was touched. Then she began to move slowly around the ballroom, her hands held out before her as if she were dancing. She closed her eyes and her voice dropped so low that Tyce had to strain to hear her words. *"I danced with my beloved Zach right here in this very ballroom on the last night I saw him. Then I lost him, Tyce. Your great-great-uncle. The only love of my life, the very essence of my soul. I waited for him to come back to me after the war, but he never did."*

She stopped her slow waltzing in the center of the ballroom, her brilliant red dress startling in contrast to the pristine white walls and floor. *"My daddy saw to that, you know,"* she said vehemently. *"He killed my Zach to steal Caroline away from Zach's family—your family, Tyce. It must be made right. And you and Delaney are the only ones left."*

"Delaney? Whoever you are, you're not making sense."

"I need Zach. As the only living Brandon son, you are my last hope. Only you can bring the Brandons and Bienvilles together again at Caroline. You must marry Delaney Bienville."

"Marry!" Tyce howled. "You're crazy! I don't even know anybody named Delaney Bienville. If you're who you claim to be, why don't you find Miss Donet and ask her where she left her new will. I'd be a lot more inclined to negotiate with you if I knew where that damned will is."

"There is nothing to negotiate, young man. And your language is most shocking. You must wed Delaney, Tyce. I insist upon it. I have been patient over these many years, but my patience is gone. I cannot wait any longer for my Zach. There is no one to stand in the way of your marriage, as there has been in the past. Delaney's father is dead. He will not interfere as Luc did with Donet and your uncle Lee. As for the will, Donet was indeed in a dither when I hid it from her. She did so want you to have Caroline, free and clear. But that would not bring

*Zach back to me. Only when Caroline at last belongs to
the Brandons and Bienvilles together can I be set free.
Delaney will be here soon, I imagine. You know what
you must do. I shall be watching you closely. Do not let
me down.''*

Tyce squeezed his eyes together. She was fading
away!

He moved toward her. "Wait a minute! Tell me where
the will is!"

She held up a hand as if to stop him. The scent of
roses drifted across the room as her image dissipated.
Her melodious voice lingered for a moment on the quiet
air. *"Free me, Tyce. Marry Delaney.''*

"I want that will!" Tyce shouted after the disappear-
ing figure.

Suddenly, cold air enveloped him, shivering cold air
that sliced like a steel knife. The room began to sway,
and Tyce felt as if his knees were about to buckle under
him. *Marry Delaney. Marry Delaney. Marry Delaney.*
The words spun in his head like a tornado, until everything went black. . . .

Tyce sat bolt upright. A thin sheen of perspiration
covered his face. Wild-eyed, he searched the ballroom.
Empty, quiet. He was braced against one of the tall columns in the center of the room—alone. Realizing he
must have dozed off after too much work and too many
beers, he concentrated on calming his pounding heart.
Picking up the empty six-pack and rising from the floor,
he shook his head.

Seeing ghosts! He was beginning to think like Miss
Donet.

"Get a grip, man," he admonished himself with a
sheepish grin as he headed for his cottage. "Get a grip!"

Chapter Two

My Dear Delaney,

How sad that I haven't laid eyes on you for most of your life. I wish it were not so. I have only the photographs of you taken by your father when you were a small child, but I remember you being as lovely as your mother and as bright-eyed as your father.

Your father, my dear nephew Joseph . . . how I wish things had been different with him. Although I understand why your mother never brought you back here, it grieves me that you had no opportunity to visit your father's birthplace, to know your family. I suppose it is wrong of me to make you come now, as will be the case if ever you are

*sent this letter—but child, poor Chloe promises
not to let me rest in my grave until her legacy is
fulfilled.*

*Forgive an old woman, dear child, but I pray
that you shall be the one to make things right
again.*
Fondly,

Your Great-aunt Donet Bienville

"Crazy old woman," Delaney Bienville muttered,
rolling her dark eyes upward as she reread the letter in
her hands from her late great-aunt. She was going to
make things right, make no mistake about that.

She planned to raze this infernal plantation her aunt
had so graciously bequeathed to her; reduce it to a smear
in the middle of a sugarcane field—and make a few
million dollars in the bargain. Amazing! She would soon
become a millionaire by doing something she had longed
to do for years. The last ties to a childhood gone wrong
would be severed. There would be no physical reminders
of her father, nothing left but bad memories, and her
therapist was well on the way to annihilating those.

Outside the tiny window of the 727 jetliner, the
ground still seemed far away, bleak, gray, and mottled.
In the distance, wisps of steam rose from the landscape,
escaping from unseen nostrils, as if some fiery dragon
lurked beneath the crust of the earth to catch the unsuspecting. Now and then a bright flame shot from one of
the tall smokestacks. Frowning, Delaney peered at the
white vapors curling into the sky. Then, as the plane
eased downward, she saw the source: chemical plants.
Molded along the curve of the brown Mississippi River
north of Baton Rouge were miles of metal pipes and

steel columns, a stark second city of industry.

The wheels of the plane touched down, bounced once, then caught the Tarmac smoothly. Delaney unsnapped her seat belt in spite of the attendant's routine warning to leave it in place until the plane came to a halt. She was ready to get on with her business. In a day or two, it would all be over. Once the papers were signed and Caroline plantation officially turned over to Gulf Coast Development Corporation, the bulldozers could do their work and a new era would be born in New Bienville, Louisiana, the likes of which that little town had never seen.

A wide interstate loop around New Orleans was projected in the near future to sweep east-west traffic well away from the congestion of the business district. Running within a mile of New Bienville, the new highway, along with the expected major development boom in the area, would put the sleepy little south Louisiana town on the map. Delaney's contribution would be the land for the huge mall and office complex that Gulf Coast Development planned to build.

Still, her aunt Donet's odd letter puzzled Delaney. What did she mean by not letting the legacy die? What legacy? And who was Chloe? Some other relic from her father's side of the family that she had never heard of, Delaney mused. She dreaded the very idea of having to meet this Chloe, who probably would not take kindly to having the family plantation destroyed. Southerners tended to cling to the past rather than embracing the future. Sentimentality left a bitter taste in Delaney's mouth. She'd had enough of that from her father before he deserted her and her mother.

As she left the airport terminal, Delaney shivered and pulled the collar of her heavy gray coat higher on her neck, snugging the burgundy scarf close against the biting February wind and rain. The moisture pasted down every errant leaf or scrap of paper that dared to rest for a moment on the cold, slick expanse of concrete and asphalt, giving the wet parking lot an unkempt look.

Shouldering her carry-on bag, she picked up her other suitcase along with the keys to her rental car. Her one o'clock appointment with the local lawyers handling Gulf Coast Development's part of the sale left her enough time to find a hotel and drop off her luggage.

It was midafternoon before Delaney finished with the lawyers. She had a little over a week until the day when she had to sign the final papers to close the deal. The lawyer informed her that the contents of the house needed to be moved as soon as possible so that the development company could begin work immediately after the closing.

She settled into the rented Camaro to study the map to the plantation that the lawyer's secretary had given her. Delaney would just as soon have everything in the place scraped away with the rubble of the house, but something in her demanded a personal visit. After all, New Bienville was her birthplace and Caroline the home of her infancy and early childhood, if nothing more. And she had a need to see the place that had stolen her father from her for most of her life. Caroline had been as seductive as a mistress to her father. He even had the effrontery to die in Louisiana, while Delaney and her mother struggled to make ends meet in New York. Delaney had never been able to tell him how badly he had hurt her by his virtual abandonment or even to say goodbye to him before he died. For that, more than anything else, she hated this plantation she had just inherited.

From the Mississippi River Bridge, she glanced to her

right at the skyline of the city and the distant metallic gleam of the chemical plants. Rain clouds were giving way to sunshine. The light glinted off the sides of the few multistoried buildings that nested along the riverbank. On the dark currents of the river beneath the bridge, seagoing ships were anchored, taking on cargo. Tugboats labored against the treacherous current, pushing long strings of barges before them. Everything along the river seemed to move in slow motion.

Taking Highway 1 south off the bridge put her in the middle of sugarcane country. Flat land. As far as the eye could see, there was nothing but flat land.

"A person could certainly pine away for a hill here," she thought aloud, already homesick after being in Louisiana only a few hours.

She loved New York City and her apartment. Outside her broad windows, the panorama of the city spread in all directions, from the natural beauty of Central Park to the towering buildings of a pulsing, ever-awake city within arm's reach. The museums fed her craving for beautiful art, keeping alive within her that innate spark of creator whose optimistic fire disappointment and uncertainty had snuffed out over the years. Still, she hoped someday to find the courage to try to rekindle the flame and return to the art she had loved so much when she was young.

After awhile, the long drive became boring and she turned her thoughts to her future plans. The idea of monetary freedom was exhilarating. She looked forward to the day when she and her mother would no longer have to worry about what tomorrow would bring, whether there would be enough money for rent and food. Not to mention the mounting doctor bills as her mother's eyesight grew progressively worse.

Maybe now, without the pressure of having to work to survive, she could set up a studio of her own where she could make her art a way of life rather than a hobby. And there would be more than enough money from the sale of the plantation to buy her mother a nice country cottage in upstate New York or Connecticut.

Delaney's mother was slowly losing her vision from a degenerative disease and soon would not be able to see well enough to navigate the streets of New York. Too, her mother seemed to have grown weary of the city, often mentioning the old farmhouse in upstate New York that the family had shared before Delaney's father left to return to his old haunts and habits.

In the coming years, Delaney expected her mother to become increasingly dependent as she lost her sight. All they had was one another. Delaney would never desert her mother. That was one lesson she had learned well from her father—the price of desertion. After all her sacrifices, the woman deserved a peaceful retirement with a garden and trees around her while she could still enjoy them. This unexpected inheritance was like the answer to a prayer.

Now Delaney would be able to take care of her mother without the worry of having to leave her alone in order to go to work and make a living. She would have the opportunity to give back the same security that her mother had provided her in the absence of her father.

Ahead, Delaney saw what had to be the turnoff to the plantation. A dirt road, the lawyer had called it, and it certainly was that. Narrow and rutted, pocked with holes, the road jolted Delaney's car as she drove slowly and carefully toward the grove of tall, sweeping trees ahead of her. Through the trees, she caught fleeting glimpses of the old house; then, around another curve in the road, it suddenly loomed in full view. Delaney slammed on the brakes and shifted the car into park.

"Wow!"

Resting her forearms on top of the steering wheel, she leaned forward to stare in shock at the huge, rambling house before her. She had forgotten how monstrously large it was. If one used a lot of imagination, it was possible to glimpse an aura of lost grandeur behind the shabby facade of the ancient mansion.

Vague, unsettling memories seeped like fog from the recesses of her mind, tendrils curling like fingers around her heart, constricting her throat, squeezing a hint of tears into her eyes. Her tiny hand secure in her father's as he took her for long walks in the woods and fields. Riding on his shoulders to watch the cane harvest. To her surprise, she even had a momentary taste of the thick, dark molasses that oozed over her pancakes.

No! She would not cry! Not over memories faded like unrecognizable photos of a past better left forgotten. Caroline, her father's birthplace and her own, had been her home for a short four years before the family moved to New York. She was surprised she had any memory of living here. Her father had been the one who loved this old house. Stories he told her as a child still formed haunting fairy tales in her dreams sometimes. He had loved this house and now she was going to destroy it.

Spiteful? she questioned herself. Sure, it was. Her father had loved this house better than he loved his wife or his daughter. Them he could abandon, but not the plantation called Caroline. Never Caroline. So now Delaney was going to have her revenge—and enjoy every minute of it!

Maybe if her father had been strong enough to turn this house loose, along with his death-grip clutch on an unrecoverable glory that had once been, things might have been different with their family. Delaney shook off a twinge of self-pity. Nothing in the past could be changed. There was only today and the future.

Her critical eye appraised the condition of the house before her. It was grotesque in its disrepair. All three stories of it. From appearances, the house had not been painted since she left over twenty years ago. The corner-to-corner porch sagged in several spots. Blank, uncurtained windows stared back at her like ghostly eyes. A tangle of unkempt shrubbery rubbed against the gray outer walls, and massive oak limbs reached precariously across the roof, threatening to take parts of the house with them if they succumbed to a strong wind.

Even if she had wanted to keep the place from a sense of misplaced sentimentality, it would take hundreds of thousands of dollars just to make it safe. Easing the car into a parking place in a graveled area near one of the outlying buildings, Delaney got out to investigate. How had her elderly aunt even lived here? She fumbled around in her pocket for the key that the lawyer had given her.

Only one short wing of the house looked habitable. Like a pretty bow in the hair of a bag lady, its freshly painted exterior and neat entryway stood out in startling contrast to the rest of the decaying house. Delaney tried the key in the door to that section. It slipped in smoothly but would not turn. She twisted it one way then the other. Still, the mechanism would not budge. Frustrated, Delaney snatched the key out, scraping her hand on the doorjamb.

"Ow!" she cried, nursing her stinging hand.

"It's a tricky lock. I need to fix it."

The deep voice so close behind her sent a shock

through Delaney. She whirled around. A man stood just behind her on the porch.

"Who are you?" she demanded, hiding her surprise under a mask of confidence.

"My name's Tyce Brandon. Are you hurt?"

"No." Delaney tempered her abruptness with a belated, "Thank you."

"There's a trick to unlocking that door. Want me to open it for you?" the man asked, his voice as congenial and relaxed as hers was tense.

"If you can." Delaney eyed him appraisingly as he inserted the key into the lock once more.

He was probably a few years older than she, maybe early thirties. Tall, well-built under a quilted jacket and worn jeans. A broad-brimmed leather hat was pulled low over his eyes, shadowing the rugged, weathered features of his face, but his hands caught her attention as he manipulated the lock gently. They were strong hands with long, nimble fingers. She noticed calluses on his palms. Hardworking hands. He must be the handyman, she surmised, eyeing his faded jeans and muddy work boots.

"You have to pull the door tight against the frame . . ." he said, drawing her attention back to his face. He really was not bad looking, in spite of the mane of disheveled, light brown hair that brushed the collar of his jacket. Her eyes met his and stopped short.

Blue, deep, pure. Purer than the purest cerulean blue she could put to canvas. She had to force her attention away from those eyes to listen to what he said.

". . . then turn the key all the way around."

The lock clicked and Tyce pushed the door open a few inches. He handed the key back with a flourish, as if he expected applause for his trick. Then he stood there, showing no indication of leaving.

"Thank you," Delaney said, by way of dismissal.

Still, he did not move. His lingering look was growing disconcerting. Realizing how isolated the plantation was gave her an uneasy feeling in the pit of her stomach. Delaney wondered briefly if he might be dangerous.

"I don't want to keep you from your work . . ." she hinted.

"No problem," he returned. "Since you have the key, I assume you're the new owner."

"Yes, that's right," Delaney said, her hand on the doorknob. "Now, I really need to get busy. I don't have much time to spend here."

"Oh," he said, with a trace of disappointment in his voice, "then don't let me stop you. If you need anything or want to know about the house, call me. I'll be out front working."

Delaney nodded. He turned and walked off. Delaney's eyes followed the rhythmic motion of his arms and legs as he disappeared around the corner of the house. Slow-moving and nosy, like the woman at the car rental agency and the lawyers. Was every Southerner the same?

"Front?" Delaney muttered, glancing at her car parked in the driveway. "I thought this was the front. Strange handyman, strange place."

She pushed the door wide and stepped inside. Her eyes swept the room before her.

"Oh, wow!" she exclaimed, standing transfixed.

The room was incredible. Directly across from the door, a magnificent black marble fireplace gleamed in the light flowing from the floor-to-ceiling windows on either side. Brocade draperies the color of fine wine were held back to the casements with golden tassels, then cascaded gracefully downward to puddle extravagantly on the floor. Carved cornices embellished the tops of the windows; lace sheers muted the sunlight. A portrait of a man of obvious means, sitting on a black horse and surrounded by his hunting dogs, hung over the fireplace.

Delaney stared at it for a moment. The face looked vaguely like her father's, but the subject was obviously from another era. A nameplate attached to the bottom of the frame declared the subject of the portrait to be Pierre Bienville. The name was not familiar, but the man had to be one of her ancestors.

She moved to touch the arm of the nearest chair. The fabric was expensive, a chintz in muted pinks and dark greens, yet the chair was obviously old. The other furniture in the room was old, too; antique, worth a small fortune on the New York market. Delaney marveled at the perfect condition of the wood, the gleam of clean, well-preserved maple and mahogany. Underneath her feet, a carpet cushioned her steps as she neared the fireplace. Glancing down, she instinctively stepped off the rug. Aubusson! A true Aubusson, worn in spots, but not tattered. Priceless!

If the whole house were like this . . . Delaney laughed aloud. This was an unexpected bonus! She had never dreamed of finding such treasures in this old house. The adjoining rooms to the right included a master bedroom suite and two smaller bedrooms, each with its own private bath—a nice touch, Delaney thought to herself. Though not so opulent as the sitting room, they were nonetheless beautifully decorated and filled with the same costly treasures. At the opposite end of the house, Delaney discovered a modern kitchen and small, cozy dining room that looked out over what was left of the gardens and on to the endless flat fields beyond. The empty refrigerator was still running, though Donet Bienville had been dead over a month now.

The house looked huge from outside. How many rooms could it have? she wondered with excitement, looking around for another door. To her surprise, she found only one that led from the kitchen to the yard. Going back to the porch to explore, she found the explanation. The small dwelling was actually detached from the house, although that was not obvious until she turned the corner.

At one end of the porch was a set of stairs leading to the upper floor; a strange arrangement, Delaney thought, starting up the steps. On the balcony above, she cupped her hands around her face and attempted to see inside. A shade was pulled over each window, blocking her view. Her key did not fit into the lock of the upstairs door. Disappointed, she went back down, crossed to the main house, and tried the back door. It was locked, but the windows were not covered, and the dim interior of the huge mansion was visible through the dusty panes.

The large room into which the window opened was almost empty, though heavy canvas cloth covered several bulky objects in the room—more furniture, probably, Delaney thought with delight. The view through other windows that she could access was much the same. The interior of the mansion was in terrible shape; there was none of the opulence and charm of the small building where her great-aunt had lived.

Compiling an inventory of the furnishings was going to be more work than Delaney had anticipated. Remembering the long drive out, Delaney gave a sigh of frustration. Driving was unusual for her. In the city she walked or took a taxi.

Once back inside the small dwelling, she cocked her head and looked around. Why not stay here? After all, it was hers for a few more days, and it was far more appealing than her room at the hotel. This way, too, she could work as early or as late as necessary and be done all the sooner. Back to Baton Rouge for the night to pick up her luggage and groceries, and she would be set by tomorrow morning.

Her hands were dirty from peering through the dusty windows of the main house. Turning the hot water handle on the kitchen faucet produced nothing. She tried the cold. Still nothing. There was no water.

"Darn it!" The lack of water would be an inconvenience. Maybe that handyman knew how to turn the water on, if she could find him. "What was his name again?" she muttered. "Unusual name. Ty? Tyce . . . that's it."

Walking around the big house, she noticed several outbuildings on the immediate property. Some appeared to be warehouses or barns. Other, smaller ones were not familiar. Perhaps they were the slave houses, she thought ruefully, reminded that her ancestors once had been slave owners. The idea of owning other humans was as repugnant to her as that of a harem. Imagining life without liberty was unthinkable, and she felt a deep sadness for the people who had worked this land by force.

Dead leaves and branches crackled beneath her feet. Probably in summers past this had been a flower garden, but now there was nothing other than dead plants and broken limbs. She found a bricked path nearby and took that instead. Oak trees dotted the lawn, their heavy branches sweeping to the ground. There were several other kinds of trees she did not recognize, their bare limbs creating a forlorn landscape. Delaney shivered and wrapped her coat closer around her against the winter chill.

The scrape of a saw came from somewhere nearby. Following the sound, Delaney rounded the corner of the mansion to find Tyce sawing on a thick plank. Delaney watched with interest as he made powerful, confident cuts into the board with the sharp-toothed saw. The muscles of his arms flexed in steady time to the stroke of the blade. The board fell cleanly into two pieces, and the sawed-off end hit the ground.

Watching him work, Delaney realized that he was an exceptionally good-looking man: clean-cut, with pleasing features and a strong, well-made body. She was used to Wall Street types who developed any muscles they might have in a gym. The raw physicality of this man impressed her.

"Excuse me," she called into the quietness after the noise of the saw died away.

He straightened at her voice, wiped his hands on his jeans, and walked across the lawn toward her. Once more she got a creeping feeling of just how remote this place was. There was no sign of another living being in any direction.

"Yes ma'am," he said, when he reached her. "What can I do for you?"

Delaney found his drawl rather charming, though "ma'am" made her feel like his mother. "I was thinking of staying in the little house out back. I suppose that was my aunt's apartment. But there's no water."

"I turned the water off last week when it was expected to freeze. Won't take me but a minute to get it back on for you. You're going to stay out here instead of in town?" he asked with a slight frown.

"Is it safe here?" she asked. "It seems so far from anywhere."

"You're too used to the city, ma'am. It's perfectly safe. Miss Donet lived here for ninety years. Besides, I live in the overseer's house just down the road from the *garçonnière*. There's a phone in both places, if you need to call me."

"The what?" Delaney asked. "Garson . . . yare?"

"Right. The *garçonnière*. Miss Donet lived there for years, but originally, it was designed for the boys in the family. Back when the house was built, boys were considered men when they reached about thirteen, and they kept their own quarters. There were eight boys in the family and four girls."

"Well, I can see the point, then," Delaney said. "I wouldn't want eight boys in my house, either."

Tyce laughed, an easy, unselfconscious sound that filled Delaney with unexpected pleasure. It was in that moment when his face lit with laughter, that she knew this man was different from any man she'd ever known before. Not a three-piece-suit, Wall Street sophisticate but rugged and free, a man who seemed confident and happy with himself and unconcerned with what anybody else thought.

"Come on and I'll turn on that water for you. How long do you plan to stay?"

"Only until I can get my aunt's belongings out. She has some exquisite furniture. By the way, why is her apartment so modern and the rest of this place isn't?"

"The *garçonnière* has been remodeled several times since it was built. Some of the family has always lived there. For years it housed the young men of the family. Then in the forties, major renovations were made. The downstairs was gutted and rebuilt. Bathrooms, closets, and the kitchen were added. A few years ago, when the mansion became uninhabitable, Miss Donet moved in and had everything updated again. Same thing with the original overseer's house where I live. It's modern and comfortable now.''

Delaney frowned, recalling that he lived on the grounds. ''I suppose you've already made arrangements to move since Aunt Donet has been dead for a few weeks. If not, you need to find a new place to live, since I'm closing the sale on the place in a week.''

Tyce stopped and, reflexively, so did Delaney.

''What do you mean, *sale*?''

''I'm selling it, of course. What else would I do with this place? In a couple of years, there'll be a new mall right here where we stand,'' Delaney said. ''I'm surprised word hasn't gotten around. I thought gossip traveled fast in these little towns.'' She shrugged. ''What's the difference? It's a tumbledown old house that's lived past its time.''

''Mall?'' Tyce looked stunned. ''You're kidding! And Caroline . . . lived past its time? It's a grand, beautiful old house. It's as sound as any modern house you'll find anywhere.''

''Beautiful?'' Delaney repeated skeptically. ''I don't think it's so beautiful. It's an overbuilt monstrosity, and . . .''

''No! Come look at it! It's not a monstrosity.''

Tyce's reaction startled her, and Delaney took an involuntary step backward. Tyce reached out and took her by the arm and walked away from the house, pulling her along with him. Delaney's first instinct was to jerk free, but she doubted that was possible, his grip was so strong.

He was headed toward the bank of earth a few hundred feet away. Stumbling through the tall grass beside him, Delaney's shoes sank into the soft earth. She doubted her sanity for not fighting away from this madman and running like hell. When he finally turned her loose and rotated her by the shoulders to face the old house, she leaned down with hands on knees to catch her breath.

"Look!" he insisted, pointing.

"You are crazy!" she shouted at him but straightened and looked anyway. Her eyebrows lifted in surprise.

So this was the front! And it was grand, as he said. From a distance, the size and dignity of the house was unmistakable, the peeling paint and sagging shutters less evident. The proportion was true and pleasing.

"Well, I admit, it is much more impressive from up here. It's rather oddly shaped though, isn't it? I thought all plantation houses looked the same."

"Caroline's different. Classic," Tyce said from beside her. "Its design was influenced mostly by Greek Revival architecture, with a bit of an Italianate influence." His gaze roved over the mansion like the hands of a lover. "Back when Caroline was built, just about everything was expected to be symmetrical. Caroline never was intended to be."

One end of the house was gabled, set parallel to the main structure. Tall columns punctuated the front of the main house and continued around the opposite end in a graceful semicircle. Delaney thought she saw a flash of movement from the red draperies hanging at one window, but from the distance, she could not be sure. Probably the wind. God only knew how many broken windows would have to be replaced to seal the place up tight.

Delaney pointed to that end. "What room is that, the rounded one?"

"Downstairs is the grand ballroom, and upstairs, a bedroom and sitting room."

"A ballroom with red curtains. How romantic," Delaney said with a hint of sarcasm. "And how useless."

"These days, I suppose it is," Tyce said, without seeming to notice her mockery, "but back then, it was a common part of any well-to-do planter's home. Dancing and entertaining was a part of life. Why did you say it had red curtains?"

"Well, it does . . ." Delaney pointed to the window where she had glimpsed red. Frowning, she realized that all the windows were boarded up, including that one. She gave a disconcerted laugh. "Sorry, I must be seeing things. Jet lag."

Tyce fell silent. Delaney glanced up. He was staring at the house, lost in thought, with a perplexed frown on his face. When Delaney turned to look at the mound of dirt behind her that stretched out of sight in either direction, Tyce snapped out of his reverie.

"Anyway, it's boarded up now. The ballroom . . ." He followed her gaze. "Want to go up on the levee and look at the river?"

"Is that what this hill is? A levee?"

"Come on."

Once more, he took her arm, but this time more gently. He guided her up the steep slope until they stood on a grassy track that ran the length of the levee. Beyond curled the broad, lazy back of the Mississippi, like a dark snake basking in the sunshine, its scales gleaming and glittering in the light.

"The river seems much narrower from here than it did when I came over it this morning," Delaney commented.

"That's an island out there. The main run of the river

is on the other side, though you'll see the barges come around this side of it a lot,'' Tyce said. "Used to be the river was farther away. It encroached year by year until the Army Corps of Engineers put up this levee earlier in the century. Caroline once had twenty acres of gardens and orchards between the river and the house, complete with an Indian mound and a grotto.''

"You know a lot of Caroline's history,'' Delaney remarked.

"Everybody around here does. It's been a part of New Bienville since before the war. It's a part of my past, too.''

"I'm sure it is,'' Delaney said noncommittally. "Could you turn the water on for me now?''

"Sure,'' he replied, but he seemed preoccupied. Just before they reached the *garçonnière*, he turned to her with a worried smile. "Listen, this old place may seem to be some kind of outdated relic to you, but to some of us around here, it's a lot more. If you're intent on selling it, sell it to me. I can pay you what it's worth, and the mall can go someplace else. How about it? How much are you asking for it?''

"I seriously doubt you could match the offer I got. It doesn't matter, anyway. The purchase agreement is already in effect. The wrecking crew is scheduled to bulldoze the house within a couple of weeks.''

Tyce's face paled at her words. For a moment, he was speechless, as if he couldn't believe his ears, then angrily he ordered, "You can't do that!''

Delaney drew herself up to her full five feet seven inches and glared at him. "Excuse me?''

"Bulldoze the house? You can't be serious! I'm trying to get it listed on the National Register of Historic Places. You can't destroy it.''

Delaney gave an amused laugh. "Well, maybe it'll be the first mall ever listed on the historic register. And for your information, I can do anything I want to with this place, and it is none of your business!"

"By God, it's going to be my business!" He turned abruptly and strode around the corner of the building.

Delaney set her hands on her hips in frustration as he disappeared. "You've got three days to move off the premises!" she called after him.

There was no answer to indicate whether he heard her or not. It didn't matter. The lawyers could evict him easily enough. Now she just had to figure out how to turn on the water.

Chapter Three

Tyce rubbed the towel across his wet shoulders, then dried his dripping hair. He still couldn't believe the turn his life had taken so abruptly. Miss Donet was dead and Caroline had slipped through his hands before he even knew she was gone. What hurt most was that Miss Donet had double-crossed him. She had promised Caroline to him. She had known he would take care of the plantation and bring the house back to life.

For as long as he could remember, he had known and loved Miss Donet Bienville. In fact, she was almost like another grandmother to him, but just now he was reeling from the blow of losing the plantation forever. Miss Donet had changed her will to leave Caroline to him, because she knew how much the place meant to him. She had supported his restoration work completely. It was her dream as well as his to see Caroline restored to its original grandeur. After all these years, a Bienville at last understood that the plantation should be returned to the Brandons—or so he thought.

The biggest puzzle was the whereabouts of that new will. He had seen it, written in her own hand, and the letter she intended to send to her lawyer. She showed it to him the night they danced in the newly restored ballroom and told him that the time had come to make things right. Tyce had not argued that point. The Brandon men had been trying to reclaim their birthright for four generations.

Then Miss Donet died. Suddenly, inexplicably, this new will was nowhere to be found. Her lawyer claimed he knew nothing about it. Tyce had searched the *garçonnière* from top to bottom to no avail. Miss Donet's new will had disappeared without a trace, and the prominent law firm representing the new owner was not taking Tyce's word for the fact of its existence.

The painful conclusion was that Miss Donet had deliberately tricked him into patching the grand old home so it would bring more money to another Bienville heir. She had played along when he applied to have it listed on the National Register of Historic Places as if it were the most wonderful idea in the world. It grieved him to think that someone he admired as much as he did Miss Donet would do something so devious, especially when she knew it would break his heart.

Taking his electric razor from the shelf over the lavatory, he ran it quickly over his five-o'clock shadow, then combed back his still-damp hair. He pulled on a red plaid flannel shirt, clean jeans, and running shoes before going to the kitchen for his jacket.

The overseer's house where he lived was small, with

only two rooms, but it was furnished comfortably. One room was his bedroom, with a small bath he had added on after moving in. The other room served as a combination living area, office, and kitchen. The kitchen was furnished with a stove, refrigerator, microwave, and an old oak table with four chairs around it. Salt and pepper shakers and a bottle of Tabasco sat in the center of the bare table. One of the straight-backed chairs wore Tyce's jacket like a wooden soldier at attention.

As he pulled on his jacket, Tyce crossed the living room to the desk against one wall to check his answering machine for any new calls. A computer and fax machine sat nearby. Laid out across the drawing table next to the desk was a stack of detailed blueprints and sketches held down by a pencil holder filled with drawing pencils and a paper clip holder. An architect's T square was laid across the bottom edge. The first sheet was a floor plan for the front downstairs area of Caroline.

Marked in red was the section where he had intended to work next. That had been before Miss Donet died. Now there was no need to begin. Thinking of the long days and nights already spent coaxing Caroline back to life brought a pang to his heart. Now his efforts to preserve the past would be destroyed, along with the rest of the house, if this new owner had her way.

Slowly, he reached down and brushed a hand across the detailed drawing. Moving the weights off the edges, he carefully rolled up the plans and slipped a rubber band around them. A dozen or more similar rolls were stacked against the wall at the back of the table—hours and hours of work that would serve no purpose now. Wasted time! In frustration, Tyce tossed the rolled-up drawing in his hand on top of the rest.

"Damn it! Why did you have to die now?" he said

aloud, turning away from the table. "And why the hell did you do this to me? I thought we were in this thing together."

Going out, he switched on the front porch light and left the house. The new owner's car was gone, he noticed. As he stepped up into his black Chevy pickup, he reminded himself to check on the *garçonnière* when he got back to be sure it was locked.

Tires spewed gravel as the pickup leapt to life and sped along the narrow drive toward the main road. Tyce tried to keep his mind off this unavoidable twist in his plans, tried not to think of the plantation being gone, tried not to let his mind come to rest on the woman he had met there today.

Hell, he didn't even know her name. Yankee girl didn't even have enough manners to introduce herself. She was easy on the eyes, though. Dark, sassy hair that framed her face with a shining halo of waves and curls. Beautiful, deep brown eyes.

Sometimes while out very early in the morning, he would come upon a doe grazing in the field. She'd look up with startled eyes just before she bounded away. This girl had looked at him the same way. An unexpected vision of those eyes gazing at him from the pillow next to his triggered a yearning to touch the softness of her skin. . . .

Forget it! He could have tolerated the Yankee in her, but right now he had no use for the Bienvilles, any of them.

After a fifteen-minute drive, Tyce pulled up in front of a well-kept, white frame house on a quiet street in New Bienville. Several rocking chairs and a wooden glider occupied the roomy front porch. To the side of the house, a separate, open-fronted garage housed a lawn mower, a multitude of gardening tools, a food smoker, and a late-model Mercury. His sister Maddie's sporty red compact, a high school graduation gift from Tyce and his mother, sat in the driveway.

All the windows were alight from within. As he bounded over the three front steps directly onto the porch, the sound of happy chatter filtered through the closed front door. Pulling the screen door open, he stopped for a moment to listen and look through the thin curtain covering the glass window of the front door. Maddie stood in the kitchen talking, her blond hair pulled up and back into a ponytail, long legs encased in tight black leggings covered by a purple and gold striped tunic. She had grown into a lovely young woman, Tyce thought, for an instant remembering her as a precocious child.

God, he loved to come home to family. Whether he was away for months, days, or only a few hours, an age-old sense of peace and security caught at his chest when he stepped through that door. And, even after all this time, even though this comfortable white house in town was not where Tyce had grown up, even though his dad had never set foot inside, the first question in Tyce's mind would be, *Is Dad home yet?* For years now, since his dad's death, there was no need to voice the question, but Tyce always felt a lingering anticipation, a sense of incompleteness in the family circle without his father's presence. That sense of loss made the rest of his family all the more important to him.

"Tyce!" Maddie called, running to hug him when she saw him.

"Hey, sis, how's college?" he returned, gripping her and lifting her up to plant a light kiss on her forehead.

Maddie was a freshman at Louisiana State University,

caught up in everything college had to offer. She was always busy, always involved in some activity, and rarely got home more than once or twice a month. When she did, though, their mother made a fuss and cooked a dinner big enough to feed the entire community.

"Hi, Mom," Tyce said, giving his mother a peck on her upturned cheek. He usually managed to stop by at least once a week to check on her. She did like for her children to stay close.

A mouthwatering aroma filled the air. Tyce lifted the lid on the large pot simmering on the stove and breathed in the steamy goodness.

"Sauce piquant," his mother said.

He had no need to be told. It was one of his and Maddie's favorite dishes. Made from the rabbits and quail he hunted or from turtle meat that a friend of his from the Atchafalaya Basin brought by occasionally, it was a rich blend of spicy onions, garlic, green peppers, tomatoes, and the game, cooked until the meat was tender and succulent and fell apart on a fork. Of course, like most everything Ellen Crochet Brandon cooked, it started with a dark roux of flour stirred together with grease until it was almost burned.

Tyce's Cajun influence came from her side of the family; the English blood was from Tyce's father, Paul. Ellen Crochet's ancestors were members of the close-knit Cajun society that populated much of south Louisiana. Paul Brandon had been considered an outsider in her narrow world along the bayous of south Louisiana.

Generations before, Paul's English family had emigrated to Louisiana from Virginia to take advantage of the rich farmland. There had been a terrible row and a scandal when Ellen eloped with Paul. For years, she had not been welcomed back home, but before her parents died, she did make her peace. Otherwise, she could not have borne the guilt, she had told her children more than once.

Because of that rift, Tyce had grown up without knowing his Cajun grandparents very well, having seen them only once or twice in his life. Still, he was proud to be half-Cajun. Independent, self-reliant people, they loved life for itself and made no excuses for the way they believed. That joie de vivre had been passed on to Tyce through his mother. He managed to take most things life threw him in stride; but his usual optimism had deserted him today.

"I'm going to try out for the track team, Tyce," Maddie said proudly.

"Well, hell, I never could catch you. I imagine you'll make it."

"*Cher*, watch your language." Ellen slapped him lightly on the arm. "What did you do today? You're not still working on the house now that Donet is dead, are you?"

Tyce took a slice of loaf bread from a plate on the table and began to pull off the crust. He liked to eat the crust first, then the soft white part of the bread, save the best for last. It was an old habit of his. "I was, until today."

When Tyce did not offer any further explanation, Maddie asked, "What happened?"

"The new owner showed up."

"So . . . ?" Maddie gestured impatiently with her hand. "What's he like?"

"She. It's a she."

"You sound disgusted," Maddie stated with a sisterly grin. "An old hag, is she?"

Tyce smiled. "She's gorgeous, actually."

"What then?" Maddie pressed. "You obviously don't like her."

"She's a Yankee and a Bienville," Tyce said. Then, to tease his mother, he added, "A real Yankee from New York."

The Mason-Dixon line was not the measure his mother used to determine a Yankee. Anybody north of Alexandria would fit the bill. Tyce's father had not been a Yankee. His failing had been that he was a redneck farmer, and that had been just as bad to her family's way of thinking.

"Oh, New York," his mother mused, turning back to stir her stew. "That one. Her daddy was Donet Bienville's nephew Joseph," Ellen offered without looking around. "He got married to that Yankee girl. After a while, she wanted to go back home. Can't say I blame her, the way Joseph acted sometime, still he was her husband and a woman ought to stay by her husband. Poor 'Tee-Joe, he never could live up North. Grieved for home when he was up there with her, then grieved for her when he was at Caroline. Drove the boy half crazy, don't you know, having to choose between his family up North and his home down here."

Maddie began to set the table with the heavy stoneware dishes that Ellen always used for family.

"The man had more serious problems than that, and you know it, Mom. He was an alcoholic and probably brought his troubles on himself. Anyway, I don't care who she is. She's apparently already sold Caroline. I can't believe it. She claims some developer is planning to put a mall there."

"A mall? *Cher*, we gon' have a mall way out here?" Ellen seemed shocked but pleased. "No more driving to the city to shop. *C'est bon*."

Tyce fumed silently. Did no one care about the past or the Brandon legacy except him?

Ellen ladled the stew into a large tureen and set it, steaming, in the center of the table next to a bowl mounded with snowy rice. Maddie brought green salads from the refrigerator along with salad dressing and butter for the bread. When all was in place, they sat down to eat. Tyce said a short grace and there were a few moments when the only sound was the clink of serving utensils against china as they settled in to enjoy the feast.

"Good. I'm glad it's sold. I'll be glad to see it gone altogether," Ellen declared abruptly.

Tyce frowned. "I wish you didn't feel that way."

"You know I never liked the idea of you living there, anyway. You had a wonderful career and threw it away when Miss Donet snapped her fingers."

"You know what I want to do with the house."

"I know, and it would be a wonderful thing if it could happen, *cher*, but it's never going to. You're obsessed with a dream that was put in your head by your daddy and your uncle Lee. It's not going to happen, Tyce. It never has, and it never will."

"Why can't you try to understand?" Tyce tried to catch his mother's eye, but she avoided his look.

"Com'on, guys, let's don't go over all this again," Maddie implored. "We all know the answers, and nobody's mind is going to change."

Tyce fell silent, but Ellen muttered under her breath, "You both know why I feel this way."

"Yeah, I know," Tyce said sharply, "but, I'm not going to let Caroline go without a fight. It was supposed to be mine. . . ." Tyce's voice faded at the idea of an empty field where the proud, majestic plantation house had stood for over a century.

Ellen put down her fork and looked in amazement at him. "Tyce, don't you even think like that. I can't stand to see another good man ruined by that place. It killed your daddy and drove Uncle Lee away for the rest of his life." Ellen's voice rose as she warmed to her subject. "It's got a spell on you, like it did them. I thank my God that the new owner had sense enough to sell it. Now maybe you can get on with your life. You've got a whole lifetime before you, ready to be lived, and you won't see that!"

"Caroline is my life. That's the work I want to do—that I was meant to do. I can't bear to see it torn down. Bad enough the way the Bienvilles treated it, but God knows, I can't stand by and let this happen. If it costs me everything I own, I'll get it back."

"You got no business getting involved in this. You get yourself back to work. John Dennis calls me every month wanting you back. You should call him, go back to New Orleans, son. A good job, a future doing what you went to school to do. Don't throw your life away trying to save that worthless plantation, *m'cher*."

Tyce looked at his mother impatiently. "Just never mind, Mom. Maddie's right; we've been over this more than enough. I'm not going to change my mind, and neither are you. Let's talk about something else."

"All I'm trying to do is save you from what happened to your father and your great-uncle. Make a life for yourself. Don't let Caroline—"

Tyce felt the tightening of his chest muscles. He wiped his mouth and crumpled the napkin, laying it down beside his plate. "Can we talk about something else!"

"Mom . . ." Maddie said, her voice taking a warning edge.

"How much time and money and effort you already wasted out there? I knew Donet was not going to do what she said. I tried to tell you."

"I don't have to sit here and listen to this." Tyce's patience was gone now. "You know how I feel about what I'm doing. Saying it's worthless or reminding me about Dad won't change my mind. I know Caroline's value and what can be done with it." Tyce rose from the table. "Once that house is razed, our past, our roots are gone forever. Gone, Mom! I'm not going to turn my back and pretend it was never there."

"Sit down and finish, *cher*. You know I didn't mean it the way it sounded. I just worry about you." Ellen's voice softened as she tried to catch his arm. He evaded her hand and abruptly pushed his chair back from the table.

As he strode through the living room, snatching his coat from the couch where he had laid it, he heard Maddie say, "I tell you, Mom, one day you're going to drive him away for good with that nagging about Caroline. He's not going to let it go, and you know it."

The slamming of the screen door behind him punctuated his sister's words. His mother might not drive him away, but she could sure make him mad. Maybe it was like she always said: *The truth is hard to bear.* But he wasn't going to give up Caroline, not without a hell of a fight.

He drove into New Bienville, had a few beers, and shot a couple of games of pool at the bar, while his blood pressure returned to normal. The drive back to Caroline gave him more time to brood. The *garçonnière* was still dark, with no sign of the woman's return. She probably wouldn't be back until tomorrow. Tyce walked up on the porch and tested the front door. It was locked.

He started to turn away, then on an impulse he found the key on his key ring and unlocked the door.

The house was just as Miss Donet had left it, except there was a lingering trace of perfume in the air. Tyce checked each room. Since he had turned the water on for the new owner in spite of her attempt to throw him off the property, he made sure she had not left it running to flood the place.

Outside once more, he locked the door behind him. As he turned to go to his own house, something caught his attention. Frowning, he stared toward the dark, hulking shadow of the mansion. Was it a movement he had seen? Maybe the swaying shadows of naked branches cast against the house by the dim moon? A stray cat slinking among the sparse shrubbery?

Startled, Tyce's eyes narrowed as he surveyed the dark facade of the house. He had to be seeing things. A dim glow emanated from the boarded windows of the ballroom. Impossible! He had the only key to that room, to the whole house except for the *garçonnière,* in fact, and he had not left any lights on the last time he had been in there.

He strode across the open corridor between the *garçonnière* and the main house, then shuffled the keys around on the ring until he found the old key that opened the door. Cautiously, he made his way through the sparsely furnished rooms without bothering to turn on the lights. He knew every inch of the place.

Around him, the silence was unbroken except for his footfalls on the wooden floors. Bulky shapes of covered furniture kept watch like faceless gargoyles. All the old ghost stories he had ever heard about Caroline swirled around in his head like disturbed tendrils of mist in a dark alley. Common sense told him that ghosts did not exist, but the unsettling dream from a few days earlier still bothered him, and he had been raised on the legend of Chloe Bienville from the time he was old enough to remember. The hair on the back of his neck prickled as he recalled the dream.

He stopped in the middle of the front entrance hall, an expansive, high-ceilinged chamber that ran from the front to the back of the house at the second level. In the chilly darkness, Tyce looked up at the landing with a vague expectation of seeing somebody standing there, but the staircase was empty.

For a moment, his mind shifted to the amount of basic carpentry work still needing to be done before any real restoration could begin. The attic floor had a rotten spot in it the size of a small car, and some of the upstairs flooring needed replacing. The old lead pipes leading from the cisterns on the roof were blocked off temporarily until Tyce decided whether to install PVC piping or remove them altogether. Their bursting one winter had been the cause of the upstairs water damage and rot.

Once that was done, only a few minor structural repairs would be necessary before the fun work could begin: the actual restoration, bringing the old structure around slowly, painstakingly, until it was as grand as the day it was built.

As his gaze swept over the ballroom door, the dim light sifting through the cracks yanked his attention back to the present. The door was locked. He knew that for a certainty. The only key was on his key ring. Under his hand, the porcelain doorknob was ice cold as he unlocked the door and went in. The ballroom was bathed in soft light that flickered from the electric candle flames in the three massive chandeliers. The air, disturbed by the opening of the door, brought a faint scent of roses to Tyce's nose, which immediately brought to mind the apparition in red, for he had smelled roses then, too.

Tyce stepped through the doorway, his senses alert. There must be somebody inside. The lights didn't turn themselves on. He drew the door closed behind him before scanning the room, all the while listening intently for the least creak of an old board, any noise to betray the intruder. There was no sign of anyone other than him in the room. His gaze raked past the floor-to-ceiling windows that faced the river, then shot back to the first windowsill. With an eerie feeling that he was not alone, no matter how empty the room appeared to be, Tyce moved cautiously toward the red object on the windowsill.

Fascinated by the impossibility of the situation, he stooped to touch the scattering of rose petals, red as rubies and still fragrant and fresh as if just plucked from the bud. They lay like glittering jewels on top of a folded sheet of linen writing paper. Tyce gently unfolded the letter and read the first paragraph in disbelief. Donet Bienville's last will and testament! Forcing his pounding heart to slow enough for him to think straight, Tyce scrutinized the room. Surely, somebody was here, but how did they get into the room and where the hell were they?

"Who is in here?" Tyce called, searching the recesses. The echo of his voice faded quickly into heavy silence.

Where had this document been all this time? Tyce had seen it only once before, when Miss Donet had showed it to him. He had picked the house apart looking for it, and it was nowhere to be found. Now it turned up in a locked ballroom with rose petals on top!

A chill ran down Tyce's spine. He had never in his

life considered whether he truly believed in ghosts, in spite of all the old family tales. But what else could explain this priceless piece of paper falling into his hands just at this moment? This will was his future—his life.

"Chloe?" he called tentatively, hoping that he got no answer. There was a shift of the lace curtains by one of the front windows, but the woman he had seen in what he thought was a dream did not materialize. Across the stillness of the room, however, the words came to Tyce as clearly as if she had spoken them: *"I return this document to you because I must. Caroline cannot be sold, else I am doomed. In return, I expect much from you, Tyce Brandon. I expect my release from this earth to go to my beloved."*

Chapter
Four

The glint of sunshine glancing off the windows of Caroline blinded Delaney momentarily as she pulled up to the front door of her new living quarters. She blinked to clear the swimming spots from her eyes before getting out of the car and unlocking the *garçonnière*. A shiver ran up her spine as she stepped inside. Crossing the room, she adjusted the thermostat before going to the car to bring in the groceries.

She had spent the previous night in her hotel room in Baton Rouge, then had gotten up early to go grocery shopping before driving back to Caroline. Twenty minutes were wasted in the checkout line while the cashier chattered with everyone, including the bag boy, then counted Delaney's change four times before she got it right. Delaney was ready to leave the groceries where they were and board the first plane home. When the bag boy finished arranging the sacks to his satisfaction, Delaney slammed the trunk closed herself and grudgingly shoved a tip at him. The boy looked surprised and politely refused her money. Strange breed, these Southerners, all of them.

She set the last bag of groceries on the counter and opened the closest set of cabinets. Cans and boxes stood in precise rows on the paper-lined shelves. There were foods in there that Delaney had never heard of before: Trappey's okra gumbo, Zatarain's spices, and lots of rice. Delaney's cans of soup and package of bagels seemed out of place.

"Dear, dear. You should put the cold foods in the ice cellar first."

Delaney whirled around. An old woman in a tealength lace dress was peering into each sack on the table that held frozen or cold groceries.

"How did you get in here?" Delaney gasped, her hand pressed against her racing chest to keep her heart from leaping out of her body at the fright. "Who are you?"

The woman's snowy hair was pulled back in an old-fashioned bun at the nape of her neck, but there was a sense of youth in the uncreased face and luminous golden eyes.

"Oh, never mind me, child. I was very close to your aunt Donet for many years. I live on the grounds," she said, gesturing with her hand vaguely in no clear direction. *"I hope to get to know you while you're here. Donet thought the world of you."*

"Oh, really?" Delaney muttered. Nobody had mentioned a renter. Then she recalled that the letter from her aunt Donet had mentioned some relative named Chloe. "You must be Chloe then?"

The woman smiled sweetly. *"Oh, no, dear child. Chloe has been dead many years now, although I did know her very well. Just call me Auntie, like everybody else does."*

"How long have you been here?" Delaney said, meaning in the kitchen with her.

"Nigh onto a month . . . oh, no, you don't mean that. . . ." The woman stopped short, then she gave Delaney an indulgent smile. *"For a long time, dear."*

Delaney noticed Auntie's long, graceful fingers and the overall aura of dignity and graciousness from a forgotten era. From her head to her daintily slippered feet, she reminded Delaney of images of grand Southern ladies conjured up by the tales her daddy used to tell of the old South in its glory. She said she lived on the grounds. That was going to pose another problem.

"I'm sure the lawyers have told you that I've sold the plantation. You'll need to find another place to live."

"Oh, no, dear. I'm afraid I shall have to go with the house."

"What?"

"Now, now, don't you worry about that. Tyce is going to take care of everything, you know," Auntie said cheerily, still snooping through the grocery bags. She added softly, *"Besides, you might say I'm a part of this old house."*

Delaney didn't have time to argue with the woman. She smiled slightly at the thought: *FOR SALE: Dilapidated Civil War mansion. Uninhabitable, but comes with live-in Auntie.*

"No cream for coffee?" Auntie asked wistfully. *"You really must have cream."*

"No. No cream. It's loaded with fat. Besides, I drink my coffee black."

"Donet always kept cream. Tyce likes cream," Auntie continued to mutter.

Delaney began to take her groceries out of the bags.

"Here, dear. I'll help you. I know where Donet likes everything to go."

"Aunt Donet doesn't live here anymore," Delaney said sharply before she thought better of her rudeness, but the woman didn't seem to hear her. She was engrossed in checking out each carton, jar, and bottle that Delaney brought out. Delaney opened the refrigerator to put the eggs inside.

"Those and the butter go into the cold cellar," Auntie admonished.

"Cold cellar?" Delaney questioned with a frown.

"Oh, dear, as long as I've had them, I still tend to forget about these modern contraptions. In my girlhood, we gathered eggs every day and used most of them. Everything else perishable had to go into the dairy cellar to stay cool."

"Well, these days, everything perishable goes in the refrigerator."

"Yes, of course, dear child. I know that."

Delaney turned her eyes upward in exasperation. *Why me?* she thought. She loaded the coffeemaker, put the empty pot in place, and flipped the switch to begin the brewing process. She had promised to give her mother the phone number at the plantation. Now seemed to be an opportune time to send this old lady on her way.

"Excuse me. I have to make a phone call," Delaney said, hoping the woman would get the hint and go home.

"Don't be too long, dear," Auntie said with concern, then began rambling distractedly. *"Tyce will be along*

soon. I do wish you'd gotten cream. He likes cream. . . .''

Impatiently, Delaney left the eccentric woman to her muttering. She'd have to speak to her lawyers about this situation. Surely, she was not going to be responsible for this crazy aunt or whoever she was. Settling onto the couch in the adjoining room, Delaney picked up the phone and dialed her mother's house. No answer. She must be out shopping. Delaney waited for the answering machine to click on, then left a short message giving her mother the telephone number at the plantation. She disconnected from that call, dialed Mark's office, and waited for an answer. Mark had not been home the night before, but he would be at work this morning.

"McAlan and Patterson," said the friendly, familiar voice on the other end.

"Hi, Jenny, is Mark in?" Delaney asked.

"Sure, hold on," Jenny said, then added before she put Delaney's call through, "How are things in the sunny South?"

"Well, actually, it is sunny today and supposed to warm up into the 60s. Not bad for late February," Delaney replied. "Other than that, don't ask."

"Going that well, huh? I'll get Mr. Patterson for you."

"Hey, babe!" The next voice on the phone was Mark's. Tall, dark-haired, suave, and dressed to perfection, Delaney could picture him sitting at his huge burled desk in his Armani suit, swiveling his chair around to look out of the picture window at the city below while he talked. "I was beginning to believe you'd fallen off the end of the earth down there."

"I tried to call last night. No answer. No machine," Delaney returned. "I thought maybe you'd fallen off."

"Just out late with a client, and you know I always forget to turn that damned machine on in the mornings."

"I know. Anyway, I'm here, for what it's worth."

"So, tell all. How's our little gold mine?"

Delaney knew his mind had flown to that beach house he wanted to buy in Florida and no doubt he now completed the picture with a yacht tied to the dock. More than ever lately, Mark talked about getting married in the summer, even though he was aware of her feelings about marriage. She never intended to marry anybody, and she had made that clear to Mark from the beginning. At first that had been fine with him, too. They enjoyed one another's company and had money to spend on the rich variety of entertainment offered in New York and the surrounding area. Their relationship had been platonic, with no strings attached, the way Delaney liked it.

Then, over the last year, Mark had changed. Subtly, he began to press for a commitment from her. They had stopped seeing one another for awhile when she refused to move into his condo with him. There was no way she was going to give up her independence to a man. Not after what she had watched her mother go through over the years.

Then she had inherited this ruin of a plantation from her great-aunt and had contacted Mark for advice on selling it. He was a well-known, aggressive young realtor, with a reputation for matching the right people with the right property, always with a hefty profit for his client. She had agreed to go out to dinner with him and discuss the property, and after that, Mark had been a steady fixture in her life again. She wasn't sure she was totally happy about the resurrection of their relationship.

And now Mark was becoming more persistent about getting married.

Delaney was wary of marriage. To surrender heart and soul to some man who might treat her like her father had treated her mother was something she was going to have to think about for a long time. Besides, Mark wanted too many material things for Delaney's naturally frugal mind-set. Mark's habit of buying whatever he wanted had always been a source of irritation between them.

"Remember, Mark, I'm going to buy my mother a nice country house in Connecticut," she said, nipping his musing in the bud before he added a Mercedes and Jag.

"Yeah, babe, we'll do that. But that won't take even a hundred thou," Mark said happily. "When will you be finished down there?"

"I want to make an inventory. Some of the furnishings are valuable antiques that I want to keep. The rest will have to be disposed of in some way. That should take less than a week. The development company wants to start the demolition work soon. I should be back in New York by early next week."

"Listen, sweetie, don't worry about all that old shit. Just dump it somewhere and let the developers take over. We'll buy all new everything once this deal is finalized."

Delaney frowned. "But I want it. The furniture is really beautiful."

"Whatever. Just don't delay the sale trying to salvage junk, okay? Anything else?"

Delaney thought of Auntie and added in a lower voice, "Well, there is one little glitch. Some relative of my great-aunt's is living here. I'm not sure she's all there in the head, if you know what I mean, and I may have to make arrangements for her, too. I have to check with the lawyer.''

''That's fine, that's fine,'' Mark said rather absently, as if he were only half-listening.

Delaney was startled by the sound of knocking at her door. She put her hand over the phone mouthpiece and called out, ''Auntie, would you answer the door, please?'' There was no answer from the kitchen. Maybe she had gone back home, after all. The knocking came again. ''Hold on, Mark, somebody's at the door.''

Mark's voice caught her before she could put the receiver down.

''That's okay, I gotta go anyway, babe. Got a meeting in two minutes.''

The phone went dead.

A vague sense of disappointment and depression enveloped Delaney as she hung up. Always rushing, always in the fast lane, Mark was as hyperactive as any child. He worked late and went in early, ever searching for wealthy new clients whose money he could sink into prime real estate, always with a hefty commission for himself. Yet he never thought about investing his own money and made a practice of spending it as fast as he earned it. Cocksure and arrogant at times, he lived in the present moment with no thought for the future, as if he could live fast enough to outrun it before it caught up to him. Delaney was too security-oriented to be comfortable with that philosophy. Until he changed his spendthrift ways and became more discerning with his expenditures, their relationship was likely to remain the same. Delaney had no intention of jumping on a financial roller coaster for the rest of her life.

Another persistent knock caught her attention. "Coming!" she called out.

"Good morning, ma'am," Tyce said as she opened the door. The smile he gave her lit his eyes and lifted her spirits.

"Good morning." Delaney smiled in return, despite herself, finding it hard to resist the charm of those blue eyes.

"Nice day," he said. "I brought you a little neighborly offering. Kind of an apology for flying off the handle yesterday."

In his hand he held something that looked like a tray, though she could not be sure, for it was covered with a cloth.

"Thank you," she said, caught off guard. "What is it?"

"Beignets," he said.

"Ben-yays?"

"That's right, beignets," he repeated, grinning. "French doughnuts."

He offered the tray to her. Looking under the dish towel, Delaney saw delicate, golden pastries piled high on a plate. Pure, white, powdered sugar covered them like snow on a mountain and piled up in little drifts around the edge of the plate.

"They look wonderful," Delaney said with delight. "Where did you get them?" She had not noticed a bakery when she drove through the nearby small town of New Bienville.

"I made them. They're only good while they're hot, so I hope you're hungry."

"I am. I was just making coffee and was about to have a bowl of cereal. But I can't eat all these. There must be nearly a dozen."

"Well, ma'am, I love beignets," he hinted, with that bedeviling grin.

"I'll invite you in to share these *ben-yays*"—Delaney tried to pronounce the word like he did—"on one condition."

"What's that?" He cocked an eyebrow.

"That you stop calling me ma'am. It makes me feel like somebody's grandmother!"

Tyce laughed. "Well, I'd love to stop calling you ma'am, except that I don't know anything else to call you. Maybe you should tell me your name."

"Oh." Delaney felt a blush creep up her neck. "I'm sorry. Delaney Bienville—"

"Delaney? Odd. . . ." Tyce's eyebrows puckered.

"It's an old family name," Delaney interjected, having had the question asked too many times in her life, "and don't dare call me Miss Bienville, either."

"Deal," Tyce said, coming inside the house. "Coffee smells good."

"So do these." Delaney took a whiff of the delicious aroma wafting up from the pastries. She set the dish in the center of the table, leaving the towel in place to hold the warmth. Glancing around at the closed cabinets, she admitted, "I'm afraid I don't know where all the dishes are yet."

Going directly to the cupboard in the corner, Tyce brought out two cups, two saucers, and two matching plates of fine china with a delicate morning glory and vine pattern around the edges, which he set on the table. "So, does this mean my apology's accepted?"

"I suppose, but that doesn't mean I've changed my mind about anything else," Delaney said.

If Tyce heard her, he did not comment. He glanced

into the refrigerator before rummaging around in a cabinet.

"Donet usually kept real cream," he said, bringing out a jar of powdered creamer and a covered dish filled with sugar, "but this will have to do."

"I take mine black, anyway," Delaney replied.

"I like the real thing, but sometimes you just have to take what's available."

"So I heard," Delaney said.

"What do you mean?" Tyce pulled out a chair and sat down as Delaney poured the coffee. He seemed completely at home here. Delaney wondered how often he had shared beignets with her great-aunt and exactly what relationship the two of them might have had. He certainly did not act like a hired worker.

"Oh, Auntie told me a few minutes ago."

Delaney uncovered the plate of beignets. A sweet rush of warmth rose to her nostrils. "Uhm," she murmured as she looked up at Tyce. "What's wrong?"

Tyce glanced around with a puzzled frown. "Who told you?"

"Auntie, that old woman who lives on the grounds. Some friend or relative of my Aunt Donet's, I think. Why?"

Tyce looked perplexed. "Nobody lives on the grounds except me, and there sure aren't any neighbors within walking distance. What did this woman look like?"

Delaney was confused at this unexpected news. "She was very different, I have to say. Had on an old-fashioned lace dress, kind of long. . . . Her hair . . . it was white, pulled back like my grandmother used to wear hers. I . . . I don't know anything else. My aunt had mentioned some relative named Chloe in her letter to me, so

I asked her if she was Chloe, but she said no, that Chloe died years ago. Anyway, she was gone when you knocked. . . ."

Delaney fell silent for a moment. She hadn't a clue who she had been talking to or where the woman went. "Oh, well, I guess it doesn't matter. She must have been a neighbor. That's just one less thing I have to worry about."

Delaney took one of the beignets. She had it almost to her mouth, contemplating the sweet coolness of the sugar on her tongue. The worried expression lingered on Tyce's face, and he looked slowly around the room again.

"Now what's wrong?" With the slight breath of Delaney's words, the airy powdered sugar seemed to explode. Like a tiny snow flurry, it flew everywhere: on her plate, the table, her face, and up her nose. "Oh!" she cried in surprise, and another cloud of sweet dust detonated in her face.

Tyce's frown relaxed in amusement. "I should have told you not to talk while you eat beignets. It's too messy. I forgot you were from up North." He laughed as he reached across the table with a napkin to dust the sugar off her nose.

Delaney jerked away from him, grabbing her own napkin to wipe her face.

"It happens to everybody sooner or later," he said, still laughing. "Just hold your breath when you bite."

She pouted for a long minute, but his laughter was so heartfelt and good-natured that she could not stay mad. With great effort, Delaney brought the doughnut to her mouth. Tyce was holding back a grin. Delaney held her breath and took a bite. The square, holeless doughnut was delicious, rich and sweet, yet light—and hollow inside. Carefully, she lowered the confection out of breath's reach. "These things are good, but they are positively dangerous."

"Like a lot of other things, they're well worth the effort, though." Tyce's gaze lingered on her face a trifle too long for comfort.

Sipping her hot coffee, Delaney glanced out the window at the brittle sunshine. The sky was almost as blue as Tyce's eyes. Looking back, she found him still watching her. Flustered, she fidgeted, then found something to say. "Did I hear you correctly? You made these this morning?"

Tyce nodded but did not speak as he ate another beignet.

As he swallowed, Delaney asked, "What else do you cook?"

He shrugged slightly. "Mostly just the things I like best. Jambalaya, hamburgers, hot dogs. I make a mean gumbo, too."

"I've had jambalaya. My mother cooks it once in a while. I think my father liked it. He was from down here. Miss Donet's nephew, Joseph."

"I know," Tyce said.

Of course, he would know. New Bienville was a tiny hamlet and her family would have been very well-known. Probably everybody in town knew her father. He had been missing from much of her life, even before he died, and her mother rarely spoke of him. Delaney felt a pang of jealousy that Tyce might possibly know her father better than she did.

Tyce washed down a bite of doughnut with coffee before continuing. "I saw him around a lot when I was a kid."

"I was only ten when he died. He spent a great deal

of his time down here, and I really resented it,'' Delaney said, silently congratulating herself that she could actually admit that aloud now.

"That's too bad. He was a pretty nice guy, as I recall, always teasing me. We farmed a few acres of land that my dad leased from him. We were lucky, my sister and I. Both of us were older when our dad died. Dad was always there for me, and I still miss him.''

Delaney felt the old rage and sense of loss surging through her. She should have had a father, too. ''Some are luckier than others. That's why I don't want to keep this plantation. It reminds me that my father loved it more than he loved me and my mother. I just want to get it out of my life. The quicker the better.''

Tyce looked at her with a concerned frown. "I don't think your father loved this plantation more than his family. He had some problems—'' Tyce stopped abruptly, as if he had said too much, then went on more carefully, ''This place was his inheritance, after all, and Miss Donet needed help with it. With his family up North, maybe he was torn between the two. I can see where it would be hard for a man to live like that.''

Anger crept through her at Tyce's defense of her father. If anything, he was offering an excuse for her father's behavior, and she had no interest in hearing a stranger's opinion on why she had been neglected by him most of her life. Best to change the subject before she said something she'd regret.

"It doesn't matter, really,'' Delaney stated, before Tyce could defend her father any further. ''I don't know why I even mentioned it. I have a lot to do.''

"I have to get busy, too,'' Tyce agreed, but he hesitated to rise from the table, as if he wanted to continue talking.

"Thank you for breakfast," Delaney said quickly. Then, remembering that she had not been able to unlock the door to the big house, she added, "By the way, I need the key to the main house. You have one, don't you?"

"Look, we need to talk about all this," he said. "About your selling Caroline."

Delaney frowned. "There's nothing to talk about. Now, the keys?"

"I still have work to do inside. You might not be around when I need to get in."

"Actually, there'll be no more work going on," Delaney said sharply, "and I insist on having the keys, all the keys to the buildings here. I might remind you that you have to be off the premises within the week."

"Yes, so you've said before. We need to discuss that, too. As for the house, why don't you let me give you the grand tour, so you'll know your way around. I think you'll find it's a lot more than a run-down old mansion."

Delaney frowned at this unexpected passive resistance. Could it be that she would have to involve the lawyers to get the guy off her property? Still, she wanted to see the house, and the easiest way to do that right now was to play along with him, since he didn't seem willing to give up the keys without a fight.

"Now's as good a time as any," Delaney said flatly.

"Get a coat; it's still cold outside."

"I assure you, *this* is not cold." Delaney was wearing a fairly heavy cable-knit sweater in a bright crimson color. She found the cottage too warm for comfort now that she had started moving around. The brisk, cooling air would be nice. Tyce stood aside and held the door for her to go through. They walked together across the lawn to the big house. Tyce opened the door and motioned her through, following close behind.

Room by room, he took her through the downstairs part of the house, uncovering some of the furniture as he went. In one room was a huge, dark mahogany dining suite with table, chairs, and a large sideboard. In another room were an assortment of chairs, sofas, tables, and cabinets, all well cared for.

Delaney was impressed by the size of the front hall, a wide, tall room running from front to back of the second floor, the main floor, Tyce explained. The breezeway had large doors and windows on either end that could be raised in summer for ventilation. In the center of the room was a grand, wide staircase with an elaborately carved, highly polished oak railing. Beside it was a hallway that Tyce said led to a staircase to the lower regions of the house, that in the house's heyday had been the domain of the domestic help.

Around the perimeter of the room, just below the ceiling, a wide band of white plaster frieze glowed in the muted light thrown into the room by the sun. Tyce explained that skilled craftsmen had made the mud locally and molded it in place along the top of the room over a hundred years ago, and it still hung there, almost as perfect as the day it had been set.

It seemed that Tyce could answer anything she asked about the house or its history. He knew what wood was used to build the house and how it was insulated with mud and Spanish moss. He told her the house's history back to the Civil War, when the Yankees passed it by because the Union captain knew the family and had often been a guest at Caroline before the war. Still, it had not escaped damage. Tyce took her outside onto the broad front porch and showed her the large round ball imbedded in one of the massive columns, fired from a warship anchored in the river.

He said that along the river, the front of a house was the side that faced the water, not necessarily the side where the driveway ended. She recalled the day before on the levee, when he had told her the river was once much farther away. He knew so much about this house—and his eyes shone with excitement just talking about it.

"What about upstairs?" she asked, as they walked back into the grand, wide hallway. "And this room. Didn't you say this was the ballroom?" Delaney tried the doorknob. "It's locked. Do you have the key?"

"Not with me."

She laid her hand on the smooth, precisely painted knob.

"The knobs and lock covers are hand-painted glass. I'll open it for you later. You wanted to see upstairs," Tyce said abruptly, heading up the stairs. "I'll warn you, though, don't come up here alone. Some of the floor has been damaged by rot and I haven't replaced it yet. Leaks in the roof and a couple of broken pipes in the walls over the years took a toll. There's no need to replace the flooring until the roof is sound, and there's still some bad piping in one of the outside walls that needs to be repaired. I have it blocked off for the time being so there won't be any more damage."

"Why would there be piping in the walls?" Delaney wanted to know. "I thought they had to draw water from a well and bring it inside."

"Most people did, but this place had the equivalent of hot running water from the time it was built. Several huge cisterns on the roof collect rainwater, which runs through pipes that run from the roof to the walls behind the fireplaces. In the summer, the only hot water would be in the kitchen, of course, but in winter, there was hot water available in the house, as well. That's what I want you to understand. The innovations that were built into this place were phenomenal for its time. You can't replace history once it's gone.''

His stubbornness irritated Delaney. He talked as if he intended to go right on with his plans, in spite of all she had told him. Who cared if the floor was rotten or the pipes in the walls needed repair? As if the place were going to still be standing in a week.

When she didn't comment, he gave a frustrated sigh. ''I'll show you the rooms from the hall, but I still have to find all the weak places in the floor.''

Following him up the stairs, Delaney tried to keep her eyes away from the tight fit of his jeans across his backside, but she quickly discovered that he was the one thing in this house she did find interesting. Most interesting and most enticing. A strange predicament. She was far more intrigued by the handyman than she was by the house. She brought herself up short in her rambling thoughts. She'd better get rid of that idea, and fast! He definitely was going out of her life along with the house.

Delaney stopped beside him in the doorway of a large room that contained more covered furniture.

''This is the master bedchamber,'' Tyce said.

''Is that the bedroom furniture?'' she asked, indicating the fall of canvas against the far wall.

''Yes. Made in New Orleans especially for this room. Here, I'll show it to you.''

''I thought the floor wasn't safe,'' Delaney said sharply, wondering if he was just trying to scare her to keep her out of the house.

''I know where to walk.''

Again, his answer was reasonable, but Delaney still had the feeling that he was tricking her. As if he read her mind, he stepped gingerly on a board. Delaney heard the crack of wood, and watched the board splinter slightly with his weight. He drew back, gave her an I-told-you-so look, then went on to the other side of the room.

The canvas reached a good eight feet from the floor, forming a rectangle of cloth big enough to be a small room. Tyce tugged at the canvas and it began to slide down. As it came off, a massive, dark piece of furniture emerged, a huge, full-tester bed with a canopy of dark, shining, carved wood. The headboard curved gracefully to the canopy and was decorated with elaborate carvings of fruit and cherubs.

Making his way carefully around the bed, avoiding certain boards as he went, Tyce revealed a matching wardrobe and a highboy chest. Delaney was amazed at the beauty and quality of the workmanship. The bed-room suite was worth a fortune. Maybe she had more here than she had first thought.

But the furniture seemed so heavy, and Tyce said the floor was rotten. "Don't we need to get that furniture out of here and downstairs? I'd hate to see it fall through the floor."

Tyce shook his head and pulled back the canvas from the edge of the bed. "The bed's on a platform. The joists are cypress. They will be here in another hundred years. It's only the floorboards that need work. And only a few of them. I just don't want you to be rambling around up here and step through. And there are a couple of places where you could go all the way to the floor below. That's a fifteen-foot fall you'd rather not make."

Tyce joined her outside the room. They stood in a

broad, open hall that connected the rest of the upstairs chambers. Scaffolding ran along one wall, reaching to the ceiling. Following the metal braces upward, Delaney noticed that a portion of the plaster frieze-work around the perimeter of the room was missing. Water stains yellowed the ceiling in irregular patches, and paint strips hung from the rotting boards overhead. He wasn't kidding about the flooring being rotten.

Delaney pointed toward the damaged ceiling. "What's up there?"

"Just the attic. A jumble of old trunks and furniture. Do you want to have a look?"

"No, I'll do that later. Let's finish the grand tour, so I can get to work on an inventory."

"All right," Tyce said easily.

The rest of the upstairs consisted of a music room and several smaller rooms that Tyce said served as parlors and guest bedrooms. One entire wing jutting out to the back of the house was the girl's domain, he said. The door to that section opened onto the main hall just outside the master bedroom, and although there was a long veranda running the length of the extension, there was no other visible means of escape. The boys of the family might have had all the freedom in the world, but the girls certainly seemed to be prisoners, Delaney reflected.

When they went downstairs, Tyce left the back door open at her request so that she could come and go as she pleased. Thanking him for his help, she started back to the *garçonnière* to begin her inventory there.

Tyce cleared his throat. "Delaney, you and I still need to talk."

Delaney did not turn around immediately. "There's nothing to talk about. I couldn't change anything now, even if I tried."

"Would you just listen to me, anyway? Maybe we can work out some kind of arrangement where we both can win."

Steeling herself as she slowly pivoted to face him, she waited for him to try to talk her into selling out to him for a pittance.

"You told me your opinion of this place, and now I want you to know how I feel before it's too late." When Delaney did not move, Tyce went on, "You see, Caroline has been a part of my family for generations. The mansion was built by the Brandons before the Civil War. Then we lost it to the Bienvilles—I won't go into the details. Let's just say it was a bad time for both families. My family has been trying to regain Caroline ever since. We've watched helplessly as it fell into ruin as you see it now. Miss Donet was the only one who seemed to understand the significance of this plantation returning to its rightful owners after all these years. She and I had an agreement. I would begin restoration of the house while she was alive; she would leave the plantation to me after she died."

"But she didn't," Delaney said pointedly. Try as she would, she could not understand the depth of his feeling for this old plantation. It was only a rotting house on a barren tract of land. Maybe her father's obsession with his family's history had affected her adversely, for Delaney had never felt any great passion for the past or anything connected to it. The man needed to get a real life, and if he thought he was going to talk her out of a multimillion dollar deal with his pitiful tale, he was wrong. "She left it to me."

"You have the original will. There is another one."

"So I heard from my lawyer—an alleged second will that could not be produced."

"Exactly. One that leaves Caroline and its surrounding property to me."

Delaney had had enough of this guy. She wanted him off her property and out of her hair. There was no way she was going to give any credence to this wild story of his. Caroline was rightfully hers, by blood and by law, and she could do with it what she pleased. "Well, until you can produce that elusive will, I'd say you'd better find another apartment quick. After Monday, the overseer's house is going to be gone, just like the rest of the buildings here."

"I don't think so," Tyce said, with disconcerting confidence. "You see, I found the second will."

Chapter Five

Tyce's words were like a slap in the face. Delaney stared at him in momentary shock, which quickly changed to fury.

"I can't believe your arrogance!" she snapped. "What makes you think you can waltz in here and take my family's house from me? I want you off my property today!"

"Look, Delaney, be reasonable. Your aunt and I had—"

"I don't want to hear anything else about it. Talk to my lawyer if you've got something to say." Delaney spun around and stalked away to the *garçonnière*, where she wasted no time calling her lawyer.

He heard her out, then confidently assured her that Tyce's newfound will would easily be proven fraudulent. After hanging up, Delaney calmed down and promised herself not to let Tyce get under her skin again. Taking an apple from the bowl on the counter and opening a ledger bought in Baton Rouge the day before, she started in the bedroom, carefully going through each compartment of the bureau and chest of drawers.

Aunt Donet had excellent and rather expensive taste in clothes. No frumpy old spinster had lived in this house, judging by the dozens of silky scarves, neatly arranged pairs of dressy gloves, and carefully boxed jewelry that Delaney discovered. An array of dresses and suits hung in the walk-in closet and shoes of all sorts were visible in separate see-through plastic boxes stacked in neat rows.

Carefully, Delaney marked down every item. Some of the jewelry she would be happy to keep for herself or her mother. Maybe the lawyer could suggest a charity that would want the other articles.

Delaney sat down on the side of the bed and pulled out a drawer in the bedside table. Inside were a few notepads and pens, a copy of a Mary Higgins Clark mystery, and a small wooden box that held an assortment of photographs, some recent, some old and yellowed. Delaney took up the old ones first, studying each one in an attempt to determine which person might be her great-aunt, for she had only vague childhood memories of her. Unfortunately, there was only one photograph of an elderly woman, and that one was of old Auntie, who had visited her earlier. Maybe Aunt Donet was camera shy.

Delaney picked up a picture of a teenage boy. The photograph was taken at a distance, and Delaney had to bring the picture closer to determine that the boy was a much younger Tyce. He had on a cap and gown and proudly held a diploma in front of him with one hand.

Delaney scrutinized the picture, then dumped the other photographs out onto the bed, looking for more of Tyce. The only other snapshots of interest were two or three of herself shot when she was a toddler. She scooped up all the photos and jiggled them back into a semblance of order so they would fit in the box.

As she was about to put them in, a frayed place in the corner of the box's liner caught her eye. It looked like a little tab. Pulling gently on it, Delaney lifted out the stiff liner. Underneath were two more photographs. Delaney took them out. Both were yellowed and fading. The one on top was of a young man and young woman standing side by side, looking rather self-conscious and not touching one another. The girl looked aside at the tall young man with loving pride. He wore a hat pulled low over his eyes. That, combined with the age of the photograph, made his features hard to distinguish.

Delaney laid that one aside, her attention suddenly captured by the second picture in her hand. It was Tyce again. His light eyes shone with happiness, his mouth drawn back with the laughter that Delaney already knew well. The clothes were old-fashioned and loose on his broad shoulders. He wore boots and held the reins of a horse's bridle in the hand that was jauntily propped on his hip. When was it taken, Delaney wondered, turning the picture over. Scrawled across the back were the words "Lee Brandon, 1920."

Nineteen twenty? Delaney flipped the photo over again and looked more closely. In the background was Caroline, miraculously transformed. Glistening white in the sunlit day, the house was in no danger of falling down. It stood proud, strong, and well-maintained, with a full, blooming garden surrounding the front of the house. And now that she reconsidered the picture in that light, this could not be Tyce; but there was no doubt it was a relative of his. Comparing the two men in the hidden photographs, she saw from the clothes that they were one and the same and probably taken on the same day. Turning over the picture of the couple, she discovered an inscription on the back of it as well: "Lee & Donet."

So this was Aunt Donet when she was young! And her great-aunt had been in love with Lee Brandon, of that Delaney was certain from the look on her aunt's face. Intrigued, Delaney kept the two photographs out, as well as the one of the old woman, placing them carefully in her purse so they would not get bent. She put the rest of Aunt Donet's pictures back and tucked the box away in the drawer.

By the time she finished documenting the rest of the little house, late afternoon shadows slanted through the tall windows of the parlor. She had heard Tyce's truck come and go several times but did not stop her work to see what he was doing. She assumed he was moving his things out of the overseer's cottage, and she didn't want to delay him in any way.

Hunger pains gnawed at her stomach. Delaney poked around in the cabinet, looking for something simple to fix. It figured. Nothing in there looked appetizing, although she had bought groceries only yesterday. At home, she could have called out for Chinese or Mexican or walked a few blocks and found any kind of food that suited her fancy. *What could a person expect, out in the boondocks like this?* she thought impatiently. Clam chowder would have to do.

She took down the can of soup, opened it, and dumped the contents into a small pot, which she set on the stove, adjusting the heat to low so that the chowder would not scorch the bottom of the pot. Humming quietly to herself, she set out a soup bowl and spoon.

"Dear, that smells just wonderful. Whatever is it?"

"Oh, my gosh, you scared me half to death!" Delaney whirled to face the old woman, who was sniffing at the aroma of the chowder. "How did you get in here?"

"You must have left the back door unlocked, dearie."

"I certainly did not. Nor the front one, either. If you have a key, I'd like to have it, please," Delaney demanded. She distinctly recalled locking both doors earlier. And she didn't like these surprise appearances. "While we're at it, what is your last name? Tyce says nobody lives nearby."

The old woman shrugged. *"Well, that Tyce, he is a nice young man,"* she said, then added in a conspiratorial voice, *"but he doesn't know everything."*

"Who are you?" Delaney demanded again. "What's your name?"

"Why, I've been called Auntie for so long that I wouldn't answer to my real name. Are you cooking enough for two?" She peered into the pot.

"I hadn't intended to, but if you want to stay, I could add some milk to the chowder," Delaney offered half-heartedly. Frankly, she did not care to spend the evening with this loony visitor, but the old lady seemed intent on staying, so Delaney decided to make the best of it. "Do you live close? You must walk over here."

"Oh, yes, I live nearby. Very close. Now, you really must make more supper. There's not nearly enough for two."

With effort, Delaney held her irritation in check. How much could a frail thing like that eat? She brought out another bowl, spoon, and napkin. "Well, this is all I'm preparing tonight. It will have to do. What would you care to drink?"

"Oh dear, nothing for me. Nothing at all for me."

"Then for whom?" Delaney wanted to know. *Crazy woman!*

Before Auntie could reply, somebody knocked at the front door.

"Would you mind getting the door?" Delaney said, as she arranged a setting for Auntie on the table.

The old woman just smiled. *"Why don't you get it, dearie."*

With a huff, Delaney tossed the napkin and spoon down. "Fine. You turn off the chowder so it doesn't burn."

Not in the best of moods now, Delaney twisted the dead-bolt knob and yanked the door open. Tyce stood on the tiny porch.

"Busy?" he asked, as if they were the best of friends and he wasn't trying to steal her inheritance from her.

"Yes, I'm cooking dinner," she replied sharply.

"And what are you having?" he inquired, looking around her toward the kitchen.

"Clam chowder. There's only enough in the can for one." She didn't want him getting any ideas about staying for dinner.

"From a can?"

"Yes, if it's any of your business, I like it. Now, I'm hungry." She attempted to close the door, but Tyce braced his hand against it and she could not budge it.

Tyce curled his lip in a gesture of disgust. "You've got to be kidding. I'm hungry, too, but not that hungry. Come on, we'll go get something."

"No thanks."

"Lighten up, Delaney. Where's the harm? Maybe we

can get to know each other a little better. I know you think I'm out to get you, but I'm not. I just want to work out a compromise so that Caroline's not destroyed. Anyway, since you're down here, the least I can do is to introduce you to real food. If there's one thing we have in south Louisiana, it's great food.''

''That might not be a good idea. Sometimes this is all I have time to fix.''

Tyce shook his head solemnly. ''They just don't make girls like they used to, who can cook and clean house and take care of a dozen children at the same time.''

Delaney's eyebrows shot up in surprise as she put her hands on her hips and glared at him. ''Well, thank God. I thought maybe down here they still did.''

Tyce grinned broadly and she saw he had been teasing her.

''Nope, they're ruined everywhere. Get your coat and come on.''

''No thanks, I said. I have my food ready.''

Tyce glanced over her shoulder, then pushed past her, striding toward the kitchen. ''I'd say more than ready. Looks like you've got a fire.''

To Delaney's horror, thick smoke was curling around the door frame separating the living room from the kitchen. ''Oh, my gosh!'' she cried, running after Tyce. ''I told her to turn that stove off.''

The milky chowder was bubbling over onto the stove, sizzling and smoking as it hit the red-hot burner. Tyce grabbed a cloth to wrap around the pot handle, then set the boiling mess down in the sink. He sopped up most of the liquid from the stove top, careful not to let the cloth catch fire. Delaney grabbed a roll of paper towels, catching the scalding chowder as it oozed over the edge of the stove, coughing as she inhaled smoke. Tyce opened the window next to the stove, letting some of the smoke escape into the cool air outside. When there was no more danger of fire or scorching chowder on the stove, he threw the saturated dishcloth into the sink.

"What were you trying to do? Burn the place down just to keep it out of my hands?"

"No! H-honestly," Delaney stammered, "it was supposed to be off."

"If you say so," Tyce said, with a hint of skepticism. "Anyway, I guess you'll have to come with me now—or starve."

"I'll stay and clean this up. Thanks for your help."

Tyce shrugged. "No problem. Just be more careful next time."

"I told Auntie to do it. That'll teach me to check things myself next time."

"Auntie?" Tyce repeated in surprise. "Where do you come up with this Auntie business?"

"She was just here. In here with me. I thought she wanted to stay for dinner, so I . . . She was right here just . . ." Tyce's strange look stopped Delaney midsentence. "Why are you looking at me like that?"

"Because, frankly, I don't understand what's going on here. Somebody's playing a trick on you, but I don't know why—and I don't know who."

"A trick? What do you mean?"

"There's nobody around here called Auntie. I want to know who this woman is. Where is she now?"

"She must have gone out the back door."

Tyce checked the door. "Delaney, it's locked."

"I think she has a key. I asked her to give it to me, but she didn't. Then you knocked, and all this happened. I guess she just went home." Delaney felt a chill run down her spine in spite of her confident words. She was not imagining the strange woman she had seen twice now.

Quickly Tyce searched the other rooms, then came back into the kitchen and shrugged. "Nobody here. Do you believe in ghosts?"

"No, certainly not!" Delaney declared, but she felt shaky inside. She cocked her head to one side, studying Tyce's expression. "Do you?"

He lifted an eyebrow. "They do say this place is haunted. But not by some old woman named Auntie. Chloe's supposedly the resident ghost around here, and I'm not sure she'd take to trespassers."

"And you believe in this Chloe?" Delaney asked skeptically, amazed at this man's audacity in trying to scare her away with ghost stories. Seemed he'd stoop to any depths to get rid of her.

"I was raised on the legend of Chloe. I guess I've always believed in her in a way."

"And you've seen her? You've seen a ghost?"

"I hope not," Tyce muttered, then spoke up, "but Miss Donet claimed Chloe was very active in the months before she died. There were some odd things that happened. Objects out of place, tools hidden, that sort of thing. I didn't pay much attention at the time. I thought Donet was getting senile."

"Well, I'm not senile."

"Never said you were."

"And I'm not seeing ghosts, either."

"Right. I understand. We'll find out who's playing pranks."

"Fine."

"Come on, grab your coat. You can't breathe in here until this smoke clears some. We'll leave the door and windows open so it can air out while we're gone."

When Delaney did not agree at once, Tyce added with a wicked grin, "Or, if you're afraid of ghosts, you can come stay at my place the night. I don't mind."

Delaney narrowed her eyes at him. "You wish," she retorted. She was hungry, and she didn't have a clue where to get anything to eat nearby. Like he said, where was the harm in going to dinner? "Let me change. I can't go like this, in jeans."

"I'm going like this. Trust me, you look great in red."

She really hated to go out to a restaurant in jeans and a sweater, but what the heck, she told herself, when in Rome . . . She got her coat and went with him.

"You've probably never ridden in a pickup, either, have you?" he said, his eyes twinkling like a sun-shot sky.

"No," she said dubiously, "but I suppose I'm going to have that pleasure, too. Where are we going?"

Tyce opened the door of the truck for her and she climbed in. "You'll see."

Delaney gave a wry smile. Tyce went around the truck and got in on the driver's side. The engine fired up easily, then purred like a big, contented kitten until Tyce put it in gear.

Within a few minutes, they were on the interstate, traveling west. Delaney asked twice where they were going and both times Tyce told her she'd see. After that, she contented herself with gazing out the windows at the flat scenery in the gathering dusk. The sun gradually set far across the fields, turning the streaks of wispy clouds into a kaleidoscope of crimson, pink, and gold, ever changing and fading as the light died beyond the horizon.

When they had driven forty-five minutes, with only

trivial conversation between them, Delaney tried again. "Where are you taking me? Am I being kidnapped?"

She was only half joking. Her uncharacteristic trust in this man worried her now that they were in the middle of nowhere. Without question, she had come with him, like an innocent child lured by a seemingly kind stranger. She had no idea where they were headed, and nobody knew they were together.

In fact, when she thought about it, he was not exactly on her side, in spite of his outward geniality. He made no pretense about his intention to take her plantation. Prickles ran down the back of her neck at the thought of what he might have on his mind. What was wrong with her? she thought with a touch of panic. Never would she have taken such a chance in New York and become so complacent with a complete stranger, even one as charming as this one.

He glanced at her with a devilish glint in his eye. "Just be patient. Where's your sense of adventure?" he said with a soothing tone that only set her nerves more on edge.

"I left it in New York. Either tell me where we are going, or put me out!"

He slammed on the brakes so hard that Delaney was thrown forward against her seat belt as he pulled onto the emergency lane. "Here?" he asked with surprise. "Are you sure you want to get out here?"

Tyce nodded toward the window. Lost in her thoughts, Delaney had not noticed where they were. Around her was swamp—nothing but swamp and gathering darkness as far as she could see. The truck was sitting on an endless stretch of elevated highway. Cars and eighteen-wheel trucks whizzed by with such force that the parked pickup rocked with their passing.

"Do you want to get out or not? Let me warn you before you decide, there are alligators in that swamp and worse predators on the roads that might stop to pick you up. You're really safer in here with me." Tyce was grinning. Delaney was furious.

"You're crazy! What do you think you're doing?"

"I'm trying to take you out to dinner. Now, do you want to go, or would you rather try to hitchhike back?"

"I'll go!" Delaney sat back and scowled out the window as he pulled back into the flow of racing traffic as the last light of dusk faded.

They rode in tense silence for a mile or so, then Tyce's voice came to her across the cab of the truck. "I didn't mean to make you angry. I just thought I'd surprise you. It's a little café off the beaten track, owned by an old friend of mine. Thought you might be interested in seeing some of the Cajun culture down here. It's better than sitting home alone in a smoky house with nothing but burned chowder to eat."

Delaney relented a little. "I had some bagels I could toast."

"Oh, brother, I'd hate to see what damage you could do with a toaster," he remarked sarcastically, then grinned at her.

Delaney allowed herself the luxury of laughing. She had to get used to his easygoing, teasing nature. Mark never teased. If anything, he was overly concerned with being serious. And Tyce never seemed to be serious at all—except when it came to Caroline. An interstate sign flashed by: LAFAYETTE 10 MILES.

"Lafayette. Is that where the café is?"

"No, it's before Lafayette. Outside a little town called Henderson. There are several good seafood restaurants in Henderson. We're going to Dupre's. It's a few miles away from the rest of them.''

They left the interstate at the Henderson exit. Tyce drove under the interstate overpass and turned down a road that led past tiny houses with cluttered yards, an old store or two, but mostly flat fields and scattered woods. Finally, ahead, the glow of lights came into view.

One after another, restaurants squatted next to one another, their parking lots filled to varying degrees. The last one, a large, rambling building with a sign outside announcing Pat's, was overflowing with cars. Hoping they were going there, Delaney waited expectantly for Tyce to slow down. He didn't. Instead, he gunned the engine and sent the truck scrambling up the levee. Delaney grabbed the door to steady herself as the truck bucked and slid, finally finding traction on the dirt road that ran along the top of the levee.

She dared not risk being put out in the dark of night on such a desolate stretch of road by asking again where they were going. Had she not seen a sign that actually advertised Dupre's Basin Café, she would have been wary of his intent. In fact, she was, anyway. But she was not going to advertise that she was worried. Not again. Not to him.

For what seemed like ten miles, they bumped along the road. The moon was up, a tiny sliver among the pinpoints of stars. There were more lights in the heavens than Delaney had ever seen before, but there were certainly no lights on earth around here, so far as she could tell.

Wait, did she feel the truck slowing? Surely not. Why would he stop now when he was obviously taking her to the end of the earth for some devious purpose? No, wait. They were slowing down. Delaney looked around. There was nothing here that she could see. No restaurant. No house. No living soul other than Tyce and herself.

The truck lurched over the edge of the levee. For a second, it felt like free fall, then Delaney felt the thud as the tires found ground again. In the pitch dark, the dim squares of buildings stood silhouetted against the faintest twinkle of moonlight on water. But a restaurant? She didn't think so!

Her heart thudded against her ribs with something akin to terror, as six o'clock news scenarios of rape and murder flashed before her eyes. How had she ever let this happen? A woman's worst fears crowded in on her until she could scarcely breathe. Frantically, she searched the darkness for some means of escape, but there would be no chance in this strange place filled with water, swamp, and worse.

Tyce pulled into an open, graveled area and parked the truck. There were two other vehicles nearby, both trucks, and both sported loaded gun racks across the back glass.

"If you think I'm getting out here . . ." Delaney began, trying to sound more in control than she felt.

"Suit yourself. You'll miss the best étouffée in Louisiana, though. And the bread pudding is indescribable."

Tyce came around the truck and opened the door, propping his foot on the running board and looking at her with that reasonable look of his that infuriated her and replaced some of her trepidation with angry bravado.

"And who am I going to dance with after dinner?" he cajoled.

"Dance? Where are you going to dance? Where are you going to eat? There's nothing here!"

"Trust me," he said, his eyes locking onto hers.

"Where? I don't even see a light."

"Trust me."

Delaney attempted a look that expressed her exact feelings. Her stomach rumbled with hunger, protesting her stubbornness. Maybe she would at least get out of the truck and go inside. It was not that those delving blue eyes of his could charm the alligators out of the swamp. It was just that no other rational choice presented itself, and she was too hungry to sit in that cold truck and starve while he enjoyed himself inside—if there were really a restaurant tucked away somewhere in the darkness among the other buildings.

She slid out of the truck, then felt Tyce's hand touch the small of her back, guiding her gently across the expanse of gravel. As they turned the corner of the building, Delaney saw steps and a porch, with a single lightbulb burning in the middle of it, which had very little effect on the night. Beyond that, a long breezeway ran down the side of the building, with several windows along its length. Muted light flowed from them onto the ground beneath. Going up the steps, Delaney braced for whatever other surprises might befall her that night.

A rush of rich aroma met them as Tyce opened the door. Seafood, spices, coffee. She breathed in the wonderful air and looked around in pleasant surprise at the interior of the café. It was quaintly rustic, with rough-hewn, exposed wooden beams overhead and an occasional mounted fish or cheap poster on the walls. Two couples were laughing and talking at a bar on one side of the room, while their young children played underneath the bar stools.

As Delaney and Tyce came into the room, the men and women glanced their way. The looks lingered curiously on her, she noticed, though everyone, including the children, greeted Tyce amiably. All the tables were empty, and Tyce led her to one by the windows, though nothing could be seen outside in the unbroken night.

A man came to their table from behind the bar and cordially extended his hand to Tyce.

"Hey, Tyce, long time, man," he said, his words having a strange inflection that Delaney had never heard before. His gaze fell momentarily but appreciatively upon Delaney, then wandered back to Tyce.

"This is Delaney Bienville," Tyce said. "Delaney, Alphonse Dupre, the owner. This is a real Cajun, in case you ever want to say you've met one. And he'll be happy to introduce you to the best food in the world and the best dancing afterward. When's the band coming?"

"Be along 'fore long, don't you worry none. Me, I got my squeeze box and Cousin René's here already. Time you finish you étouffée, we'll be cooking."

"Good. Bring me a bowl of turtle soup to start, and bring the lady a sampling of all the good stuff," Tyce said.

"Sure 'nuff. You kin to the Bienvilles from Caroline?" Alphonse asked, his dark eyes studying Delaney without apology.

"Yes, Miss Donet Bienville was my great-aunt."

"Ah, den you got to be 'Tee-Joe's daughter."

"I beg pardon?" Delaney said in confusion.

" 'Tee-Joe. That means little Joe," Tyce explained.

"Yes, that's right. Joseph Bienville was my father," Delaney said, trying to be courteous in spite of this man's forwardness. However, she did not offer any further information. She certainly did not want to get embroiled in a conversation about her father here with this stranger.

"So, you still gone have Tyce restore the old place? You seen what he's done to the ballroom? *Mais chére*, ain't it somethin' else what he done to that room?"

Perplexed, Delaney turned to Tyce. He had acted like the ballroom had been locked for years. He avoided her look.

"We're starving, Alphonse. How about that food?" he said with emphasis. As if by some code, Alphonse cut his questions short and left for the kitchen, sending over a waitress who had been leaning on the bar, talking.

"What about the ballroom?" Delaney pressed, ignoring the waitress who brought a basket of bread and glasses of water.

"Nothing," Tyce said. "Alphonse was just talking."

"I thought the ballroom had been locked for a long time. You said the key was gone."

"No, I said I didn't have the key with me. I'll have to find it or try to pick the lock. You'll get in, don't worry."

"Oh, I know I'll get in, one way or another," Delaney said with determination. "Not that it matters much. It'll all be gone in a few days."

Tyce gave her a glowering look, but the waitress set dishes of coleslaw in front of them, and he did not comment. By the time they finished the last of the tasty coleslaw, the waitress was back with huge plates of steaming food. Delaney could not identify anything on her plate, but there was enough of it for three people. Tyce's dark, thick turtle soup was in a bowl that resembled a tureen in size.

"I can't eat all of this!" Delaney said, though as hungry as she was and as delicious as it smelled, she thought she might come close.

Tyce began to identify the different dishes to her: seafood gumbo in a cup beside her plate, sausage and chicken jambalaya, crawfish étouffée on steaming rice, a mound of fried crab claws, a half dozen boiled shrimp, and stuffed crabs baked in the shells.

"I would have ordered you a little fried alligator, but I didn't think you were ready for that yet."

"Thanks for your consideration," Delaney said with caustic sarcasm. "I'm not sure I'm ready for all this."

"Try it. If you don't like it, I'll eat it and order you a grilled cheese or something ordinary like that. Alphonse might even have a can of clam chowder back there somewhere." Tyce took a piece of bread from the basket, broke and buttered it, then started on his soup.

Delaney glared at him for a minute, but he ignored her. She picked up her fork and poked around on her plate, deciding at last to take a tiny nibble of the concoction he had called étouffée. It was spicy and laden with bits of green pepper, onion, and small pink lumps that resembled shrimp, but which Tyce said were crawfish. The taste of the stew was delightful. After that, trying the rest of the food was easy. Everything was equally good, and to her surprise, she finished every last bite, including the gumbo. Tyce, in the meantime, downed his soup, a platter piled high with étouffée and rice, and two beers.

While they were eating, other customers came in. Alphonse went personally to each table, making friend and stranger equally welcome. He dropped by their table a couple of times to ask how Delaney liked his cooking. She assured him it was some of the best food she had ever had. He seemed pleased and joked with Tyce, though he never mentioned Caroline again.

"Now for the bread pudding," Tyce said, as the plates were being taken away and Alphonse came by again.

"I can't eat another thing," Delaney protested.

"Sure, you can. You don't want to miss this. Besides, I'll see that you work it off in a few minutes."

Delaney shot him a look. Surely he did not think that just because he had invited her out to eat that she would . . . would . . .

Tyce grinned at her, then nodded his head toward the corner of the room. "The band's about to play. I meant we could dance."

Why was she always reading something bad into what he said? Why not just relax and enjoy the night? Why not? Because there was something about being around him that made her uncomfortable. She was not accustomed to such relaxed familiarity from anybody, much less the raw masculinity that exuded from his very being.

He was a perplexing blend of physical strength, confidence, and a gentle chivalry foreign to her. And lord, he was attractive. The more she saw of him, the more obvious that became. But she couldn't let her guard down. This was just another of his ploys to trick her into relinquishing Caroline.

The bread pudding was brought, and though she was about to explode from all the other food, there was no way to resist the slab of heavy, rich, moist cake with brandy-laced sugar sauce ladled over the top and running down the sides.

As they were finishing dessert and coffee, the band struck up. Delaney listened with interest. The sound was totally alien. There were drums, a fiddle, a guitar, and of all things, an accordion. The music had an odd, thumping beat, and Alphonse was singing in French. Two songs later, Delaney realized that all the music had a sameness to it: a high-pitched cacophony, almost a wail, punctuated now and then by a shrill yell that sounded like *aye-eeee*.

A man and woman from the bar ambled over to a spot of bare floor where there were no tables. They began to dance. Delaney stared. The man held the woman's hand far out beside them, and his other hand was placed carefully at her back as he led her around the tiny floor in a shuffling two-step. Now and then he would release her back and twirl her around and catch her again in their original position, or she would step beside him and skim along with him for a few steps.

"Come on, are you ready to dance?" Tyce asked, scraping his chair back from the table.

Delaney hesitated. "I don't know how to do that."

Tyce took her hand and led her onto the floor. "Just follow," he commanded. "It's nothing but a two-step."

Within minutes, Delaney had mastered the movement well enough to enjoy it. The warmth and strength of Tyce's hand holding hers and his firm guidance at her back was reassuring and comforting.

When Tyce asked if she wanted to dance again, there was no hesitation in her yes. The music played and they danced again and again. After almost an hour, the band took a break. Tyce and Delaney walked out onto the porch that ran around three sides of the building. Looking down over the railing, Delaney realized that the structure was elevated on pilings, and that they were standing over the black water of the swamp. Delaney could make out the barely visible outline of trees and stumps forming a distant, jagged horizon. She shivered at the thought of the desolation of that expanse of water. Tyce's arm slipped around her shoulders.

"Cold?" he said quietly. "Do you want to go back in?"

"No, I'm fine. I was just thinking about how lonely the swamp looks at night. I would hate to be out there."

"It's not so bad, as long as you know where you are and what to do."

"Do you go out there?"

"I used to trap and fish in the summers for the restaurants around here. Worked several summers for Alphonse's daddy. Once in a while, I'd be out too far to come back in, so I'd make a camp for the night. Actually, it's peaceful until the alligators start bellowing. Then it's hard to sleep."

"I wouldn't like it, so don't plan on a swamp excursion," Delaney said at once, before he got any ideas. She heard the strains of the band starting again.

"Where's your sense of adventure?" he teased. "Let's go back in and dance."

There were no dining customers left in the restaurant, though several people were still at the bar or dancing. By now, Delaney had figured out that most of them were either regulars or relatives. Alphonse called them all "Cousin." They seemed to know Tyce well and Delaney could feel their unspoken curiosity about her. Apparently, these people considered it some sort of honor that Tyce had brought her.

Around midnight, people began to drift out of the building. Soon, only Alphonse, the waitress, and two others besides the band remained. As she became more accustomed to the unfamiliar dance steps, Delaney realized that sometimes she and Tyce were two-stepping and other times, waltzing. When she mentioned it, Tyce confirmed that a Cajun band generally alternated two-step and waltz numbers.

They danced almost every dance, skipping one or two to get a drink and stand at the bar in conversation with the locals. The counter was clean, the tables wiped and made ready for the next day. Alphonse told the waitress she could go home and sent the cooks off as well. When he came back into the dining room, he picked up his accordion, his squeeze box, as he fondly called it.

"Say, Tyce, man. I know how you like all that rock and roll. Here's the one you like 'bout the lady in the red dress. This last one's just for you and your lady in red."

Alphonse winked and grinned at Tyce as he turned and said something in a low voice to the other musicians. As the chords of the guitar sounded, the fiddle turned into a concert violin in the hands of the masterful player. Alphonse's deep, melodious voice began, his thick Cajun inflection all but lost as he sang the words to "Lady in Red."

Without a word, Tyce took Delaney into his arms. Close. So close that she breathed in his clean, earthy scent as he swept her slowly across the floor in smooth rhythm to the beautiful melody. His body moved against hers with tantalizing firmness, hard muscle against yielding softness. In her ear, his breath sent shivers down her spine as he sang the words softly along with Alphonse.

Delaney closed her eyes and listened to his voice, enthralled by the mellow words of the song and the warmth of his breath on her face. Tyce never missed a word. He knew the song as well as Alphonse, his voice pure and clear.

Captured by the mood, Delaney moved willingly with him, content in his arms, responding to his caress as he drew her hand up, still enclosed in his own, to brush her cheek with the backs of his fingers. If the song and the night had lasted forever, Delaney thought she might gladly give up a few decades of her life to stay there. She had not felt so carefree in years.

The last notes died in the quiet air of the café. For a long minute, Tyce simply kept on dancing in the silence, his face pressed against her hair, their hands still clasped together, drawn into the warmth between their bodies.

Alphonse cleared his throat. Delaney started at the sound. Opening her eyes, she realized that every person in the café was watching them. Embarrassed, she pushed away from Tyce.

"*Mais,* yeah, Tyce! You better watch what you got there." Alphonse laughed. "She got you by the tail, man."

"It's your own damn fault, Alphonse. You know not to play that song," Tyce joked in return. "Anyway, I'd better get her home, else she'll never go anywhere with me again."

"You come back here with Tyce again, you hear? You always welcome here," Alphonse called to her.

"I will if I have time," Delaney said, hoping the dimness of the café hid the warm blush that she knew covered her face. Tyce brought her coat and they said good-bye and left. As they walked toward the truck, he put his arm around her again and drew her close to his body. She didn't resist, wanting to prolong for a few minutes more the secure warmth she felt when she was close to him.

"My surprise wasn't so bad after all, was it?" he asked.

"It was a very nice night. Thank you," Delaney said honestly. "I just didn't know what to expect."

"Next week, we'll go to New Orleans."

"I doubt I'll be here next week. I have to get everything finished at the house as quickly as I can. I didn't expect to find so much to take care of."

"It'll take you longer than a week," Tyce said, his voice confident. "I'll see to that."

Not a chance, Delaney thought, realizing just how much she had enjoyed Tyce's company that night. *I can't afford to stay here another week.*

He opened the truck door and helped her in. The drive down the levee was not nearly as long going back as it had been getting to the restaurant. It had been a thoroughly enjoyable experience, an adventure Delaney would not forget. Tyce was an interesting man, and she wanted to understand more about him.

"You know, all of you have me at a disadvantage. Everybody seems to know who I am, but I don't know anything about them—or you," she said.

"Where do you want to start?"

"I'm not exactly sure," Delaney said, caught off guard by his apparent willingness to talk about himself. "Are you from New Bienville? Where is your family? How did you get to know my aunt?" She thought of the pictures in her purse and was about to ask him, but he started talking and didn't give her a chance.

"I was born in New Bienville. My mother still lives there and my sister Maddie goes to LSU in Baton Rouge. I've known Miss Donet all my life. She's always been at Caroline. What else?"

"How long have you lived at the plantation?"

"Almost a year now. Miss Donet had a dream to see the place put right again, restored to what it once was. She had me file an application to place it on the historic register, but those people have been dragging their feet for months. There was a lot of work that needed to be done, and she couldn't really afford to hire outside people, so I agreed to move in and do the work—in return for the plantation after she died.''

''Are you a carpenter, then?'' she asked, not wanting to follow that lead into another argument.

Tyce gave a low grunt. ''Yeah, you might say that. Jack of all trades is what I've become lately. Doing everything myself's not as fast as having a crew come in, but at least I know it's done right.''

''Why?'' Delaney asked pointedly. ''Why bother? The place looks like it's about to fall down. Why not just let it?''

''I told you before; it's not about to fall down. It's as sound as a dollar. Granted, there's a hell of a lot of work left to do, but it's far from falling down.''

''Well, I wish things could have worked out for you.'' Delaney nestled against the seat and leaned her head back drowsily.

''Caroline has stood almost unchanged since before the Civil War. The walls, the ceilings, the roof, the cellar. Nothing much has been modified, almost everything is original. That can't be said for most of these old plantation houses. They have been remodeled and modernized until they are ruined. Caroline deserves better than that.''

''So, what would you do if it were up to you?''

''I'd restore it. Make it just the way it used to be in its glory days. It was a fabulous plantation, Caroline was. The most modern house of its time. It had hot and cold running water, unheard of in the 1850s when it was constructed, and the craftsmanship that went into building the house was phenomenal. That's why it has endured. It's a sin to destroy that.''

"Be that as it may, I can't keep it. I don't want to live in it, and even if I did, I don't have the money to fix it. Is that what you wanted to do? Restore it and live there?" Delaney knew that there was a trace of smugness in her voice, though she did not mean to be unkind. But it was unrealistic for anybody to harbor such grandiose ideas, especially if he had no expertise in restoration. Besides, how could he afford such an undertaking if he had not been working for months?

Tyce caught the insinuation. "You saying there's something wrong with that?"

"No. It seems like a grand, impossible dream. Can you pay for all that work?"

"Nothing's impossible," Tyce said shortly. "It would take time, and I would have to do most of the work, but I can make it happen."

"Just how would you go about it, then? What about the research and the skilled work that would have to be done? How would you pay for all that? I mean, does a carpenter make that much money down here?"

"I have money in savings. How much is the offer you got for it?" he hedged.

"Three million."

She heard the whistling intake of breath from the other side of the truck. "Jesus," he said softly.

She sensed a change in Tyce's manner, a terseness in his voice that had not been there before and knew instinctively that he could not match that offer.

"I can't believe you would sell this plantation to some . . . some outsider who has no more inkling about its real value than you do!" Tyce automatically turned off the interstate at the correct exit. He braked hard at the stop sign at the end of the exit ramp. When the truck stopped, he turned to her.

"Let's find some compromise, Delaney, between you and me. I may not be able to come up with as much money as some corporation, but I can sure do a damned sight better by Caroline than anybody else can. You're a Bienville. Your history is part of that plantation as much as anybody's."

Delaney turned away to look out into the darkness. She didn't understand. And regardless of Tyce's deep emotion over this plantation, she could not afford to pass up this opportunity just to appease his yearning for a past that was dead and gone.

When she did not respond, Tyce stomped the gas pedal to the floor, leaving a shrieking trail of rubber on the highway. They rode the rest of the way to Caroline in stony silence. Tyce walked her to the door without a word, but just as she was going inside, he caught her by the arm. "I want to work this out, Delaney. I want a solution that's fair because you and I belong here, both of us. But, understand me well, I will not let you destroy Caroline, even if it means fighting you to the bitter end. I won't give up—and you won't put a mall here."

"I'm sorry, Tyce. I have to consider my best interests. I just don't feel the same sentimentality toward the place as you do. I want the money."

"You're destroying a link to the past that can never be recovered! To your past and to mine," Tyce shot back angrily. "I guess I shouldn't have expected any better from a Yankee!"

"Yankee? That's stupid. That war is over, Tyce, and has been for a hundred years! Why can't you people put it behind you and get on with life?"

Between gritted teeth, Tyce growled back, "Because the destruction never ends. It just never ends."

Chapter Six

Restlessly, Tyce rolled over in bed again. Morning already! His body was tired, but his fuming mind had not let him rest during the night. Confusing and aggravating thoughts of Delaney materialized whenever he closed his eyes to sleep.

Dancing with her the evening before, he had felt an overpowering urge to kiss those inviting lips. The memory of how she felt in his arms lured his mind to more intimate ideas. He had hoped for a more fulfilling evening, intending to get to know Delaney better, to comprehend what was driving her to sell Caroline without a second thought.

The mere mention of the plantation started up another argument. It was going to be difficult to come to any understanding when the one thing they needed to discuss rationally was the one thing they could not mention at all without a flare-up of temper on both sides.

Tyce sat up in bed and ran his fingers through his hair. Damn it, he didn't have time to play games. He could not stand by and let all his dreams disappear before his eyes. Whether Delaney Bienville agreed or not, losing Caroline forever was unthinkable.

The sound of thunder rumbling outside cut through his drowsiness. Pulling on a pair of jeans, he went to the front door to watch the rain pour down. Gushers of water spouted from the gutters and drains. Puddles had already formed in the driveway and low areas of the neglected gardens. Rain soaked into the furrows of the sugarcane fields nearest the house, nourishing the second-year stubble in the ground as it waited out the winter, ready to send up tender shoots in the spring.

This land was a part of Tyce. He had lived almost all his life in the shadow of Caroline. His grandfather had been a sugarcane planter until Gran moved to New Orleans society and forced Grandpa to go with her. Then Tyce's father Paul had taken over, leasing the fields from the Bienvilles so that he could stay on the plantation. Tyce's father could barely scrape a decent living from the land, but he wouldn't have been happy anyplace else. The family had subsisted at poverty level most of the time, for Paul Brandon was too proud to beg money from his own mother who, over the decades, became wealthy dealing in the New Orleans antiques trade and who did not share her son's passion for Caroline.

When he was growing up, Tyce wouldn't bring friends home to the tiny, unpainted shotgun house where he lived in the shadow of the mansion that should have been his ancestral home. There was no way to explain that all this—the land, the house, the heritage—should have been his, that it was stolen from his family a century ago. He was too proud to play that game, using the might-have-been that was changed by a twist of history to pretend he was something that he obviously wasn't.

His father worked as hard as he could to keep the family fed and clothed. Paul Brandon's eyes, when he stared wistfully at the old house for minutes at a time, were the only gauge of the loss he felt, the emptiness of soul that he had inherited from his father and his uncle Lee. But Tyce had seen the sadness, had felt the loss along with his daddy as he helped work the land that should have belonged to them.

In order to satisfy his father's need for Caroline, the family had settled for a spartan, difficult life, but Tyce's parents gave him and his sister an abundance of the important things—love, attention, discipline—and they always managed to scrape up enough money for one special interest for each child. For Maddie it was piano lessons; for Tyce, baseball.

What kept him from bringing all but his one close friend home was the cruelty of other kids. He heard them make fun of his father when Paul came to Tyce's baseball games straight from the fields in his dirty work clothes and heavy boots because it was important for him to be there.

Only Alphonse had been admitted into Tyce's private life. Alphonse could come to the tiny house and act as happy as if he were in a mansion, and Tyce could go home with him to his shack on the bayou and feel the same way. That as much as anything had cemented a friendship between them that had lasted over the years. Tyce was glad Alphonse was doing well with his café on the Atchafalaya Basin. If anybody deserved good fortune, Alphonse did.

Tyce had been nearly grown when his father died in a farm accident. Soon afterward, his mother moved the family into New Bienville, renting the small house she still lived in. Tyce had taken whatever jobs he could find in order to help his mother pay the bills.

His grandfather had always expected him to go to college and had set up a trust fund before he died to provide the money. His grandmother made sure that Grandpa's wishes were carried out. Tyce had graduated in record time with a degree in architecture and design and had risen quickly in the architectural arena, able within a few years to pick and choose his projects. When he was able, Tyce had bought his mother's house and given it to her.

A partnership in a prominent New Orleans firm had promised a secure future, but it wasn't enough. Although his mother never missed Caroline—in a way she even blamed the plantation for her husband's death—Tyce felt as if a piece of him were missing, as if he were no longer grounded but cut loose and drifting.

When the opportunity to work on Caroline had come up, he had taken an extended leave from the firm, over his family's shocked objections. Having lived from hand to mouth all their lives, his mother and sister expected him to starve to death within a short time. But he had plenty of money stashed away to live well for a long time—just not enough to match Delaney's offer for Caroline.

It seemed sometimes that from his earliest memory, Tyce's self-image had been linked to Caroline—or rather, to the loss of Caroline. Regaining the status his family had once enjoyed in New Bienville had dominated most of his life decisions from the time he was a child, and to give up now would be utter failure. Tyce was not ready to face that possibility. He didn't know if he ever could.

The haze of rain clouded Tyce's eyes as he watched the gentle readying of the land for its annual rebirth. How would he survive away from this place? It was his land, by God. His land by rights. And he was going to have it!

Glancing toward the mansion, he noticed that there were lights on downstairs. Delaney must already be in there, cataloging everything inside for disposal to perfect strangers. Tyce set his jaw in determination. He was going to slow her down any way he could, either by charm or by force.

In his strange dream, Chloe had mandated that he marry Delaney. He still thought it odd that Delaney's name had come to him in a dream, but maybe he had heard it someplace else and forgotten. He could just imagine her reaction to that idea; besides, she was willful and stubborn, and she'd probably make life hell for a husband. Marriage between the two of them was not a likely option, which meant that Tyce's most pressing problem was how to keep a close eye on her so that she did not pull some slick trick that would destroy Caroline before he had a chance to interfere.

He closed the door, took a quick shower, and made coffee, hoping the rain would let up before he went out into it. Half an hour and two cups of coffee later, he resigned himself to the fact that he was going to get wet. Grabbing his umbrella from the rack by the door, he ran the distance from the cottage to the house. The door was unlocked. He had made a duplicate key for Delaney so she could get in when she wanted to.

Searching for her, Tyce made his way as far as the front parlor, stopping in the doorway. Delaney sat in the middle of the floor with a notepad in one hand and a pencil in the other, writing. All the furniture in the room was uncovered, and she had brought out dishes and serving pieces from the butler's pantry nearby.

Her hair fell in loose, silky curls around her face, glistening in the light like the rich mahogany of the furniture. Concentrating on her notes, she did not realize he was there. He took the opportunity to study her face, a lovely, sweet face, when she was not on her guard. Tyce felt a surge of arousal as she bit her lower lip for a thoughtful moment before her pencil scratched across the paper again. A dark fringe of curling lashes brushed her smooth skin. Tyce wanted to do the same. Her skin had been soft to his touch last night when they danced, her smell exotic and tantalizing, the womanliness of her so very enticing.

He wished she were somebody else, that she did not stand like a rock barrier between him and his dreams. Because, as much as he tried to deny it and in spite of their differences over Caroline, he was drawn to this woman with a force he had never known before.

She looked up and caught him staring.

"I didn't hear you come in."

Tyce looked around the room at Miss Donet's treasures. "Doing your inventory?"

"Yes, I've made a good start," she said, getting up and dusting off her jeans. She wore a pale yellow knit shirt that molded to the lines of her body better than the red sweater had and made the contrast of her dark eyes and hair startling.

When she smiled at him, Tyce felt something melt inside. Damn it, he didn't need his feelings getting in the way of business, but he knew instinctively that he was in trouble.

"You know, if you want any of the furniture or dishes or anything, you can have them. That seems only fair," she said.

Fair? Tyce thought ruefully. *Fair was getting Caroline.* But all he said was, "We can work that out later."

"Actually, I'm glad you're here. I'm almost finished with the downstairs, and you said not to go upstairs without you. Do you have time to show me the bad places in the floor?"

"Sure. Today's a good day. Nothing to be done outside."

Delaney brought her pad and pencil and went with him up the stairs. She glanced back at the locked doors of the ballroom. "I need to get in there, too. Have you located a key yet?"

"No, not yet," Tyce replied evasively. "Exactly what are you doing? Just writing down everything that's here?"

"Yes, and trying to assign some sort of value. But I have to admit, I'm out of my league on that. I have no idea what these old pieces might bring. I get the feeling from looking at the condition in which they've been kept, that some of them are priceless."

"No doubt." Tyce didn't bother to tell her that no amount of money could match their value, as far as he was concerned. To him they were pieces of history, of his own history and that of the people who had lived here in another era. To her, they were just sticks of furniture, going to the highest bidder. Lost in thought, he had not been paying attention to what she was saying, but her last few words tolled in his head.

". . . finish by tomorrow, then I'll be able to book a flight home by the end of the week."

Tyce felt a knot form in his stomach. He had thought

how nice it would be if he had never met her, but now that he had, he did not like the idea of her going back to New York. In his mind, he began to believe that as long as she stayed, Caroline stayed. At least the legal complications posed by his possession of the new will would detain her a while. He'd call his lawyer to make sure the new documents got to Delaney tomorrow. That should give her something to think about.

"Listen, you shouldn't just sell this furniture at any price. Like you said, some of the pieces are valuable. You need to get them appraised first."

Delaney looked doubtful. "I don't know. I can't spend weeks doing this. Maybe I'll just take my chances."

"My grandmother's an expert on antiques. Why don't I take you to New Orleans to meet her? I might be able to persuade her to send somebody up to have a look. She might want to buy some of these things herself."

"Well, that sounds sensible. Can we go tomorrow?"

"No," Tyce hedged. He wanted to keep her in Louisiana as long as possible. "Probably not until Saturday. Gran's usually busy during the week."

"Saturday," Delaney said with an edge of disappointment. "I'd hoped to be home by then."

"Well, have it your way, but it would be well worth staying a few extra days, trust me. You'll kick yourself later when you find out how much money you lost selling these antiques without knowing their true value."

"Oh, all right. I'll stay the weekend."

"Fine. I'll call Gran and tell her we're coming on Saturday," he said, relieved to have a few more days to work on Delaney's resolve.

Room by room, they went through the upstairs. Around noon, they stopped and had a sandwich and a soft drink, then went back to work. By four o'clock, Delaney had jotted down every piece of furniture, every knickknack, everything even remotely notable about the old house.

"Now I want to go up in the attic," she announced, opening the door that led up the stairs.

"Today?"

"Yes. Why not? Are you busy?"

"No, I'm not busy. Like I said, there's not much to be done in the rain. But there are dozens and dozens of trunks up there. Let's save that for later."

"I don't have time to wait. You're just trying to stall me. Either come with me, or I go by myself," she said firmly.

She was the most willful girl ever born! But Tyce wanted to placate her, so he went up the stairs into the dark attic and found the cord to the light. A dull glow filtered down around them. The floor of the attic had been severely damaged over the years by leaks in the roof. Tyce had been afraid the floor was going to give way, so one of the first things he had done was to build a walkway and lay temporary plywood flooring around the perimeter of the room to support the heavy trunks.

He tested each board before he allowed Delaney to step off the stairs. Around them and piled far back into the recesses of the attic were large leather-bound trunks, furniture, children's rocking horses and wagons, and box after box stacked on top of one another around the perimeter of the sloping roof.

Gazing around him, Tyce blew out his breath. "Are you sure you want to do this?"

Even Delaney looked daunted by the sheer amount of stuff up there.

"Well, let's at least have a look in some of the

trunks,'' she said. ''I'd like to get an idea what's in them. We may find they are not worth the effort it will take to go through them. In that case, they can go with the rest of the house.''

Tyce winced. ''I wish you'd stop saying that. This house is not going anywhere.''

''Give it a rest, Tyce. You know you're not going to win. My lawyer told me you won't even say where you found that so-called second will. It's going to be thrown out as a fake, and you know it.''

''It's not a fake. You and I are going to have to come to terms on this.''

Without waiting for her protest, Tyce pulled one of the heavy trunks over to where she waited. The floor creaked beneath the weight of it. He situated it so that it sat over the supporting joists, then pried the latch open. Inside were old newspapers dated from around 1860. Beneath those were clothes. Delaney began to pull out the articles of clothing slowly and carefully.

''Look how lovely!'' She held up an intricate lace shawl and wrapped it around her shoulders.

Tyce thought it was indeed beautiful on her. He was surprised to realize how much he enjoyed being around her when they weren't fighting about the plantation.

Bending over the trunk, she lifted out other shawls and handkerchiefs and a pair of satin shoes whose leather soles were worn thin. Digging deeper, she discovered letters and ledgers, but nothing else.

''Bring another one over,'' she entreated, her face alight with the pleasure of discovery.

Tyce smiled at her enthusiasm. He had not expected her to be interested in the contents of the trunks any more than she had been in Caroline itself. He enjoyed seeing what was in the trunks, too, for he had not had time to prowl around the attic.

One after another, he dragged the nearest trunks over and they went through them together. Most of the items inside were mundane, but an occasional treasure was unearthed among the worthless.

"This will have to be the last one. My back's about to break," Tyce told her as he replaced the trunk they had just finished repacking and started to drag another one out.

"All right," Delaney said reluctantly. "But I want to come back tomorrow."

Tyce did not comment, but inwardly, he was pleased. He positioned the trunk safely, then opened it. A faded and tattered woolen sash and an old sword in a cracked leather scabbard had been placed carefully on top of the other articles. This time it was Tyce who reached in and brought out the sword, turning it over in his hands as he examined it in the poor light. It was a Civil War officer's sword. He slipped it out of the scabbard a few inches. The steel blade was as clean and sharp as the day it was made.

"Look, Tyce."

Pushing the sword back down into its protective sheath, Tyce laid it aside to see what Delaney had found. In her hand was a bundle of scarlet satin. The cool, slick surface of the cloth stood out against the ordinary clothing in the trunk. Slowly, she loosened the red material from its meticulous folds, then stood to display her discovery completely. As the voluminous dress unwound to the floor, a dainty, white leather-bound book dropped at Delaney's feet with a soft thud. Tyce picked it up.

"It's magnificent," Delaney cried, holding the satin ball gown against her waist and up to her shoulders. "It needs a bit of work to get the wrinkles out, but isn't it beautiful?''

"It is," Tyce agreed. Red was this girl's color, he realized at once. Her face was glowing with delight over the dress.

"What's that book?" Delaney held out one hand for the white book in Tyce's hands.

He turned it over and looked at the engraving. "I don't believe it," he muttered, closing his eyes against the sudden rush of apprehension that flooded through him. He knew without even looking at it again where he had seen that dress before and who must have been wearing it. But that had been a dream. It had to be a dream when he had seen the magnificent gown on the stranger in the ballroom—on Chloe Bienville.

He didn't want to believe in ghosts anymore. Not even Chloe. Not even after Miss Donet's will had turned up so mysteriously. He couldn't explain what was going on, but he was not going to admit to seeing ghosts.

"Let me see the book," Delaney pressed, reaching to take it from his hands. She still held the dress across her body. "Chloe Delane Bienville."

"Who is Chloe Delane Bienville? She had my name."

"Or maybe you have hers? She lived here after the Civil War," Tyce explained, enthralled by Delaney's doe-brown eyes, alight with curiosity as she waited for him to go on. "I told you that people say she haunts Caroline, waiting for her lost lover to return from the war."

"Oh, really?" Delaney asked skeptically. "You keep trying to scare me off with that haunted house tale, don't you?"

"No, I swear it," Tyce said, crossing his heart with

his hand. "You see, according to family legend, almost every generation of our families has seen a Brandon man in love with a Bienville woman. And it began with Chloe Bienville. Just at the start of the war, she was in love with Zach Brandon, one of the sons of a wealthy planter who had left Virginia to settle in Louisiana. Zach's father built Caroline, then died a few years afterward. When the war broke out, young Zach, zealous like the rest of the Rebels, couldn't wait to join the fray. There was a grand ball here at Caroline to send the boys off with glory. Chloe had a red ball gown made, maybe even that one you've got."

Delaney glanced down at the red satin she still held against her, then looked back to Tyce with fascinated eyes.

"Chloe danced with Zach the whole night long, and during that time, he proposed to her. Her father, Pierre, was totally against the union because of a long-running dispute between the two families over a piece of land claimed by both. I would imagine he also considered the Brandons to be unacceptable because they were of English ancestry and the Bienvilles, French. Undeterred, Zach supposedly gave Chloe the priceless Brandon rubies as a betrothal gift and promised to return and marry her in spite of her father. Then he went off to war the next morning. She waved good-bye to him from one of the windows at Caroline, still in her red ball gown."

"Poor thing," Delaney murmured, sitting down with the dress still clutched in her hands. "So what happened when he returned? Did they get married?"

"Zach didn't come back. They say Chloe could never accept that he was dead. Rumor was that old Pierre killed him in a drunken rage in New Orleans because he would not give up the idea of marrying Chloe."

"Surely not!" Delaney protested softly. "A father would never be that cruel."

"Well, that part was never proven. But old Pierre wasn't a saint by any stretch, I assure you. Times were harsh after the war. Most of the remaining planter families were physically and financially devastated. Pierre had managed to hold on to his wealth by hook and crook, sucking up to Confederate or Yankee, as the occasion warranted. After the war, he paid the exorbitant taxes on Caroline, moved the Brandon women out into the street, and brought his own family here to live. They say Chloe slowly lost her mind, living in the very house she would have shared with Zach. Every day she put on a red gown and went to the window to wait for Zach. Until the day she died, she stood by the window, waiting. And she went to her grave without ever revealing the location of the fabulous rubies, if she ever had them."

Delaney looked at him intently for a long moment. "You like that story, don't you?"

"Yeah, I guess I do, in a way. At least, I used to." Tyce was beginning to wish he had never heard the tale.

"You'd like a woman to pine away for you like that? Go crazy waiting all her life for you?"

"No. Not necessarily. But it would be nice to think she'd wait a little while for me before she gave up."

"Well, don't think I'd ever do that for anybody!"

"No? Not even for me? I'm crushed. Whatever happened to true love?"

"I don't call that true love—expecting somebody to sacrifice her entire life waiting for something that's never going to happen."

"It was Chloe's decision, I'd think. Anyway, don't

worry about it. I certainly don't expect that from anybody. Not anymore," Tyce said sharply.

"What do you mean, 'anymore'?" Delaney asked, her eyes boring into his.

Tyce shifted uncomfortably, wishing they had never begun this conversation. "Never mind; that's another story. Try it on," he said, to change the subject.

"Try it on?" Delaney repeated in surprise, drawing the dress snugly around her waist. "I don't know if I should. It might tear."

"It looks like it would fit. Try it on. Let's see what you'd look like if you did decide to pine away for me," Tyce encouraged. "Go behind that stack of boxes and put it on. I promise not to look."

"Sure."

She spoke sarcastically, but he could see that she was intrigued by the gown.

"I won't move, I swear. I want to see it on you. Seems like a shame to let tradition die with us. I mean, I'm the last Brandon man left, and you may well be the last Bienville woman. Chloe might be pleased if we got married, finally brought the Brandons and Bienvilles together." Tyce said the words jokingly, but all too well he recalled the woman in his dream practically demanding the union. But if that was her ghostly plan, Chloe was out of luck from the look on Delaney's face just now.

"Good grief, you talk nonsense! But I do want to see what it looks like."

Delaney hesitated for a moment, then rose and took the gown with her behind the tall stack of boxes near the wall. Overhead, a hard clap of thunder rattled the rafters and the rain began to drum harder upon the roof just over their heads. The attic grew chilly with the approach of night.

"Need any help?" Tyce asked suggestively. "Fasten the buttons, maybe . . . or unfasten them?"

"No, I certainly do not! I thought you were a Southern gentleman."

"I never said that." Tyce leaned back on one elbow to wait for her.

"I don't see how women ever got dressed back then," Delaney complained a moment later. "All these hooks and buttons."

"They had help in days gone by. I offered my services."

Still attempting to fasten the top hook, Delaney shot him a scathing glance as she came from behind the boxes. Finally, she mastered it and put her arms down to her side.

"Jesus, Delaney," Tyce breathed, sitting upright on the floor.

She was gorgeous! The gown fit perfectly, cinching her tiny waist and pushing her breasts up into soft, irresistible mounds. The color of the material gave her smooth skin a delicate flush.

She smiled self-consciously, and Tyce knew he couldn't stand up at that moment without embarrassing them both. As enchanting as the dress was, he had an overpowering impulse to take it off of her and wrap himself around her, and his body heartily agreed.

"It's lovely, isn't it?" she asked, then added with a deep blush, "Stop looking at me that way."

"I can't help it. You are incredibly beautiful in that dress." The only problem was the dress itself. He knew it was the one worn by the woman in his dream, although how he had dreamed every detail about it was beyond him. Maybe Miss Donet had shown it to his mother when he was a child, and he had seen it then. That reasoning was far-fetched, but right now, he was willing to accept anything that would explain away a ghostly visitation that might be repeated.

"Such chivalry, sir," Delaney said, with something akin to a Southern accent, holding out her hand as if she expected it to be kissed. "Whatever am I going to do with you?"

Tyce had no intention of disappointing her. As he rose, he pulled the Confederate sash from where it lay across the open lid of the trunk and tied it around his waist, sticking the sword underneath the waistband the sash created.

He bowed gallantly and placed a light kiss on her small hand. "My lovely lady," he said, looking up at her, "whatever would you like to do with me?"

Their eyes met. Dark mirrors of the soul, ageless, timeless. Hers could have been Chloe's glowing eyes, loving him with a passion that even death could not still.

"Wait for me by the window, Chloe," Tyce whispered, drawing her hand to his lips again.

"Don't call me that," Delaney protested weakly, her breathing shallow and fast.

Tyce brushed his fingers across her cheek, and she closed her eyes. Her lips parted a tiny bit. Her face pressed ever so slightly against his hand. The sensation was more than he could endure. Slipping his hand behind her neck, he drew her face toward his. She came to him willingly. Tyce leaned down, covering her mouth with his, pulling her against him with both arms. Hungry, hard, he kissed her. Reason faded, replaced by a maelstrom of uncontrollable yearning.

He did not want to fall in love with her. She had the

power to destroy him and planned to do it. He felt her fingers run through his hair, her soft hands at the back of his neck holding his lips to hers. The urge to fight temptation dissipated as the surge of blood through his groin seemed to wash all the sense from his head.

Delaney's neck was so smooth, so long, so graceful, as his lips slid down its length. He pushed the sleeve of the low-cut gown off her shoulder. His lips touched the firm swell of her breast as his hands fumbled for the hooks on the back of the gown. Now he inwardly cursed the old ways, for the stubborn hooks would not give.

"Tyce," Delaney whispered, "Tyce, stop. Please stop."

Tyce could not stifle the low groan that came from deep within. He slowed down, but he could not stop. Not just like that. She pushed against his chest with her hands. He kept her in his embrace, his hands motionless on the back of the dress, reluctant to turn her loose. His lips still touched her hot skin. Finally, he eased his grip on her a bit. She stopped resisting then and let him hold her. He could feel the slight trembling of her body, and he knew that she was affected by what had happened, too. He laid his forehead against hers for a moment.

"Do I have to stop?" He forced a slight smile.

"Yes," Delaney said, her voice low with a husky breathlessness. After a moment, she drew the gown back on her shoulder and pulled away, avoiding his eyes. "I'm going to change back into my clothes before I ruin this gown. It's too lovely to spoil."

"I'll wait for you downstairs," Tyce said, needing to put some distance between them. He sat down on the bottom step with his head in his hands. What had he done? All he wanted was to get Caroline from her. To do that, he needed to keep his distance from her emotionally. Well, he had just blown that part of it to hell.

He rose as he heard her coming down the stairs, the white book in her hands.

"I turned off the light," she said, meeting his eyes for only a moment before she looked away. Then, to his surprise, she said, "Do you want some coffee? I think I could use a cup . . . or maybe a stiff drink."

"So could I," Tyce said, with a short laugh.

Tyce sat in silence at the table in the kitchen of the *garçonnière* while she made the coffee. She poured it into their cups and sat down. He didn't know what to say to her. She was quiet, too, and would hardly look at him. Finally, she lifted her dark eyes to his.

"We don't need to get involved with one another," she said softly. "I'm not Chloe, and you're not Zach."

"You're right," Tyce said, though he didn't really sound convincing, even to himself.

"I mean, we've got nothing in common. We'd both get hurt in the end." She lowered her eyes to study the coffee in her cup as she held it in both hands.

"I know."

"And besides, I have to go back to New York next week and—"

"You don't have to," Tyce said.

"Yes, I do. It's my home. My life is there."

"You could make a life down here. And look at the practical side. You already have a house."

Delaney laughed softly. "This house is far too big. I hate housework."

"I love housework," Tyce lied, just to keep her talking.

"I'll bet."

"No, really, I'm great at housework. And I'm a hell of a cook, too."

"I know that already. Still, it wouldn't work. What would we do with Mark?" she joked.

"Who the hell is Mark?" Tyce wanted to know.

Delaney met his eyes, as if anticipating his reaction. "He's the man I've been seeing in New York. He wants to get married this summer."

"We could always use a butler."

Delaney burst into surprised laughter. "He would die first!"

Tyce was glad she was still talking to him, but he didn't like this talk of her leaving anymore.

"Besides, Tyce," she said softly, "it's already sold. It's gone. There's nothing either of us can do about it now. Maybe, if I'd come down here first. . . ."

"There's always something that can be done," Tyce offered, jumping on the first sign of indecision he had seen in her.

"It's too late. And I have to consider my mother. I don't think she would like to come back here. I'm sure she has bad memories. She doesn't talk about that time in her life. She hardly talks of my father at all. I'm going to buy her a nice place in the country in Connecticut."

Tyce rose from the table to leave. It was getting late, and he didn't have the heart to argue with her about the plantation. He'd do what he had to do to save Caroline, but it was not going to be as easy now as it would have been yesterday. As he opened the front door, he turned back to Delaney.

"By the way, I'd keep Chloe's gown, if I were you, even if you don't wait for me by the window. I've never seen anything as beautiful as you are in that dress."

Chapter Seven

After Tyce left, Delaney sat for a while at the table, staring out the window, wishing she had never seen Louisiana. Life had been relatively uncomplicated before, but now, Tyce was quickly becoming a problem, and not only because of his claim to her inheritance.

In spite of everything, she liked him. She reminded herself of the threat he posed, and still she was attracted to him. So much so that her feelings were eating away at the hardness inside her, a steel core that kept emotions at bay, that allowed her to believe that the love of a man, whether he be father or companion, was not necessary to make life complete. Now, like never before in her life, she was going to have to fight the weakness within, to bolster the framework that sustained her. Her first priority had to be to take care of business here without emotional involvement, then get away before this man corrupted her most basic beliefs.

But deep inside, the question nagged: What would it be like to feel love, true love, such as Chloe Bienville must have had for Zach Brandon? How would it feel to have Tyce Brandon love her with all his heart? Somewhere within, in a dark, hidden place, she felt a sudden stirring, a thrill of excitement, a longing to know that feeling, which she had never known before.

"No!" she cried aloud, slamming her fist down on the table. "I won't!" Abruptly, she pushed the chair back and went into the parlor. Her bravado was a pretense, and she knew it. Her insides were crumbling, and she was afraid.

Ordinarily, she would have called her mother around this time of night, but just now, she was too upset, and her mother would pick up on her mood immediately. She'd wait a little while before making her call.

On the coffee table lay Chloe's diary. Delaney picked up the leather-bound book and opened it at random, disappointed to find that the pages were so yellowed and stained that she could not read most of the words. A sound came from the kitchen. She started at the noise. All this talk of ghosts had her jumpy. It didn't help when old Auntie appeared in the doorway. Delaney shuddered and wrapped her arms across her chest as a chill passed over her.

"Don't be afraid; it's only me, dearie," Auntie called. *"I thought you might like some company tonight."*

Delaney was on the verge of a rude "Not really," when she decided fellowship was better than being alone with her feelings. Oddly, she was growing used to the old lady's uninvited calls, although the sudden appearances were unsettling.

"Auntie, you are simply going to have to give me your key to this apartment," she said. "Otherwise, I'm going to die of heart failure one day when you sneak up on me."

"Oh, dear. Have I given you a turn? I do apologize. I am just so used to coming and going, don't you know. However, I promise I shall not do it again, since it bothers you. I will announce my presence and wait outside until you invite me in."

Now Delaney felt badly for chastising her, sweet old thing. "Never mind," she said. "Stay and have a cup of coffee."

"I never developed a taste for the drink, myself," Auntie replied, *"but you have some, if you'd like."*

Delaney brought a steaming cup of coffee from the kitchen and found Auntie seated in a wing chair. Delaney curled up on the couch nearby. The heat from the cup was comforting, for the room was much cooler than it had been earlier. It promised to be a cold night, with frost expected in the morning, or so Delaney had heard on the early-morning weather report.

"Don't you worry, walking around in the dark?" Delaney asked. "And it's so chilly out. I'll drive you home when you get ready to go."

"That's all right, child. I can make my own way just fine. I'm accustomed to it. I hardly feel the weather anymore."

Auntie's gaze fell upon the white book on the table. Curiously, she leaned closer, squinting at the embossing on the leather cover. *"What are you reading?"*

Delaney lifted the book, leafing through the brittle pages. "It's an old diary we found in a trunk in the attic. Unfortunately, it's unreadable from age. I was interested in learning more about this Chloe who Tyce said once lived here.''

"Oh, yes. Chloe was a fascinating woman."

"That's right, you said you knew her well."

"Indeed. Many's the time I sat at her knee, listening to her yarns."

"Oh?" Delaney questioned, trying to figure out where this old lady had fit into life at Caroline. "Are you a member of the family, then?"

"In a manner of speaking, I suppose so," she replied. *"Donet's father treated me as if I were his own child."*

Delaney wasn't sure she knew any more than before she asked. The old lady seemed to be talking in riddles on purpose, and Delaney was not in the mood tonight. She decided to pry later. "Tell me a little about Chloe, then."

Auntie seemed to turn inward, her face taking on a lovely, faraway look as she gathered her thoughts. Delaney settled deeply into the soft couch, nestling her warm coffee cup in both hands as the old woman began to speak.

"Chloe . . . dear Chloe. Her story is tragic, you know. Of course, that was only after she had grown into a woman. Her childhood was charmed, one might say. Growing up as the only daughter of wealthy Pierre Bienville, she was petted and indulged. As she changed from child into young lady, all the eligible Frenchmen in south Louisiana came calling. Chloe had her choice, had she wanted any of them. But she had fallen in love with someone else—a handsome, gallant young man of English descent."

"Zach Brandon," Delaney murmured.

"That's right," Auntie confirmed. *"Zach Brandon was the son of Robert Carter Brandon, descended from*

the famous Carters of Virginia. His father had emigrated from Virginia, settled on a choice tract of land, which of course later became known as Caroline, and made his fortune here. Zach was well-bred and dashing, and he stole Chloe's heart the first time she met him. But he was unacceptable to her father because he was English and there had been a row about a parcel of land that Pierre claimed, but that Robert Brandon eventually proved was legally his.''

"But if the land legally belonged to the Brandons," Delaney mused, thinking of her own situation with Tyce, "why would Pierre hold that against Zach?"

"Pierre was a rather spiteful man. He never forgot the least slight if he found an opportunity for revenge. And, as I said, Zach was of English rather than French descent. That made all the difference to old Pierre.''

"Poor Chloe and Zach, it must have been awful for them to be kept apart."

"As you know, child, a father's disapproval has failed to stop more than one romance from blooming, and despite Pierre's admonition to his headstrong daughter, she found ways to see Zach. They wanted to marry. Then the war broke out. Zach, being as patriotic as the next young man, was anxious to join the fracas. The Brandons held a ball in honor of the departing soldiers here at Caroline. Chloe, knowing that Zach loved the color red, had a fabulous scarlet ball gown made for the occasion, over her father's objections. Indeed, for once Pierre was right. Red is not the color of choice for a chaste young maiden. But Chloe was spoiled and as stubborn as Pierre, and she prevailed in the end.''

"I saw the dress. At least I think I may have seen it," Delaney said. At Auntie's questioning look, she explained, "We found a red ball gown in the same trunk as the diary. Tyce thought it might be Chloe's.''

"Well, dear, perhaps it is, indeed. I'm sure she would not have parted with that gown."

"I didn't mean to interrupt. Do go on," Delaney encouraged, eager to hear more about Chloe.

"Of course, Pierre Bienville would never have attended a ball at Caroline under ordinary circumstances. He and the Brandons were on opposite sides of the political fence on most issues. However, the war brought together many strange bedfellows, and Pierre was induced to attend because the governor would be present. Pierre had high political aspirations, don't you know. Indeed, he envisioned himself as a future governor, if he could cultivate the right backing and support. Pierre spent the night wringing the hands and bending the ears of Louisiana's most influential—failing to notice his daughter's constant dance partner. Until, of course, Zach approached him to ask for Chloe's hand in marriage."

"That must have been interesting," Delaney commented, imagining the young couple waltzing blissfully together.

Auntie nodded. "Pierre made an awful scene, as one might expect. As an engagement gift, Zach had presented Chloe with a set of magnificent rubies—jewels that could have bought and sold old Pierre's entire holdings. In a fury, Pierre flung the priceless necklace to the floor at Zach's feet and spat upon it.

"'Never,' he thundered, 'will a daughter of mine marry a Brandon!'

"No amount of begging, pleading, or cajoling could sway him. Only the intervention of the governor himself kept old Pierre from striking down Zach Brandon on the spot for his audacity, and taking his family home at *once. But politics prevailed, and the Bienvilles stayed on into the night. At some point, Zach and Chloe managed to slip away into the garden, where he secretly returned the jewels to her and pledged his undying love. He promised to return after the war and marry her, with or without her father's blessing. As a token, he kept the ruby ring that matched the set, vowing to place it on Chloe's finger upon their marriage."*

"But he never came back," Delaney said.

"That's right," Auntie said with a slight frown. *"Do you know the story already, dear? I don't want to bore you with it again."*

"Oh, please don't stop," Delaney urged. "I want to hear the rest. Tyce told me who Chloe was when we found the dress, but you seem to know so much more about what happened. I'm very interested."

The old woman seemed pleased and went on with her tale. *"Zach was on his way back after the war ended. He got as far as New Orleans. From there he sent Chloe a letter by the hand of her cousin Remy. Zach and Remy had grown up together and were as close as brothers, so Zach knew he could trust his friend's discretion.*

"Chloe was elated that her beloved was coming back to her at last. But the days passed with no sign of Zach. At first, Chloe did not worry. Young men often dallied in New Orleans for the entertainment, and Zach had been at war for two years and might be much in need of entertainment, she reasoned. Never for a moment did she doubt his love for her or his promise to return. Still, after a week and more, her joy diminished in proportion to her impatience. Understand, child, she did not love her Zach any less, but felt a pang of disappointment that he did not fly to her arms sooner, as she would have done to his.

"It was only when Remy returned in the middle of the night and crept into her bedchamber that she learned the worst. There was a rumor that Zach had been killed over a card game in New Orleans—his body presumably thrown into the roiling Mississippi River and washed to sea. At first, Chloe refused to believe her cousin, but he was adamant. He did not see the murder, but he had been with Zach only hours before he disappeared, and Remy knew that there had been an argument. And, horrible though it was to hear, Remy warned Chloe that her own father, Pierre, was among those at the card game who might be suspected of killing Zach. Pierre was very drunk that night, according to Remy, and had threatened young Zach more than once in the course of the night.

"Denying even to herself the possibility of Zach's death, Chloe still watched for him for days. When her father returned from his business trip, she discreetly questioned him, but he seemed completely innocent in his answers. In fact, he was overly jolly. He laughed off her concerns about Zach. 'Now, daughter, you know a Brandon can never be trusted. Chances are he's bedded with some *fille de joie* in New Orleans, and has not a thought of *une vierge* such as you,' he told her."

"What a heartless man," Delaney said, setting her empty coffee cup on the table to listen with rapt attention as Auntie continued her tale.

"At long last, official word of young Zach's death at some unknown murderer's hand reached Chloe's ears. She had no choice then but to accept the truth, but still she could not fathom that her father would have killed the man she loved. She had to know for sure. The search for some sign of Pierre's guilt at last led Chloe to her father's room one afternoon when she was supposed to be napping.

"Her father and his manservant were absent from the house for the day. Her mother had gone to a neighboring plantation to spend the week nursing a woman confined to her sickbed. Careful not to disturb his belongings, Chloe went through coat pockets, trouser pockets, wardrobe drawers. Just as she finished fingering through the jewelry in his jewel box, Chloe was startled by a noise outside. In her haste to put the box back, she dropped it to the floor with a crash. Running to the window, she saw that the noise she had mistaken for her father's early return was only one of the few loyal Negroes remaining after the war, bringing a horse from the stables. Rushing to replace the spilled jewelry box, she discovered that the bump had dislodged a panel, revealing a secret compartment. Sliding the panel open, she found hidden money and another small object wrapped in Confederate gray.

"Loath to confirm her worst fears, she procrastinated a moment before slowly unwrapping the cloth-bound object. When the last fold of cloth fell away, Chloe broke down and wept. In her hand was Zach's ruby ring. The one he had vowed to put on her finger at their marriage. Her father, the man she had loved and respected all her life, the man who had bounced her on his knee when she was a babe, the man she deemed most honorable of all men, had murdered her love and had lied to her face about it."

"How horrible," Delaney whispered, Auntie's words giving life to the scene in her mind. "What did she do?"

"Chloe was not a weak girl in mind, body, or spirit. Her grief was enormous, but her anger at the injustice her father had done was stronger. Knowing that he soon would return, she slipped from her finger the sapphire ring that her father had given her for her eighteenth

birthday. Wrapping that in place of Zach's ruby ring, she replaced the jewelry box just as she had found it, her way of telling her father that she knew his horrible secret.''

''Why didn't she turn him in to the authorities?'' Delaney wanted to know.

''Oh, no, she couldn't do that. By then, the Yankee carpetbaggers had taken over Louisiana. It would have been akin to treason to turn her father over to them, and it would have thoroughly disgraced the family. And Chloe knew it would have done nothing to bring Zach back to her.

''Pierre, however, was not finished with his devilment. He took advantage of the Brandon women's helplessness. The only surviving Brandon male was infant Robert, Tyce's great-grandfather. When the women could not raise enough money to pay the exorbitant taxes levied on the plantation after the war, old Pierre simply paid the taxes and took possession. Finally, he had the tract of land he had lost to Zach's father and more. He had the fabulous Caroline plantation. But even that was not enough for Pierre. Without an ounce of remorse, he turned the hapless Brandon women out on the streets with little more than the clothes on their backs.''

''How would they survive? Could women support themselves back then by working?''

''Gentlewomen could not, I'm afraid, without sacrificing their social status. Of course, survival overrides pride, and Mrs. Brandon might have taken in sewing or laundry for a few pennies. Still, she had her daughters and her infant son to care for, and she was not strong after the birth of the baby.

''Her father's hardness toward Zach's family hurt Chloe deeply. She felt a keen guilt at having the price-

less Brandon rubies in her possession, but they were the only tangible reminder she had left of Zach, and she could not bear to part with them. Nonetheless, she could not stand by and watch his family perish in those harsh times. Pierre had managed to hold onto his wealth, in part by ingratiating himself with the Yankee scoundrels who took over during the Reconstruction. In reparation for her father's sins, Chloe began secretly sending money to the Brandon family to support them, even if it meant slyly selling valuable possessions to the coarse and vulgar carpetbaggers. Because of Chloe, the Brandon family never went cold or hungry. With Chloe's beneficence and her father's increasing wealth, the Brandons survived the ordeal, although they never returned to Caroline.''

"Poor Chloe, to have to bear such a burden all her life.''

"Chloe had a brave heart and a quick mind. She never recovered from the loss of her Zach, but in time, she did have her revenge. She had a bit of her father in her, you see,'' Auntie said with twinkling eyes. *"However, it is growing late, and that story can wait until another time.''*

Unexpectedly, Delaney felt tears sting her eyes. She looked down quickly so that Auntie would not notice. A wave of shame washed over her that her family, no matter how long ago, could have done such a wicked deed. She thought of her own father and wondered if he had not done something just as cruel as Pierre when he deserted his wife and child and fled back to the South.

"What's wrong, child?'' Auntie asked with concern, her dark eyes fixed on Delaney.

"Nothing,'' Delaney said quickly.

"Something is amiss. You are crying. Over my story? I didn't intend to upset you."

"No, it's not that," Delaney protested. "Really."

Auntie remained silent, obviously not satisfied.

"It really wasn't your story," Delaney said, feeling foolish now. "Only that it made me think of my own father and how he left us in the cold when he deserted us, much like Pierre did to the Brandon women. It must run in the family."

The old woman frowned deeply. *"Your father? Joseph? Oh, dear, did you really believe that?"*

"What? That he deserted us? He most certainly did."

Auntie shook her head and leaned forward. *"Please don't ever think that, Delaney. Your father loved you dearly. Why, you were his pride and joy. The stories he told about you! We all knew you were a little princess."*

"Yes, well, the little princess grew up, and there was no daddy there to see what she did," Delaney said bitterly. "This place, Caroline, this was his pride and joy. This is what he chose ultimately."

"Because he became very ill. He didn't want to burden your mother or you. He drank heavily, Delaney. His dark secret was an addiction to alcohol that has always afflicted Bienville men. Whenever his drinking got out of hand, he could come back here to regain control. It was not something your mother could fix, and he loved her so much. He did not want her to have to deal with his devils."

Delaney was not ready to hear excuses, but Auntie's intensity seemed to cast a spell over her, quelling her protests before they found voice. Finally, she managed a weak, "But we would have taken care of him. After a while, he never even came back at all."

"I know. Donet wrote your mother and told her how

*ill he was. She came down to fetch him home, then saw
for herself his condition and thought it would be better
to leave him here where he was happy.''*

"I don't understand," Delaney said. "Why was he
better off here than with his family?"

*"His mind and body simply gave out. The alcohol
destroyed him, dear,"* Auntie said, her voice profoundly
sad. *"He developed cirrhosis of the liver. In the final
stages, his memory began to desert him. He forgot at
times who he was or that he had a wife or a daughter.
Your mother, knowing how he loved his homeland, admitted him to a hospital down here that could care for
him until he died. It was all for the best, child.''*

"Mom told me once that he was too sick to come
visit," Delaney said, closing her eyes against the flood
of memories that threatened to break loose and drown
her. "I said she was lying. I was a teenager, full of
myself and on the verge of rebellion against everything
I did not understand. I refused to believe her, and when
she asked if I wanted to visit him, I said no, if he cared
enough, he would come to me. After that, I refused to
talk about him at all. I began to pretend that he didn't
exist. How selfish can a person be?" Delaney wiped the
moisture from her cheeks with both palms and looked
up at Auntie, trying to explain. "I had seen him drunk
off and on all my life. Whenever he got really bad, he
would disappear for months. But I never saw him when
he seemed to be sick. I just never considered—"

*"It's all right, dear child. You had no way of knowing
any different. Young people have an idealistic view of
the world.''*

"That's no excuse," Delaney said. "I should have
listened to Mom, at least."

"The past can't be changed, Delaney. Only the future.

You have the power to amend the past, if you so choose. You hold the fate of the Bienvilles and the Brandons in your hands right now, child.''

''Are you trying to tell me something?'' Delaney said, narrowing her eyes at the old lady in sudden suspicion. It was beginning to sound as if Tyce had put her up to this whole storytelling bit to weaken Delaney's resolve. ''Like maybe I should give Caroline back to the Brandons just to make up for what my ancestor did? I don't see how that's going to rectify anything. If Tyce sent you over here—''

''Tyce? No, I haven't spoken to Tyce in quite a while. And I didn't say that you should give Caroline back to him, dear,'' Auntie said calmly. *''Not at all. But you are responsible for your own future. The decision is yours how best to live it. Now, you simply must get some rest. It is very late.''*

Delaney glanced at her watch, surprised to see that it was half past two in the morning. ''I didn't mean to snap at you,'' Delaney apologized. ''My father is a touchy subject with me, as you saw. And there's just so much going on right now with the sale of this plantation, that I'm beginning to feel the stress. I do want to hear the rest of Chloe's story. Will you come back tomorrow and finish it for me?''

''Of course, I will, dear. Around the same time? Shall I knock?''

Delaney laughed. ''No. If I'm expecting you, I'll leave the door unlocked. You can't walk home this late. Let me get my keys, and I'll drive you.''

''That's not necessary, dearie. I shall make my way just fine.''

''No, I insist. You stay here. I'll be back in a second.''

Quickly, Delaney picked up her keys and coat from

the adjoining bedroom. When she returned to the parlor, the old woman was gone. Looking out the front door, then the back, Delaney saw no sign of her walking away. She went outside and called but got no answer. Her shoulders slumping in confused disappointment, she went back into the house, hoping Auntie would get home safely, wherever home was.

"What a strange old bird," Delaney muttered, as she locked the doors again and went off to bed.

In spite of having gone to sleep only a few hours before, Delaney awoke early the next morning with that quivering excitement deep inside her that she had tried to squelch last night after Tyce left. For the first time in a long while, she felt an eagerness to start the new day. Sitting up in wonder at the awakening sensations inside her, Delaney caught a glimpse of the sunshine threading its way through the shuttered windows and smiled. Stretching like a limber cat, she threw the covers back and put on jeans and a sweatshirt. No way was she about to question her delightful disposition on such a beautiful morning. One thing she had learned in her life was to be grateful for small pleasures and enjoy them before they disappeared—as they always did.

In fact, she was in such a good mood, and the morning sun slanted across the facade of the old mansion creating such a fascinating interplay of light and shadow, that she decided to pull out the sketch pad that she habitually took with her everywhere and make a morning of sketching the plantation before it was gone forever.

"I'm beginning to think like Tyce," she admonished herself softly. "And where will that get me? Nowhere, I'm afraid."

She had not put pencil to pad in months, always blaming her busy schedule for lack of time. Deep inside, however, she knew the truth: She no longer enjoyed her art because Mark made fun of it.

"Don't quit your day job, babe," he told her once, with a mocking laugh. "You'd starve to death as an artist."

She might not have paid so much attention to his criticism had she not failed at her first attempt at making a career in commercial art. That had destroyed her self-confidence and set the tone for the ensuing years. She simply would not think about all that today. She would pretend to be that innocent child she once was, who was convinced she had the talent to make her mark on the world.

Within a quarter of an hour, she was settled against a towering oak tree on the perimeter of the garden, with a clear view of the plantation house and *garçonnière*. As always, the pencil became an extension of her hand and mind. Line and shadow fell into place as quickly and easily as she saw them before her.

Her drawing had always been that way, and studying art in college had only honed and refined her natural talent. This was what she had always wanted to do, what put her at peace with herself. Before now, she had never had the luxury of putting aside working for necessities for herself and her mother in order to pursue her art. Something like that took courage and confidence in one's ability, two things she found hard to muster when the reality of surviving faced her every day. She hoped that the sale of Caroline would bring her enough financial security to summon the nerve to follow her dream. That, along with her other important goals, was the reason it was so hard to even consider Tyce's argument.

As the old house took shape on her pad, Delaney

found herself sympathetically softening some of the harsh damage done to the mansion by age and weather. She ignored the peeling paint in favor of catching the dappled sunlight and shadow on the face of the house. She left out the overgrown brambles in the garden but included the wild rose vines tangled around one corner column of the back porch. The sun climbed higher, chasing the chill from the air. Delaney lifted her face to the bright warmth, letting the continuing euphoria wash over her; then she bent to her work once more, soon becoming engrossed.

"You're very good."

Delaney's head snapped around toward Tyce at the same time that her hands pulled a blank sheet over her work. Mark's ridicule had made her self-conscious and wary.

"Don't put it away," Tyce said. "I want to see it."

"It's nothing. Just doodling," she countered.

"I don't care. Let me see it." Tyce held out his hand for the pad. "Please?"

Delaney hesitated, then handed it over, turning her back to him while he opened the cover. There were other drawings on the pages before the plantation house. She had forgotten those. A heated flush of embarrassment crept across her face as she realized he was looking at every one.

"These are fantastic, Delaney," he said, as he slowly turned the pages. "Really good. You have a lot of talent."

Delaney waited, holding her breath, for the sarcasm she had come to expect. She should have known better from Tyce.

Stooping beside her, he blew gently across the sketch of Caroline, dislodging a few traces of eraser crumbs.

"You have a true artist's eye," he said, thoughtfully studying her work. "You embellish the strong points, selectively leave out the worst, and still manage to bring out the strength of the house. You make reality beautiful."

Delaney couldn't look up at him. She was struggling with the tears that welled in her eyes. "Thank you," she managed to whisper, as she regained her composure.

"I know a few firms that would love to have you on staff. If you decided to stay down here, I could put in a word for you."

So that was it. He was flattering her to get her to stay. At least Mark was honest with her and didn't try to trick her. She held out her hand for the pad. "Thanks, but no thanks. I doubt my amateurish work could hack it in the real world. It's just a hobby."

"Trust me; you wouldn't have any trouble making it. You've got more talent than most. And there's nothing amateurish about your work. I'm surprised to hear it's a hobby. I assumed you must be a commercial artist."

"From those sketches?" Delaney asked in surprise. If only he knew how much she wanted to believe him.

"You've obviously studied, even if it was on your own. Nothing wrong with that. Don't you do this for a living?"

"I tried once, when I was young," she said hesitantly. "It didn't work out."

"What happened?"

His words stirred long-repressed dreams. For a moment, she relived the optimism and overconfidence of her youth, when she thought she could accomplish anything.

"When I was just out of college, I was so eager to get started that I took the first job I was offered, with a seedy greeting card firm in the Bronx. My boss was an overbearing, chauvinistic prick. He didn't like women, especially women with a college education. He had brought himself up 'by the bootstraps,' as he liked to say, and thought anybody who got there any other way was cheating. So he set out to make me pay my dues, which included disparaging my work and lying about my deadlines. Finally, I took all I was willing to take of him and quit. Only later I realized that the bastard was using my work for profit, and I gained nothing."

"So, you got a better job somewhere else and went on," Tyce said, turning back to look at the previous sketches more closely.

"No, I chose not to. I had lost a lot of confidence in myself because of his criticism. And about that time, my mom's eyesight began to fail and she was diagnosed with an eye disease. I needed a sure source of income, not something as iffy as the art world. So I got a 'real job,' as they say. At least there, you know how much you're going to make on your next paycheck, and you know that if you do this and that, you'll get a raise and promotion in two years. It was the best thing to do at the time."

"You gave up too easily. Never give up on a dream."

"Like with Caroline? Even when you know you're not going to make it come true? Maybe I'm more of a realist."

Tyce looked wounded for a moment, then recovered. "I'll give up when I'm forced to and not a second earlier," he said, his tone harsher than it had been before mention of Caroline.

"Well, I was forced to give up, in a way," Delaney said in self-defense. "After Daddy deserted—left us, we didn't have much money to live on. My mother's eye problem is degenerative and needs expensive care. We needed real money, not just the possibility of it. I made the decision to get a dependable, paying job to keep our heads above water."

Tyce stared at the ground in silence for a moment, then said seriously, "That was then. What about now? Do you still support your mother?"

"No, of course not. She has a good job with the city as a librarian, but her eyesight is failing faster now. The problem was stable for several years, but it has flared up again. I want to see her comfortably retired, with a home of her own, where she can putter around and enjoy herself for a change."

"That's understandable, but there comes a time when you have to do what your own heart tells you to do. If you wait too long, it begins to seem impossible, and you stop trying. I'd hate to see that happen to you. You've got so much more to give. What do you do in New York, anyway?" Tyce eased down onto the grass beside her.

"I'm an account manager for a marketing firm. It pays well, good benefits, the whole nine yards."

Tyce arched an eyebrow and whistled softly. "An artist with business sense. That's a rare combination. Do you enjoy marketing?"

"Sure, most of the time. It could be worse."

Delaney told the truth, at least the part she was willing to admit. She did enjoy the job. It was challenging, secure, and she was moving up the ladder at a good pace. It simply was not satisfying. It did not feel like what she should be doing with her life. She wanted more and was afraid to go after it. That was the part she tried to deny, that she would not admit to Tyce. He would not have understood, she was sure. He was the type to bully ahead with whatever he wanted to do. Like with Caroline.

Without a thought of how it might affect somebody else. Delaney had never known the luxury of that sort of self-centered drive. She was not like that, anyway. Her mother was important to her, and she would do the same thing again if she had to.

" 'It could be worse' is not my idea of enjoyment. What would you do if you had the choice, without worrying about finances or failure? What would you do?"

"I don't know. I haven't given it much thought. I do what I need to do, not necessarily what I want to do." Delaney did not want to delve any deeper into her feelings. She felt the crack in her armor widening with each of Tyce's questions, so she dodged the issue by challenging him. "Is that what you've done all your life, exactly what you chose to do?"

Tyce gave a low grunt. "Not exactly."

"What then? What did you do that you didn't want to do, and how did you stop?" Delaney expected him to clam up or change the subject. It was really none of her business, but then his probing questions were none of his, either.

"I worked the fields of this plantation most of my life alongside my daddy, because that's what he thought he had to do. He couldn't buy the place, even if Miss Donet had been willing to sell it. But he couldn't leave it, either. We were dirt poor, you might say, and I hated it. I was determined that I never would be in his position."

"Yet here you are, clinging to the same thing." The words were out before Delaney realized the innate cruelty in them. She wanted to take them back and apologize for her rudeness but did not have the chance.

"No, you're wrong on that," Tyce said, the defensive anger evident in his voice. "I'm not at all where my daddy was. He didn't have a chance to make his dreams come true, but I do. My grandfather saw that I got a good education and a good job. I haven't always stayed on a straight path, but I've always gone in the direction I want to go. And that direction is right back here. I left my job when Donet wanted me to start restoring Caroline. I had been living for that opportunity for a lifetime, and I finally got it. And I'm not giving it up.''

''What work did you do before you came here? It sounds as if you chose a career you wouldn't enjoy so you'd be eager to give it up.''

''No, not at all. I was an architect with a firm in New Orleans. I enjoyed my work, but this was more important to me. Reviving Caroline is the embodiment of everything I've worked for over the years, but on a grand scale. It's a dream, Delaney, a life's work, not a job, not a career. My life's work.''

''You don't see the reality, do you? You are as trapped here as your father was, just on a different economic level.''

Tyce's eyes glinted and anger tightened the muscles of his jaw. ''Think whatever you want to. There's no reason you should understand.'' Abruptly, he handed back her sketchbook, then looked away while he regained his composure. ''Anyway, I'm serious about your talent. If you ever decide to change careers, I'll be glad to put in a recommendation for you.''

''I'll keep that in mind,'' she replied, putting her pencils away. ''I guess I'd better get busy inside. I still have a lot to do.''

Tyce stared at the mansion in contemplative silence, then closed his eyes for a long moment. When he looked back at Delaney he asked, ''Will you do a sketch of Caroline for me? From the front? I'd love to have one.''

Delaney searched his face. He was in earnest. "Sure, if I have time."

"Thanks. Come on, I'll walk back to the house with you." He pushed to his feet, then turned and offered his hand to pull her up. When she was on her feet, he held to her hand for a long moment, looking into her eyes. She thought he was going to say something, but he let go of her hand and looked toward the mansion. "It looks a lot better in your drawing," he said.

Together, they turned and walked toward the *garçonnière*. As they approached, Delaney noticed that the curtains at one of the windows were parted. Squinting, she recognized her visitor.

"Oh, look, Tyce, Auntie's back. You can meet her."

"Good. I want to meet her. I have no idea who it could be, though. Where is she?"

"There, at the window," Delaney said, pointing. To her surprise, the curtains had dropped back into place. "She was there, at the window. Oh well, I'm sure you must know her. She's very knowledgeable about Caroline. She stayed a long time last night, telling me about Chloe and Zach. I hope she will be in the mood to finish her tale tonight. I wanted to hear the rest of the story. You should stay and listen, since you're so interested in Caroline's ghosts."

Tyce frowned deeply, as he reached for the door to the *garçonnière*. "I think I will. Let's see who this is who knows so much about Caroline."

Chapter Eight

"Auntie," Delaney called, as she came through the door ahead of Tyce.

No answer.

"Auntie!" she called louder. "Where are you? I have someone who wants to see you."

Silence. Delaney checked every room. Nobody was in the *garçonnière*. Yet she had seen Auntie looking out the window, of that she was positive. Sheepishly, she returned to Tyce. "She seems to have left."

"So it would appear," Tyce said skeptically.

"You don't believe me, do you?"

Tyce gave a slight shrug. "I have to admit, I'm puzzled. I can't imagine any reason you would have for outright lying to me."

"Well, thanks for that vote of confidence," Delaney snorted as she removed her coat and laid it across the back of the nearest chair.

"But," Tyce continued, "I can't figure out who this woman is. There's not anybody fitting that description within walking distance of here. The only people living nearby are two families of sharecroppers, and they're both young black families. Maybe she drives over, or someone drops her off."

"Maybe, but I don't think so. There never seems to be a car around when she appears. She can certainly come and go quickly," Delaney admitted. "One minute she's here, and the next, she's gone. She really knows a lot about Caroline's history. That's why I assumed she was close to the family."

"Like what?"

"Everything, it seems. She told me all about Chloe and Zach's ill-fated love and how Chloe's father killed Zach. And how Chloe helped the Brandon family after her father took Caroline and put them out." Delaney noticed Tyce's deepening frown. "What?"

"Nobody ever knew for sure that Pierre killed Zach. Even at the time, it was mere speculation, and nobody ever found any proof that I know of."

"Auntie didn't indicate that. She was certain of it, because Chloe found Zach's ring hidden in a secret compartment of her father's jewelry box."

Tyce's brows knitted in further confusion. "I've never heard any such thing. This old woman's telling tales. Next time she drops in, I want to see her. Make sure she stays until I can get here."

"I'll try. I'm sure you'll recognize her when you see her." Tyce was obviously disconcerted by what she had told him, and she couldn't figure out why. The old woman was harmless, and maybe she was embellishing Caroline's history, but she certainly told an interesting story, and Delaney wanted to hear the rest.

"I doubt it," Tyce replied. "I'm going into Baton Rouge this afternoon. Anything you need?"

"Sure. Let me make a grocery list for you, if you don't mind shopping."

"I don't mind."

Tyce waited for the list, then left. A few minutes later, Delaney heard his truck rumbling down the driveway headed for the main road. She made a cup of hot chocolate, planning to head to the house to continue her inventory. Instead, she sat down on the couch and picked up the white diary that had belonged to Chloe.

If only she could read the faded writing, she could prove or disprove what Auntie told her. She peered closely at the yellowed pages and found that she could make out a few words here and there. Going for a pad and pen, she began to transcribe the diary bit by bit, jotting down the words she recognized and drawing blank lines in between. This was going to be slow going, she realized after half an hour's work produced a dozen words and ten times as many blanks. Still, one or two sentences began to make sense, and she continued, losing herself in the work for the rest of the afternoon.

When she could no longer make out the words on the page by the fading natural light, she stopped long enough to stretch her legs and heat another mug of chocolate. The diary enthralled her. Not only had she transcribed enough to confirm Auntie's story, but she had come to like Chloe Bienville very much. The young woman was never at a loss for spirit, as Delaney found when at last she made sense of one of the entries.

In it, Pierre Bienville had pressed his daughter

strongly for the location of the Brandon rubies, so rather than disappoint her father, Chloe told him that she had buried them beneath the rambling rosebush at the far side of the back garden. Unfortunately for Pierre, that was the very same rosebush he had ordered cut down so that the new privy could be built there. Not to be deterred by a bit of a stink, especially when he could force his laborers to do the filthy work, he set about having the entire privy moved and the waste-sodden ground underneath dug up.

For days, the men worked, their lower faces swathed in vinegar-sprinkled kerchiefs to ward off the stench, while Chloe watched diligently from her post by the window of the ballroom. After a while, it became obvious that nothing more than maggots and dung beetles were to be found in the soil. Pierre was furious. When confronted, Chloe merely shrugged and said perhaps she had been wrong. Perhaps she had thrown them down the well.

"Good for you," Delaney said, laughing with admiration at Chloe's spunk.

Laying the book aside, Delaney leaned her head against the back of the chair, trying to imagine the misery Chloe suffered, but she found it difficult, for she had never loved anyone enough to sacrifice her life for him. When she and Mark had broken up, she had been lonely for a while, or maybe it was mostly boredom. Soon enough, she recovered and went on with her life. In fact, it was more a bother than anything when he began calling again. Things were different with Chloe, that much Delaney understood perfectly, for Chloe had loved Zach to the bottom of her soul.

A noise on the front porch caught Delaney's attention. "It must be Tyce with my groceries," she muttered, pushing up from the chair. Without warning, a thread of excitement wove its way through her. What was wrong with her, that the mere anticipation of seeing this man thrilled her? This was not a good sign. She should send him on his way as soon as she got her groceries inside, instead of thinking of reasons why he might linger a few minutes to talk.

Opening the door with a smile, she found Auntie waiting on the porch. The warmth in the pit of her stomach subsided along with the excessiveness of her smile. She put on a pleasant face, however, for she didn't want to hurt the old lady's feelings.

"I promised not to intrude," Auntie said.

"Oh, Auntie, come in out of the cold. I didn't hear you knock. How long have you been out there?"

"Only a moment. You anticipated me, I see."

"I heard a noise and thought it was Tyce. He's supposed to come by. I hope you'll stay. He really wants to meet you. He can't seem to place you. How do you know him?" Delaney wanted Auntie to stay, not only for Tyce's reaction, but also because her interest in Chloe's diary had become insatiable and she wanted to know all about the woman in red.

"Why, I've known Tyce all his life. And, believe me, dearie, he would know me." Auntie moved to the table where the diary lay open with Delaney's notes on top. *"What is this? Have you been able to decipher it?"*

"Only a small part," Delaney said eagerly. "I pieced together a section where she told her father the rubies were hidden under the privy."

"Oh, yes," Auntie said, nodding. *"Chloe was not above a good prank. That was only one of many she played on the Bienville men."*

"Please sit down and tell me all about them," Delaney begged. "Do you like hot chocolate better than coffee?"

"Nothing for me, dearie." Auntie waited until Delaney was settled onto the couch like the night before. *"Where shall I start?"*

"Where else did she say she hid the rubies?"

"Let's see." Auntie mused for a moment. *"After her father's death, she convinced her brother Jean-Pierre that she had dropped them into the well. Where Pierre had learned his lesson from the privy incident, young Jean-Pierre was still naive and greedy enough to be duped. The servants from the mansion had to tote water from the river for nigh onto a month after Jean-Pierre muddied the well trying to find the jewels. One thing about the Bienville men, they never burned themselves twice. They soon learned to leave Chloe to herself. Everyone was of the opinion that she was looney, of course. But she wasn't. It was only her way of dealing with what was left of her life."*

Delaney stared into her mug of chocolate. "It's so hard for me to comprehend that she was willing to just stop living because she lost a fiancé. Surely there would have been other men she might have married if she had given herself a chance. You said she had many French suitors before the war. Were none of them left?"

Auntie frowned slightly. *"Really, dear? I understand her feelings very well. She loved Zach with all her heart. Many of the young men of the area were killed or maimed in the war, it is true. However, Chloe would not have married any of them, had they wooed her. She had no heart left to give another man."*

"I think that is foolish. I would never love a man that much, that I could not recover if he were gone."

"Have you never been in love then, my child?"

''No. And I never intend to be, either. I don't like that sort of vulnerability.''

''Then you may lose more than Chloe did in the end. I hope you learn to love, because that is the most important part of living.''

''Sorry, I find it hard to believe that,'' Delaney said abruptly. ''Please tell me more about Chloe's pranks.''

Auntie gave a protracted sigh, but she continued her story. *''The last time Chloe played her little joke was with her nephew Luc. And that was the worst time of all. She hinted to her nephew's overseer that when the new sugarcane mill was being built, she dropped the jewels into one of the foundation holes. The workmen got wind of the rumor, and before Luc could stop them, they tore down and dug up every square inch of the mill, destroying their very livelihood in their frenzy to find the treasure.*

''Soon after that episode, Donet was born, and at sixty-three years old, Chloe's heart began to feel love once more. She doted on the baby girl, and as she was considered harmlessly demented, she had all the freedom in the world to spend with the child. She became, in effect, another grandmother as Donet grew up. And loving Donet as she did, Chloe did not want to hurt anyone Donet loved. So she told Donet's older brother, Louis, that she had long ago thrown the jewels into the Mississippi River to return them to Zach. Everyone thought that was probably the truth. But I never did. I still think they are hidden here somewhere. Chloe never breathed another word about them, however, not even to her precious great-niece Donet.''

''Why do you think they are still here? It makes sense for her to want to give them back to Zach, doesn't it?'' Delaney asked.

"Maybe. But the reason I believe differently is because of what happened when Donet fell in love. If she had picked any man except the one she did, things would have been different. But she fell in love with Lee Brandon. Donet's father, Luc, could not tolerate Lee and threatened him more than once when he came calling on Donet. But, like Zach, Lee was headstrong and tried to get Donet to elope with him.

"Chloe did all that she could to soften Luc's attitude toward Lee, for she wanted Lee and Donet to be together, as if that might atone for her own loss, I think. She even had Luc commission a set of paste rubies like the ones Zach had given her, for Donet's eighteenth birthday. I believe that she intended to switch the real jewels for the false ones when Lee and Donet married. But Luc finally frightened Donet badly enough that she refused to run away with Lee and told him never to call on her again.

"Lee was brokenhearted and begged her to reconsider, but Donet feared for his life and would not be swayed."

"Do you think Luc would have hurt Lee?" Delaney asked.

"I would not have put it past him. He was quite protective and overbearing at times, a controlling man like many of the Bienville men. I believe Donet did the only thing she knew to do, even though she would never love again. Not long after, Chloe passed away. We always thought this second wounding of her heart was more than she could bear."

"What a sad and tragic history I seem to have," Delaney said with a wry smile.

"Yes, it is. But your future could be very different from the past."

"What do you mean?"

"Well, dearie, I was just thinking, you could marry Tyce Brandon and there would be no objection from either side, I daresay. He is a wonderful young man, honest and true-hearted. He needs a wife. He's been alone for too long. I think you two would make a fine match. Think of the romance. The Bienvilles and Brandons united at last. Don't you think it sounds lovely?"

Too astonished to reply at once, Delaney could only stare at Auntie. "Marry him?" she sputtered. "What ever gave you that idea?"

"I think you make a lovely couple. Have you really looked at him, dear? He is quite handsome, like all the Brandons. And he will love you well, I can assure you."

"All he's interested in is what he can get from me— like this plantation. That's what he really loves, in case you haven't noticed, and I don't care to be involved with another man who has a plantation for a mistress," Delaney replied sharply. "When did you see him, anyway, to know what he's thinking? He says he has not seen you. If I discover this is some ruse he cooked up to trick me—"

"My dear Delaney, you are such a skeptic," Auntie said, waving her hand as if to dismiss Delaney's concerns. *"There is no plot between Tyce and me. I just know the young man quite well. But you are right about Caroline. The plantation is a part of him, like it has been a part of all the Brandons. And it is breaking his heart to lose it, but if you think that he would sacrifice true love to have Caroline, I believe he will prove you wrong. The boy could soon realize what is truly important in life."*

Delaney gave a short, skeptical laugh. "I think you would be the one surprised by his attitude. He has never shown any great interest in me other than the times he's tried to talk me out of my inheritance.''

"It may seem that way to you, and in truth, he may not yet have discovered the true depth of his love for you, but Delaney, dear, you are his destiny and he, yours. I believe that in my heart.''

''Well, your heart is wrong,'' Delaney began. The thud of footsteps on the porch caught her attention. Both she and Auntie stared at the door. Delaney smiled sweetly. ''Well, there's Tyce now. Why don't you tell him what you just told me? I bet he'll be surprised to know how much he loves me or will when he discovers his true feelings.''

Delaney got up to open the door. Tyce stood there with a bag of groceries in each arm. ''Good timing. Thanks,'' he said, as he came through the door.

''Really good timing,'' Delaney agreed. ''Auntie is here, and we have had the most interesting conversation tonight.''

Tyce glanced into the room, then back to Delaney. ''So, where is she?''

''Right there,'' Delaney said, turning to point to the chair—the now-empty chair—where Auntie had been sitting. ''She was right there!''

Tyce shook his head slightly, then went past her to deposit the bags on the kitchen table. Delaney rushed into one bedroom after another, even checking the bathroom in each one. There was no sign of Auntie anywhere, and this time, she could not have gone out of the house, because Tyce and Delaney were between her and both doors.

''I don't understand,'' Delaney said, when she joined Tyce in the living room again. ''Where did she go? Is

there some secret staircase in this old house that you
didn't tell me about?"

"Nope. The only stairs are outside, and I know she
didn't go up those because I was out there."

"You don't believe me, do you?"

"Afraid not," Tyce said.

"I read some of the diary. What she told me is true.
Chloe wrote the same thing. She was here!" Delaney
insisted. "Tonight and last night. Right here . . . Wait, I
have a picture of her! I found it in Aunt Donet's drawer.
It's been in my purse, and I forgot about it. Wait here."

"I'm waiting."

Delaney returned in a moment with the three pictures
she had taken from the photo box. "Here," she said,
handing them to Tyce, with the picture of the young man
on top. "I thought the guy in this one was you at first.
Then I saw the name Lee Brandon and the date on the
back. I assume the girl in the other photo with him is
my aunt when she was young? Auntie says Aunt Donet
was in love with Lee Brandon."

"Yes," Tyce said, looking with great interest at the
two pictures he held side by side. "This is Lee Brandon,
my great-uncle. He was my grandfather's twin. Tyce
took the third photograph from underneath the others. A
perplexed frown crossed his face. "This is the woman
who's been visiting you?" he asked, looking from the
picture to Delaney for an explanation.

"Yes, I said it was."

"What are you trying to pull on me?"

Delaney bristled at his sarcasm. "What do you mean?
I'm not pulling anything."

"You know who this is," Tyce said reasonably, holding the picture up.

"Yes, I know. Auntie. The woman who keeps coming

to visit me. Who sat in that chair not half an hour ago, telling me the most ridiculous things I've ever heard. Now, who is she?''

''When's the last time you saw your aunt Donet?'' Tyce asked out of the blue.

Confused, Delaney thought for a second, then said, ''When I was four. When we moved away from here.''

''Never been back?''

''No.''

''Never saw a picture of her later?''

''No! What are you getting at?''

Tyce stared at Delaney for a long minute as if he still did not believe her, then the frown took over again. ''You really don't know what your aunt Donet looks like, do you?''

''Of course not. I can't remember back that far.'' Delaney felt a wave of uneasiness wash over her as the blood slowly drained from Tyce's face.

''If this is the woman who's been visiting you, then we've got problems, because I went to her funeral.'' He held the picture out toward her. ''This is your aunt Donet.''

Chapter Nine

Delaney's knees weakened. She might have sunk to the floor if Tyce had not caught her. She leaned on his strong arm as he guided her to the sofa and sat down beside her.

"I don't believe in ghosts," she whispered.

"Might be a good time to start."

"How can you take this so lightly?" she demanded, then saw the ashen color of his face. "It worries you, too, doesn't it?"

"You kidding? Why would I worry about a ghost?" Tyce put his arm around Delaney's shoulders and pulled her against him comfortingly.

"You once thought this was a prank. Don't you still think it might be?" she asked hopefully.

"How?" Tyce replied. "There was no way for her to

get out of here except to come by us. She just disappeared, like I suspect she's done in the past, but we were too busy making up explanations to see the truth.''

"My God, you talk like you think she's really a ghost!" Delaney sat up enough to look into his face.

"Got any better ideas?" he said, with a slight grin. "I know I don't."

Delaney settled against his chest again to think this out. She still was not ready to admit she was nutty enough to be seeing ghosts, but for the life of her, she couldn't come up with any other explanation.

"You mentioned earlier that she was saying something ridiculous. What did she say?" Tyce asked after a few moments of silence.

Delaney hesitated. What was the harm in telling him what the old woman had said? He'd get a laugh out of it and deny it. Maybe that was it, she didn't want to hear him say he didn't care for her. She didn't want the truth. She shrugged. "Nothing of importance, just some silly notion of hers."

"What?" Tyce insisted. "Tell me what she said. Maybe it will give me a clue."

"All right, fine. I'll tell you. Just remember, it was her idea not mine. She said you were madly in love with me but just didn't know it yet and that we should get married. That it was our destiny."

"She's in cahoots with Chloe," Tyce muttered.

"I beg your pardon?" Delaney said, not sure she had understood right. Now there were two ghosts in the bargain? Then she realized Tyce hadn't laughed nor had he denied anything—yet.

"I had this dream," Tyce said seriously, "a day or two before you arrived. At least I thought then it was a dream. Chloe came to me in the ballroom. She even called you by name, but at that time, I'd never heard your name before.''

"Didn't you hear it at the reading of Aunt Donet's will?''

"I wasn't invited to the reading of the will," Tyce said with a note of bitterness, "because I wasn't mentioned in that first will, remember? Only the second one, which couldn't be found at the time. Afterward the lawyers just called you Miss Bienville or 'the new owner.' ''

"Oh, I see. So, what did Chloe say in your dream?''

At that, it was Tyce who hesitated. His arm tightened around her. "She demanded that I marry you, to bring Caroline back into the hands of both families, so that she could be free to go to Zach.''

"And that's what you've been trying to do?" Delaney asked skeptically. "Could have fooled me.''

"Actually, I've been trying to get possession of Caroline by legal means. I've never been inclined to coerce somebody into marrying me. Anyway, you haven't exactly been receptive when I have mentioned your staying. But, that aside, I think we've got a problem, and I'm not sure what to do about it.''

"What do you mean?''

"Well, if we can suspend our skepticism for a few minutes and accept the possibility of the existence of ghosts, then we've got two of them here, working together to get us married. If Chloe's visit to me wasn't a dream, then I can tell you that she was not kidding about us having to marry to free her. And she appeared most anxious to be gone from here. Now, if it's possible, she must have shanghaied Miss Donet for her purposes—unless Miss Donet's trying to get to Uncle Lee as well. That love affair was broken up by Donet's father. Uncle Lee was devastated. He roamed the world, searching for adventure—or death—for the rest of his life. Never came back to Louisiana at all. But never for a minute did he forget her, I guarantee. Brandons don't forget Bienvilles, and I sure as hell don't want to live the rest of my life like my ancestors have.''

''I don't intend to be another Chloe, either, so don't even think along those lines. What do you suggest we do?''

''Get married?'' he said with a mischievous grin.

''Forget it. This may just be another trick of yours to be sure you get Caroline.''

''You have to admit, though, it would solve the problem,'' Tyce teased. ''And it wouldn't be so bad. I'm a decent guy. Ask anybody around here. I could teach you how to use a hammer and saw, and we could spend our days rebuilding this place together.''

Delaney looked heavenward for divine intervention. ''Oh, brother! Just what I had planned for my future!''

However, she already knew that he was a decent guy, and more than that, a really nice guy. And he probably wouldn't make a bad husband at that, but even if she wanted to get married, which she didn't, the whole idea was just too bizarre. He was teasing her, anyway, and she refused to taunt herself with the impossible idea of being married to him. ''Somehow, I don't think it will work.''

''Well, are you going to be the one to tell Chloe? I can say, frankly, I don't plan to carry bad news to her. She's got a real bad reputation for revenge.''

Delaney had to laugh, recalling some of the pranks Chloe had pulled, according to Auntie . . . Aunt Donet . . . whoever. ''I haven't seen Chloe. She seems to prefer Brandon men. But if I do, I'll give her our regrets.''

"Be sure you tell her I gave it my best shot. That you're the one who didn't want to get married and set her free."

"Excuse me? I don't recall being swept off my feet since I've been here. If you gave it your best shot, I want to know when, because I obviously missed the attempt!"

"Right now." Tyce leaned over and took her face in his hands, his lips caressing hers like a whisper.

"Stop that!" she protested, pulling away slightly. But her body remembered the day before in the attic when she had felt as if she belonged in this man's arms. Instead of relinquishing his hold on her, he drew her closer. She breathed in the masculine scent of his body mixed with a subtle, heady cologne.

"How can I give it my best shot if you don't cooperate?" he asked, nuzzling her neck.

A shudder of pleasure ran down her body at the touch of his lips. *Stop,* she wanted to say again, but she couldn't get the words out. Instead, she closed her eyes and savored the tiny currents of electricity shooting through her, warming her insides like nothing had ever done before.

When his lips sought hers again, she gave in willingly. He laid her back gently on the sofa, pressing his body against hers as he kissed her. Delaney felt the play of muscle in his body as he moved, recognized a rock-hard erection forming as he kissed his way down her neck, skillfully unbuttoning her shirt as he went. Now was the time to stop him. She was not naive, she knew the routine, where this was going to lead. Delaney was not one to tease men, but she didn't want this to end. In that moment, she wished that he did love her like the old woman said, because what she was feeling for him was far from anything she had ever felt for any other man.

Her blouse was open now, hanging loose on either side of her body. Tyce's hands enveloped her waist, his tongue tracing a path down her breastbone. Delaney sucked in her breath and arched toward the pleasure. Her whole being suddenly ached for this man. She knew that if they came together now, her life would change. Even if he did not love her, nothing would ever be the same for her again. If she gave in to him now, she would be giving herself completely—and that was something she had never done before.

Tyce moved upward, his lips finding hers again. He drew back just slightly, gazing deeply into her eyes for a moment as if in search of an answer to the age-old question. She offered her lips in response, and he accepted her decision wholeheartedly, releasing the passion he had been holding in check.

This time, Delaney sought him out, too, pulling the knit shirt over his head to get to his wide, tanned chest. Her hands roamed the broad shoulders, thick with muscle, slid down a smooth, flawless back and under the waist of his jeans, pulling him closer against her.

He responded with a low moan, the tension in his body increasing palpably. His hands slipped behind her to unclasp her bra. She moved to make it easier. Tyce pushed the lacy undergarment upward, his fingers brushing her breasts, triggering an immediate response. His breathing quickened as he ran his hands gently down her body, then lowered his head toward her breast.

Delaney trembled in anticipation of his touch, her fingers entwining in his thick hair. Feather-light, his lips covered her nipple. A throaty moan escaped her as she came to meet him.

Abruptly, the phone on the table by her head jangled.

Delaney jumped as if Chloe herself had grabbed her. Tyce froze momentarily, then whispered, "Let it ring."

The next ring sounded in Delaney's ears like an alarm.

"It might be my mother. Something might be wrong. I haven't spoken to her since the day before yesterday."

"Let the answering machine catch it," Tyce begged.

"It's not on." Delaney reached over her head for the receiver. As she brought it to her ear, Tyce raised up off her.

"Hello?"

"Hey, babe, what's going on? You sound out of breath."

Mark! Jesus! Delaney tried to clear her head, to think of something to say as she pushed Tyce away enough to sit up. "Mark. H-hello," she stammered. "Oh, I was just doing aerobics. You know, go for the burn."

She hoped she sounded casual, but she had her doubts. At the other end of the couch, Tyce laid his head back and closed his eyes. To his credit, he didn't grin at her awkward lie. With her free hand, Delaney fumbled to rebutton her shirt, as if Mark could see through the phone what she had been doing.

"Yeah, well, that's good. Listen, I got a damn restraining order on the sale today. What the hell's going on down there? Aren't those hick lawyers doing their job?"

"I'm sure they are, Mark. The new will has put everything on hold, like I've already told you. You should have known the sale couldn't go through until everything's settled."

Delaney didn't want to talk in front of Tyce, but he made no effort to leave. She felt torn now between what she was doing and how it was affecting Tyce. At the mention of Caroline, he opened his eyes slightly to watch her.

"Well, I'm about to get them back to business. Stir things up a bit."

"What are you going to do?" Delaney's stomach churned with dread, for she knew Mark's methods too well.

"I'm going to offer the judge a little incentive to get off his ass. I hear those officials down there tend to look for the highest bidder. I'm going to be that bidder."

"Don't do that, Mark. Please just let things be. It will all work out in the end."

"Damn right. I just intend for it to work out my way. Besides, I'm ready for you to come home. Get this thing over and get on with life. I thought maybe a June wedding? What do you say?"

Delaney couldn't meet Tyce's eyes. He sat up on the couch, sensing the change in her.

"I don't want to talk about that on the phone," Delaney hedged. "I still have a lot to do here. Tomorrow"—she almost said "we," then thought better of it—"I'm going to New Orleans to get an appraisal on the furniture."

"I told you to let that junk go with the house. That's wasted time."

"Fine. Don't worry about it, then."

"So, when do you think you'll be back? I'm missing you, babe."

"I'm not sure," Delaney said, still avoiding Tyce's eyes.

"You miss me?"

"Mark . . ."

"Doesn't sound much like it," Mark wheedled.

"Sounds more like you want to get off the phone. What's the hurry?"

"Nothing."

"Something's wrong. What's going on? Somebody there?"

"No, that's not it. I guess I'm just tired. I've really been working hard to get everything done."

"You want me to come down and take care of things? Get it finished faster?"

"No!" Delaney said. "That's not necessary. I mean, there's no need for you to take time away from work. I'm doing okay."

"Baby, pretty soon, I'll be able to take all the time off I want. I don't mind starting a little early. As soon as this deal is finalized and we're married, things are going to be different. It's going to be the good life for us."

Delaney knew Mark's idea of the good life. Before the year was out, they would likely be penniless, no matter how much money they started with. She had never been so blind as to think she cared enough about Mark to marry him. Her vision of what their marriage would be like was about the same as living apart, except they would be legally and financially bound to one another. That, she did not care to contemplate.

Until tonight, however, she had never allowed herself to consider how empty life might be without love. She had thought all her life that was what she wanted, but sitting there with Mark on the phone and Tyce on the couch beside her, she was not sure of her feelings at all. She wished she could clear all this up with Mark right now, but she was not crass enough to give him the brush-off on the phone, especially with Tyce listening. It was just a muddle that she had to get through until she saw Mark again. Though she had never made a commitment to him, still she wanted to explain how she felt and say good-bye in person.

Tyce's fingertips touched her hair, immediately sending a warm eddy of delight through her. These new, wonderful feelings awakening within her felt like an incomprehensible miracle. Emotions, long repressed, were opening like a blossom to sunshine. Tyce was responsible. She leaned her head back into the curve of his hand. She wanted more of what Tyce was offering. Maybe even take a chance on loving somebody someday.

"Let's talk about all that later, can we?" she said to Mark. "I'm really exhausted."

"Sure. Get some sleep, then. Talk to you tomorrow."

"Bye, Mark." Delaney replaced the phone in its cradle and looked up at Tyce, knowing that their moment together was over. They couldn't go back now, not right away. She felt guilty, and judging from Tyce's face, he wasn't too happy, either.

After a heavy silence, Tyce reached out and laid his hand on hers. "I'm sorry. I shouldn't have done what I did. I'll get going. We'll start for New Orleans around ten, if that's okay." He got up from the sofa and reached for his shirt, pulling it over his head, but not bothering to tuck it in.

"Sure, that's fine," Delaney managed. She didn't want an apology. What happened was as much her doing as his, and she wasn't sorry, but she couldn't bring herself to tell him that. She just didn't know how to say what she felt.

"You going to be all right here alone? You're welcome to sleep at my place. I promise it's not haunted."

"I'd better not," she said.

"If you're worried about me bothering you—" Tyce began.

Delaney stopped him. "No, I'm not worried about that. I just want to be alone. I'm sorry. I'll be fine. Auntie doesn't scare me, just puzzles me."

"See you in the morning then," Tyce said.

There was no hint of a smile on his face or in his eyes as he turned to leave. He looked totally dejected, and Delaney didn't feel any better herself. Maybe a long night of contemplation would help, because she suspected she wouldn't be getting any sleep.

Chapter Ten

Tyce would be there any minute, and Delaney was late getting dressed. A sleepless night had resolved nothing in her mind. Finally, just before daybreak, she had dozed, which caused her to sleep through her alarm. She did not want Tyce waiting in the other room while she dressed. Last night had been as much as she could handle at the moment.

Lying in his arms had seemed as natural as breathing. The strength of his arms, the passion of his caress did not feel unfamiliar. In fact, it was as if she had known him for an eternity. She was coming too close to falling in love with him, and she didn't know how to handle that. She should get back to New York. There she had a life, a career, a mother who needed her. Tyce was a complication she could not afford in her life.

From the closet she pulled out a flowing, off-white knit skirt that she loved to wear because of the way it swung freely around her legs when she walked. The matching, long-sleeved knit top had a wide neckline that was very sexy when worn off the shoulders. The only problem was that she could not wear a bra or camisole under this top because the straps could not be hidden. Delaney pulled the neckline well up on her shoulders. She did not want to be sexy today. She just wanted to get her business done and get away from Louisiana— away from temptation.

Temptation knocked as she was putting on a pair of dangling gold earrings.

''Coming,'' Delaney shouted, slipping around her neck a heavy gold chain with a seahorse pendant. She snatched her purse from the bed and left the bedroom.

Tyce was waiting on the porch for her. She was so used to seeing him in jeans and work clothes that she did a double-take at his attire: a light blue shirt with burgundy and navy pinstripes and a glove-soft leather jacket; pleated navy slacks; shining, expensive oxblood loafers instead of his usual running shoes or work boots. His hair was combed back, the golden highlights streaking through darker brown layers underneath.

Delaney took one look at him, standing there, straight out of *GQ*, with a patient smile on his handsome face, and wished she had a plane ticket back to New York that day. How would she keep her mind off him and on business long enough to escape the pull of pure, undiluted sex appeal that hung about him like a seductive aura? She was edgy enough about the situation with the plantation and Tyce as it was, without adding an extra stick of dynamite to the pile.

She had a sudden, unbidden vision of Mark and Tyce

standing side by side, stripped of Armani suits and common work clothes—two men reduced to the very core of masculinity. Delaney sucked in her breath and blushed at her wicked thought. But, Lord, if she was honest with herself, there was not much she'd like to do more than to strip Tyce Brandon and compare him—or do whatever else came to mind.

"Ready?"

Thank God, he could not read her mind, Delaney thought as she locked the door behind her. "Let's go."

The drive to New Orleans took a little over an hour. The skyline of the city looked comfortably familiar after so long in the country, but she felt an odd pang of homesickness—odd because it was not for New York but to be back at Caroline. She frowned slightly at that idea. She hated Caroline and what it stood for, didn't she? Her mind spun with all the changes of the last week. Maybe she had begun to soften toward her father after what Auntie told her.

What Auntie told her! *Geez,* she thought in exasperation, *now I'm being influenced by a ghost or something. I must be cracking up!* To get her mind off these perplexing new developments, she began to ask Tyce questions about the city.

"I'll take you on a short tour," he offered, as he exited the interstate near the space-age hemisphere of the New Orleans Superdome.

Tyce knew the streets well and negotiated the traffic easily without a break in their conversation. They drove through parts of town that would have made Delaney nervous if she had not been with him. Surely, she hoped, his grandmother did not live back in here. But he had said he grew up poor, so maybe she did. Then, almost without her realizing it, they were cruising down a broad, tree-lined boulevard with a streetcar track down the center, a world apart from the squalor they had just passed through.

"The Garden District," Tyce told her. "One of the oldest parts of the city."

The houses were grand old structures, almost all of them well-preserved and much larger than they looked from the front. Delaney could see from the houses that sat on corners that they ran far back from the street. Tyce showed her several different types of architecture, his interest mostly on the ones with Italianate or Greek design. She recalled him telling her that Caroline's design had the same influence.

His knowledge of the region's history and architecture was impressive. Yesterday's revelation that he was an architect made his interest in Caroline more understandable and more materialistic to Delaney. She had given it a lot of thought overnight and concluded that he probably wanted the place for its resale value after he had restored it. He was hoping she would sell to him for a pittance, then he would make a showplace of the mansion and sell it for a fortune. If anything, his occupation cemented Delaney's resolve not to sell Caroline for less than what she had already been offered. Let him meet her price or find some other ruin to work on.

She could not fathom why it would make a difference to him that his ancestors had once owned the place over a century ago. What did that have to do with the present? Nothing, as far as she could see. And Tyce was an intelligent, rational man. It probably meant no more to him than to her, but it was a good sob story to soften her into selling out cheap. *Try again, Tyce,* she thought, looking aside at him as he drove along and described points of interest.

He stopped for a traffic light at the intersection of another long boulevard with a street sign announcing Canal Street. On the other side stood a row of hotels and department stores. From what Delaney could see, there were only alleys and dilapidated old buildings beyond that.

"This is the French Quarter, *le Vieux Carre*," Tyce said, driving straight across and down one of the alleys, a narrow, cluttered street infringed upon on both sides by ancient, squat buildings.

"Seriously?" Delaney looked about with open curiosity. "I expected it to be different, more sophisticated, I guess."

"Don't judge it on first sight. Wait until you've seen more of it," he said. Finding a parallel parking spot, he deftly maneuvered the truck into the narrow space.

When he switched off the motor, Delaney gathered the courage to broach a subject she had been trying to bring up since they left Caroline. "Tyce, about last night—"

Tyce caught her hand in his and gave it a slight squeeze to stop her. "Let's not talk about last night right now. I want to show you New Orleans and have a good time. We'll discuss last night later. Deal?"

"Deal," Delaney agreed, relieved to have that pressure off her for a while, anyway. But it was something they had to talk about sooner or later. She needed to know him better, to know how his mind worked. If, contrary to what she chose to believe, Tyce really did have a deep emotional interest in Caroline, Delaney knew she was going to be in a quandary, because she didn't want to see him hurt. And she didn't want to see herself hurt, either. Something had to give, one way or another.

"We'll stop in at Gran's shop first. Sometimes she works on Saturday mornings."

"Your grandmother works? I thought she was just a collector of antiques. How old is she?"

"Close to eighty now. She'll work until the day she dies, if she has any say in the matter. She's quite a character."

Delaney walked beside Tyce down the narrow sidewalk, staring at the aged buildings around her. Almost every door had burglar bars over it. Occasionally, beyond the barrier of iron gates, the greenery of a courtyard could be seen. Tyce stopped before an antique shop.

"Here, this is my grandmother's shop," he said, walking behind her through the open shop door.

The place was a tiny cubbyhole, every inch of it crammed with collectibles and furniture. There was nobody in sight inside the shop.

"Gran? Where are you?" Tyce called, making his way between the closely situated displays.

From the back, a high-pitched voice called out. "Tyce, is that you? Come back, come back. I'm surrounded by all this junk and can't seem to get out easily."

They discovered she was indeed hemmed in by stacks of half-unpacked shipping boxes, their contents of old books, figurines, whatnots, dishes, and silver strewn on the floor among foam peanuts and shredded newspapers.

"There's nothing like boxing oneself into a corner, is there?" the old lady said gleefully.

Tyce's Grandmother Brandon was petite and wiry, with shimmering gray hair done in a fashionable style. She was sitting on a small stool in the midst of her merchandise, wearing a royal blue tailored silk suit with a carnation bud in the lapel. Hanging from a chain about her neck was a pair of gold-framed bifocal glasses, which she picked up and brought to her eyes to examine Delaney as closely as she probably did her wares.

"So, this is the little Bienville girl, is it?"

The woman's face was noncommittal, her smile neutral and unreadable.

"Make me a way through here, Tyce, so I can get out and visit with you two." Tyce's grandmother took his hand and got up from her stool to come through the opening he made in the boxes.

"And you, Tyce, what have you been doing with yourself, you naughty boy? John Dennis was asking about you the other day. Why don't you get yourself back where you belong?"

"I am where I belong, Gran. Let's not get into that today. Delaney needs you to appraise some of the furniture at Caroline for her."

Delaney pulled out her list and handed it to the woman.

"Does she? Well, let's see," she said, going to sit down at her desk in a back corner of the shop. Suddenly, the old woman was all business. Slowly, she went down the paper, jotting notes in the margins, and assigning a value to each piece. "These question marks mean I'm not quite sure of a reasonable price. It would depend on the condition. I haven't seen these pieces in decades. Somebody would have to take a look at them. If you intend to sell them, I could send my assistant around to have a look."

"Yes, that would be fine, Mrs. Brandon. I'll be at Caroline another few days."

"So you're selling the place, are you?" the old woman asked.

"Yes, I plan to, as soon as the legalities are worked out." Delaney hazarded a glance at Tyce. "I made arrangements to sell it to developers for a mall before I came down here."

"Well, Tyce, that should make your mother happy, anyway. I know she agrees with me that you should get back to doing something worthwhile."

Delaney looked at the old lady in surprise, then noticed Tyce's face. His mouth was drawn tight and he stiffened at his grandmother's words.

"I appreciate your help with the furniture," Delaney said, taking the papers back from her. "If you would send your assistant as soon as possible and send me the bill for your services, I'd appreciate it. I plan to return to New York midweek."

"Of course. Would you two like to come around for lunch? I'm about to close up for the day and go home."

Tyce glanced at Delaney and lifted his eyebrows in question.

"No, thank you," Delaney replied at once. "Tyce promised to show me the French Quarter, and I am anxious to see as much of it as possible."

If she sounded a little rude, so be it. She simply didn't want to share Tyce that day.

"Thanks," Tyce said, when they were a few blocks away from his grandmother's shop. "I wasn't in the mood for her kind of lunch."

"What do you mean?"

"She likes tofu and bean sprouts."

"I'm glad I said no then. I hate tofu." Delaney laughed. Then, recalling his grandmother's words, she asked, "Your mother doesn't like Caroline?"

"No."

"Why?"

Tyce was quiet for a few moments, then he caught Delaney's hand again. "She's seen it destroy too many Brandon men, I guess. My daddy among them, in a way. And she thinks like you and Gran, that I should get a real job."

"I never said that," Delaney said. "I said I had to have a real job."

"Let's not argue today. Come on, I'll show you the French Quarter."

They walked the streets of the Quarter the rest of the day. Tyce knew the history of the old city from its inception. He showed her what was left of the crumbling red-light district that had been the sole domain of madams and prostitutes. He took her for a horse and buggy ride, and they browsed the offerings of the street artists set up around the spiked wrought-iron fence of Jackson Square. Finally, as late-afternoon shadows slanted across the faces of the buildings, they stopped at Pat O'Brien's.

"It's a tourist trap, but the courtyard is nice," Tyce said, "and if you went anywhere else, your friends in New York wouldn't be impressed."

Delaney was content to be able to sit for a while. She slipped off her shoes under the table and looked around the peaceful courtyard with its tall, gurgling fountain in the center. Thick vines covered most of the crumbling brick walls separating the courtyards of the buildings on either side. The Court of Two Sisters restaurant was just behind them, Tyce told her. She could hear the murmur of diners enjoying their evening, and from somewhere nearby, the melodic tinkle of a piano drifted across the evening air. A quiet solitude slipped over Delaney. She studied Tyce's strong, pleasing face as he ordered Hurricanes for them.

"You have to have a Hurricane, too," he said, when

the waiter had gone. "It's mandatory for newcomers. Then you can order whatever you like."

"Why aren't you married, Tyce?" Delaney gazed into his eyes, made even bluer by the shirt he wore, and thought how pleasant they were. "I can't imagine you've gotten away from these Louisiana girls this long."

"Why? You think I'm a catch?" he said with his familiar grin. "You seem to be resisting me well enough."

If you only knew, Delaney thought wryly. "Have you ever been married?"

Tyce shook his head.

"Surely you've been in love a few times."

"Really in love? Only once. When I was in high school."

The waiter brought their drinks in the tall, distinctive glasses that had made the bar famous. Delaney sipped hers and found she liked the fruity sweetness of the red drink. Tyce settled back into his chair, studying her face.

"So. What happened to you and your high school sweetheart?" she pressed.

Tyce was quiet for a long time, his eyes focused on the table between them. "It didn't work out," he said at last, quietly. "We fell in love too young. But then, if we had been older, we probably never would have gotten together at all."

"Why did you break up?"

"I graduated from high school and she wanted to get married. My father had died two years before, and I had been working almost full time in addition to school. I was tired of working. I was restless. I didn't want to get married in that mood, discontent from the beginning. Besides, she was just a senior in high school the next

fall. Even I knew that was too young to be married."
Tyce seemed caught in his reminiscing. Absentmind-
edly, he swirled his drink and stared at the play of lights
within its depths. "I told her I wanted to have a little
time to get my mind straight. I wanted a bit of adventure
before I settled down. She didn't see the need. I went
anyway. Took the summer off and backpacked through
Europe. Got as far as Russia before I ran out of time
and resources. When I got back, she was married to an
old sports rival of mine."

"Geez, that was fast," Delaney commented, thinking
about the irony that she herself didn't want to marry at
all, and this girl Tyce had chosen seemed eager to marry
whoever was available at the time. "Is that what you
meant the other day in the attic when you said you didn't
expect anybody to wait for you anymore?"

"Yeah. It took me a long time to get over the fact
that she didn't love me enough to wait a few months for
me, or at least have the decency to wait until I got back
to dump me. My mom told me what happened as soon
as I got off the plane, because she was so mad with
Amy. I couldn't believe my ears. I went to her house
and her mother cried on my shoulder and said how sorry
she was. She said she tried to talk sense into Amy, but
she went on and married Buck anyway."

"Where is she now? Do you ever see her?"

"Nope. I never went to see her after that. I couldn't
stand the thought of her with him, and I didn't want to
see the look on his face that he'd finally won it all when
it counted most. That was the first inkling I had that you
could love somebody as much as I loved her and still
lose. Last I heard, she lives in Baton Rouge, has about
four kids, and her third husband owns a beer joint."

"Are you like your great-uncle? Still in love with her

after all these years?'' Delaney asked, trying to sound nonchalant, but unreasonably preoccupied with his answer. She had always kept up her guard, protecting her feelings, keeping a certain distance from those who might pierce her armor, avoiding the possibility of being hurt like her mother had been. This Brandon-Bienville penchant for pining away after lost loves was new territory for her. She never intended to fall so completely in love with anybody that she lost her own strength and independence. With Mark, that was easy. He was as aloof as she was, focused on himself and money. Logically, she should be happy with him because they were so self-reliant. They would be able to keep their own interests, go their separate ways when they wanted, and come together when they chose. But, she suspected, her life was never going to be that simple again.

And Tyce . . . she had the feeling Tyce was just the opposite. He probably offered everything, his heart and soul. She sensed that from his single-mindedness toward Caroline, the intensity of his determination to save the old plantation. He would be the same way in love, she suspected. He deserved somebody who could give his devotion back full measure, and she was not sure that she could.

''No. We didn't have much in common, anyway, I realized as I picked up the pieces and tried to get on with life. I went to college and immersed myself in that, then, later, in my job. After a while, I saw how unhappy we both would have been as we grew apart. I'd be her ex by now, too, I'm sure. Even so, losing Amy was a tough lesson. One I haven't wanted to repeat in my life.'' Tyce finished his second drink and looked her in the face. ''How about you? You and this Mark known each other long? When are you getting married?''

Delaney did not like having the conversation turned around. She didn't want to talk about Mark or their plans, because, frankly, as far as she was concerned, they really didn't have any plans. Still, Tyce had answered her question, and she could not very well refuse to answer his.

"We met two years ago at a party. A driven guy, preoccupied with making money. Why did you think we're getting married?"

"You told me you were. And he seems to be handling most of your business here."

Delaney gave a slight shrug. "I said he wanted to get married. I didn't say I was going to. He's a real estate broker. One of the best in New York. That's why I hired him to handle the sale. He found the buyer for the property."

"So you're not engaged or anything?"

"No, we're not. Mark talks about getting married, but I'm not the marrying kind. My father rather soured the notion for me."

"You know, you shouldn't let one bad experience ruin the whole institution of marriage. A lot of marriages are really good. Your father's problems contributed to the situation."

"That 'one experience,' as you say, was my whole life. Small wonder it colors my opinion of everything. I'm sure there are some fine marriages out there with happy children who are loved and sheltered. I happen not to have any frame of reference for them, unfortunately. This is the only way I know to live my life. Sorry."

Tyce sighed softly. "You're going to miss a lot in life, Delaney, unless you decide to open up a little and let somebody in. Don't you love anybody?"

"Of course I do! I love my mother. She sacrificed everything for me, and I'm not about to desert her for some man who's never proven his loyalty."

"How is a man going to prove anything if you never give him the chance?"

Delaney narrowed her eyes in irritation. She did not like these questions. Her philosophy of life was her business. Unfortunately, she couldn't be completely pragmatic with those sky blue eyes delving into hers as if they could penetrate to her very soul.

Tyce leaned forward across the small table, catching her hand in his. "Don't go back to New York next week," he said earnestly. "Stay here; let me prove to you that every man in the world is not a monster."

She avoided his eyes. He had the power to make her question everything she had ever believed in. She didn't want to give in to his charisma.

"Look at me," he commanded gently, and she obeyed. "I don't want you to go back."

His clear blue eyes were entreating her. He sounded sincere. Delaney wondered why everybody sitting nearby was not staring at her, for surely they could hear her heart thundering through her clothing. She was actually considering his words. In spite of all logic to the contrary, she wanted to stay—at least a little while longer.

"I have my job," she offered as a weak excuse.

"Take a few more days off. Don't you have vacation time?"

Delaney fought her better judgment. She knew what she should do. Just like that first time when he had dragged her up on the levee to look at Caroline, she had the feeling she should run like hell from this man. But she knew that if she did, she would never feel complete, not knowing what might have happened between them. Hesitantly, she said, "I suppose I could. Only for the rest of the week, no longer."

Tyce squeezed her hand and held on to it, and she made no effort to take it back. Delaney swore to herself that she would book a flight for next weekend—one of those that you couldn't get a refund on, to make sure she went. Why she even agreed to stay, she couldn't imagine, for she would probably be just as mixed up next week as she was now. And when the demolition crew brought Caroline down, Tyce would hate her.

But Tyce seemed happy for the moment, and that was enough. The cool of night came upon them sitting there, but the warmth of Tyce's hand kept the chill at bay, and his low voice isolated them from the rest of the world. They talked until the small hours of the morning before leaving the bar to return to Caroline.

The day had been unseasonably warm, and Delaney had left her coat in the truck that morning. The night, however, was cold. When a shiver ran down her spine, Tyce wrapped his jacket around her, then hugged her close to his body for warmth. Royal Street was deserted as they walked back toward Tyce's truck.

"Where is everybody?" she asked. "There were so many people earlier."

"I assure you, Bourbon Street is still rocking. Do you want to go over there? One block away."

"No," Delaney said, snuggling closer under his arm. She did not want to share him with anyone or anything just now.

Somewhere in the distance, a dog barked. Other than that, there was no sound except the soft tread of their slow footsteps. Delaney did not want the day to end. Strange that she always had that feeling with Tyce yet rarely did with Mark. Tyce's grip tightened on her shoulders as he turned a corner.

Delaney looked up sharply. The truck was parked a few blocks straight ahead. She was sure of it. But they had entered a dark, close, vaulted arcade off the main street.

"Where are we going?" she asked nervously.

"Where's your sense of adventure?" Tyce returned.

"Oh, God, not that again!" she cried, trying to extricate herself from his firm grip.

He caught her by both hands and would not let her go. Instead, he lifted her arms and pinned them gently against the brick wall behind her, leaning down to brush her lips with his. Delaney felt a rush of heat as her breath shortened. His body, hard with muscle and power, pressed against hers. His kiss deepened. She responded briefly, then turned her face away.

"Tyce, stop! Where are we? Somebody lives here. We'll be seen."

"Nobody lives here. This porte cochere leads to a little coffee shop back there. It's been closed for hours."

His lips nuzzled along her cheek and down her neck. She tried to free her pinioned arms, but he would not let her go. His breath was hot, his lips soft and inquisitive. She was not afraid of him and really did not want him to stop. It was just infuriating that he was not giving her a choice in the matter. She avoided his mouth and tried to jerk her wrists free.

"Don't run away from me, Delaney," he said softly, the touch of his lips burning a line of sensation across her forehead.

"Let me go!" she demanded.

"Why?" he asked, his voice soft in her ear.

"So that I can hold you, you dolt!"

Tyce laughed softly, then released her. She wrapped her arms around his neck and pulled his head downward, meeting his lips gladly now. His jacket slid off her shoulders onto the ground, but neither of them bothered to pick it up. She ran her fingers through his hair, then slid her hands to either side of his face, feeling the hard plane of his jaw, the prickly stubble of beard, the cool, firm skin at her fingertips. There was a gnawing hunger in her that demanded relief, a void that needed filling, a part of her that had always been forced to be strong but now longed to be shielded and secure.

She made no effort to stop his kisses or his exploring hands that had made their way beneath her top. The hard calluses on his palms grazed her skin lightly as he caressed her bare back. A tiny sound of pleasure came from Tyce's throat as his hands slid around to her front, lifting the white top enough that shivers of cold air crept in, giving her goose bumps.

Delaney laid her head back against the mossy bricks as his fingers touched her skin. The sensation was maddening, for he held her captive against the wall with his body. She could not get away, nor could she indulge her own curiosity easily, for his clothes were tucked in, belted and secure against meddling, though she could feel the hardness of his arousal against her thighs. She was compelled to stand there, with her insides squirming like a thousand snakes in a pit while he drove her mad with his touch.

Her breath came in hard pants as prickling currents shot through her, sparked by Tyce's hands and mouth on her body. She tugged at his shirt to release it from its prison within his pants. At last she could run her hands along the ridges of tight, corded muscle that crossed his stomach and chest. The heat of his body felt good against the cold air, yet she quivered—not from the winter night but from sheer anticipation. She wanted to take his clothes off, to explore his body, to unleash the passion that he held in check, that betrayed itself in his hard breathing.

Meeting his mouth greedily, Delaney pulled him into her body, wanting more, wanting to slide her hands downward, to feel his hardness, to drive him as wild as he was driving her.

Tyce lifted his lips a few inches away from hers. "Don't go back, Delaney."

"No, I won't. Not for a few days," she said, taking the opportunity to try to catch her breath, to get some semblance of control over her frenzied emotions.

"Not ever," he insisted, between labored breaths. "Not ever. Stay at Caroline with me."

Delaney felt the chill creep in. Felt the heat ebb. "I can't do that . . ." she faltered, ". . . can't stay . . ."

"If you wanted to." He drew back to look down at her in the dim light thrown by a streetlight at the end of the porte cochere. "If you wanted to, you could. We could make it work. Rebuild Caroline together, you and I."

Delaney shook her head.

"No, we couldn't." She twisted away from him enough to straighten her top over her skirt. "We couldn't. It's sold. It's gone, Tyce. And even if it weren't, you couldn't afford to restore it."

"But we could do it together," he argued, his voice sounding exasperated. "Why won't you even consider it?"

"It's useless to consider something that's impossible," Delaney blurted out, then turned away. "It's too late. I've already signed the place away, and I can't do anything about that now.''

She would not look at him, but she knew that he was staring at her. In a way she was glad she did not have a choice. His proposition was frightening to her. To give up everything . . . to let down her mother who counted on her and trusted her. The decision would have been impossible to make.

The feelings she had for Tyce were so new, so different from anything she had ever felt before—and they were intense and getting worse. No, she could not stay. And he would not want her without the plantation. It was Caroline that he wanted in the long run. She would just be lagniappe, as Tyce called it, a little something extra.

Just like her mother and she had been with her father. There was no need to replay that scene. It had hurt badly enough the first time around. After all the years of avoiding just such a commitment, there was no way she was going to fall into the trap being set by Tyce Brandon.

''Tyce, suppose I did stay. Then Caroline's destroyed for a mall. How would you feel about me then? How could you love me after I had destroyed your whole world? I don't think you could.''

''It doesn't have to be that way.'' There seemed to be a trace of desperation in Tyce's voice. ''There is some way to negate this deal you've made. There's always a way. Let's find it.''

''Don't you see what I'm saying? I'm not going to back out of this deal. I don't want to keep Caroline. I've resented the hold it had on my father all my life. I don't want it! I want the money! If you want me, it has to be without Caroline. That's the way it is, Tyce. That's the decision you would have to make.''

Tyce's arms dropped to his side like lead. He stared at her, all traces of passion replaced by disbelieving anger.

"You see, it's not me you want. It's Caroline. Why would you think I was a big enough fool to believe otherwise?" Delaney felt the coldness of unwanted triumph. She had been right. But at what cost? She trembled with the cold and her own confusion.

Tyce lifted his hand as if to brush his fingers across her cheek, then thought better of it. Reaching down to retrieve his jacket, he slipped it around her shoulders again.

"You're freezing out here. Let's go," he said, his voice unable to hide his keen disappointment.

Delaney fell asleep in the cab of the truck as he drove home. She woke up the next morning to the ringing phone. She was in her bed in the clothes she had worn the day before, with no memory of how she had gotten there. The other side of the bed was untouched. For the first time in her life, she felt keenly alone in a big bed. She fumbled for the phone to stop its infernal noise. Those drinks from Pat O'Brien's were potent; her head was throbbing and she was still exhausted from too little sleep.

"Hello," she mumbled.

"Where have you been?" Mark sounded extremely irritated. "I've been calling almost all night."

"I had to go to New Orleans to get an appraisal on the furniture, remember. I didn't get back until late."

"Late! I called until four this morning. That's more than late."

"It's a long drive," Delaney said. "Let's not argue. I'm not in the mood."

"So what did you find out about the furniture?"

"Not much. An appraiser is going to have to look at most of it."

"You were in New Orleans all night and still don't know what you went to find out?"

Delaney sat up rigidly in bed. She was in no mood for Mark's lecturing. "I don't like your tone of voice, Mark."

"And I don't like you out all night doing God knows what. Has the lawyer straightened out that mess with the wills?"

"No," Delaney said shortly, "not yet."

"Ignorant hicks! I told that son of a bitch lawyer what to do, how much to pay that damn judge. Maybe I need to try paying off that yokel with the fake will. That might be the easiest way out. Frankly, I'm not concerned about proving any legal points here. I just want the damn deal closed."

Delaney reacted instinctively to the surge of indignation she felt, before it dawned on her that he had rejected her for herself last night. Still she felt protective of him. "He's not a yokel, and he doesn't want money. He wants to save the plantation."

There was a brief silence on the other end; then, "Really? Save the plantation, huh? A real tree-hugger, there. Don't let him fool you, Delaney. He just knows what it's worth. He's got to be shown he can't win. Then he'll take my offer."

"No, he won't. You don't know him," Delaney replied.

"Then maybe I need to get to know him. Sounds like you know him too well." Mark's voice went a pitch higher, a sure sign he was working into a fury. "I tell you what. Since you don't seem to be making much progress, I'll fly down and get this mess straightened out.''

''You don't have to do that,'' Delaney said, feeling a knot of dread form in the pit of her stomach. ''The lawyers are doing all they can. This sort of thing just takes a little time.''

''Come on, Delaney, where are your smarts? This is not like you. We've got a multimillion-dollar deal. We could have the money in our hands, and you're letting some clodhopper bamboozle you.''

''*We*, Mark? *We've* got a deal? If you recall, this is *my* property, and I can sell it however I want to—or keep it, for that matter!'' Delaney swallowed hard at her own words. Three million dollars. Had she just suggested throwing away three million dollars? Her throat hurt, dry from the drinking last night and the shock of what she had just said. *Only a fool—*

''What's happened to you since you've been down there? The heat get to you? I'm coming down. I can't get away until this afternoon, but I'll be on the first plane out. Don't do anything stupid before I get there, do you hear? And keep in mind, you've already signed the purchase agreement. The deal is done!''

''Mark! Don't . . . Mark? Mark?''

Delaney looked at the receiver as if it were responsible for the dead air on the other end of the line. *He hung up! The nerve of him!* Delaney slammed the phone down. *Come ahead then*, she thought angrily, *and just see what you can do!* She turned back over in bed and pulled the pillow over her aching head, vowing she would never go back to New Orleans again as long as she lived.

Chapter Eleven

After another hour of troubled slumber, Delaney opened her eyes to face the day and her nagging headache. To her drink-weakened eyes, the bedroom was awash with dazzling light. The slant of late-morning sunshine mottled the floor and the mahogany furniture with a kaleidoscope of images.

This room had grown on her quickly, almost as if she belonged here. She rolled onto her side, facing toward the center of the bed, relishing for another moment the luxury of the soft sheets and downy pillows. Her eyes widened and she quickly sat up, intrigued. There on the pillow beside her was a single red rose, its petals still fresh with dew. Smiling, Delaney picked up the lovely flower and brought it to her nose, breathing in the sweet scent. Tyce. How sweet of him. Then their argument

183

from the night before came back to her. But why? Why give her a rose after that?

Her mind drifted through yesterday with Tyce in New Orleans, how relaxed they had been together at first and how much fun they had exploring the old city. Then the unpleasantness with which the night ended, as well as Mark's phone call, intruded on her thoughts.

Glancing at the clock, Delaney realized the morning was almost gone. Dressing hurriedly, she went to the front door. The morning air was humid and growing warm. Tyce's truck was gone. Delaney heaved a sigh of frustration. It was just as well. She did not want to prolong last night's argument.

After putting the rose in a bud vase, she sat down with a cup of coffee and a piece of toast, staring out the window at the barren sugarcane fields, the brown, untended gardens, the ramshackle old house that meant so much to Tyce. Unexpectedly, a lump formed in her throat that made swallowing difficult.

Against her conscious will, Caroline had come to mean something to her, too. She had always despised it for taking her father away. A week ago, nothing would have given her more pleasure than to send a wrecking ball through the very heart of the mansion. Now that thought brought with it a vision of the light flickering out of Tyce's eyes as the old plantation came crashing down. She wasn't sure she could bear to do that to him now.

But what if she lost the legal battle? There would go her inheritance, her chance to guarantee her mother's old age and the possibility of fulfilling her own dreams without having to worry about finances. Three million dollars versus doing what was right. Tough decision. Maybe, Delaney mused, she didn't need that much money. So what if she took less money and sold the plantation to Tyce? She would still have enough to buy her mother a house and add substantially to her current savings.

Backing out of the deal at this late date would leave Mark unhappy. He had put a lot of effort into negotiating this contract, and it really wasn't fair to him, but taking Caroline from Tyce was not fair, either. One of them was going to lose, either way.

After leaving a message on Tyce's answering machine, asking him to come to the *garçonnière* when he returned, Delaney gathered her drawing pad and pencils. This was a good opportunity to sketch the front of the mansion as Tyce had requested. Finding a comfortable spot on a hummock of grass along the levee in front of the mansion, she put herself into her work and tried not to think about Mark or her dilemma. Sometimes, she had found, the mind worked better subconsciously.

The warmth of the sun and the smell of early-sprouting spring grass mingled with the breeze off the river, filling her senses with the essence of Caroline. She left off the boards over the windows of the ballroom and lightly penciled the windows in the way she imagined they would look. She'd have to get Tyce's input before finishing the drawing.

As the afternoon grew late and chilly, she studied the facade of the unusual plantation house to capture it in her memory forever. Unwanted tears stung her eyes. If only she'd known about her father earlier; if only she'd opened her mind all those times her mother had tried to explain. If only she'd met Tyce a long time ago. . . . She brushed the tears away, along with useless conjecture, then put the incomplete drawing into her tote bag and went back to the *garçonnière*.

Once there, she settled into a corner of the couch to decipher more of the white diary. Chloe's story fascinated her. The parts of the diary that she could make out were engrossing, hilarious at times, with Chloe's own rendition of her devilish pranks with the hidden rubies. Other entries were so heartbreaking that Delaney could not fight back tears as she read of her ancestor's undying love for Zach Brandon and the misery and heartache caused by Chloe's father.

As the hours passed, the waning light in the parlor made reading the tiny script more difficult. Delaney switched on the nearby lamp but couldn't bring herself to put the book down. Chloe had aged in the diary into her sixties, and a new baby, Donet, was born to her nephew Luc. The tone of Chloe's diary changed subtly after little Donet's birth, as if she had a new outlook on life, just as Auntie had said.

The thought of Auntie turned Delaney's mind in a different direction. She glanced around the room, hoping to see Auntie's form. The old lady hadn't been around lately, and Delaney actually missed her. Ghosts. How could she rationalize a ghost, even if the old woman's appearances and disappearances were odd—well, maybe completely inexplicable? Still, a ghost? Maybe even her great-aunt Donet! Delaney wrestled with that concept for a long while, delving into her memory for every ghost story she had ever heard. She wanted to see the old lady again so she could ask her outright who—or what—she was.

"Have you discovered where she hid the rubies yet?"

Heart hammering, Delaney jumped up, dropping the diary to the floor. From behind her, Tyce leaned down to retrieve it.

"I knocked," he offered. "You must not have heard me."

"Sorry," Delaney said, her hand still on her chest from the shock. "I was trying to read Chloe's diary."

"So I noticed. Has she said where she hid the rubies? It's a mystery that would certainly be worthwhile to solve. It would give you a little more money for your nest egg."

The flutter of excitement at seeing him died in Delaney's chest at the sharpness of his words, his voice cutting like the edge of brittle glass.

Tyce sat down in the chintz-covered chair next to the couch and thumbed slowly through the diary. "Interesting?"

"Very," Delaney said, hoping to revive some of their former camaraderie. "I've learned a lot of family history this week. Some of my ancestors were not exactly compassionate . . . or honest," she admitted reluctantly.

"Old Pierre was supposedly the devil himself, according to Brandon lore."

Delaney nodded. "According to Chloe, too. You should read my notes when I'm finished."

"Maybe I will. See if I can find those rubies for you." Tyce handed the book back to her. "So, why was I summoned? After last night you decided you couldn't bear another hour away from me, right?"

Delaney laughed nervously. He did not need to know how much he had been on her mind since then. He might make assumptions. And he might be right.

"Thanks for the rose. It's beautiful."

"What rose?"

Delaney frowned. "The one on my pillow this morning. I just assumed . . ." Her voice dropped off at his bewildered look. Why would he bring her a rose after last night? She didn't want to know any more about that rose or where it might have come from. "Never mind. The reason I called was to tell you that Mark phoned me this morning. Naturally, he's not happy with the way things are going. He's flying in tonight."

"Coming to straighten everything out, is he?"

"He seems to think so."

Tyce leaned forward in his chair, his eyes intent upon her face. "His coming won't improve the situation. In fact, it will only make things worse."

Delaney frowned. "How?"

"Because I'm willing to work with you when I win, but I'm not going to come to any agreement with this Mark."

"You are really convinced that your will is going to hold up in court, aren't you?"

"It's a valid will, Delaney. Miss Donet wrote it herself and showed it to me a few weeks before she died."

"Then why didn't you come forward with it at the beginning and save us all a lot of trouble?" Delaney demanded.

"I did come forward, but without the will, I didn't have a case. I couldn't locate it at first. She had never sent it to the lawyers."

"So where did you find it?"

Tyce fidgeted uncomfortably. "In the main house."

"Where in the main house?" she pressed. When he refused to get more specific, Delaney gave an impatient flick of her hand. "Frankly, I find your story hard to believe, anyway. Why would Aunt Donet leave Caroline to you just because you were making a few repairs for her? It really doesn't make sense."

"You know the story now. This place was stolen from

my family years ago. Maybe Miss Donet wanted to make restitution.''

''Oh, come on! By the time Aunt Donet was born, that was long past. I can't believe she cared.''

''She cared. Trust me.'' Tyce studied his hands for a long moment, then looked up at her again. ''I'll show you what I was doing, why she wanted me to have Caroline.''

Delaney hesitated. ''Where are you taking me this time? I'm not going back out in the swamp with you again.''

''We're just going over to the main house.''

''I've been there, done that,'' Delaney said, not recalling anything she had seen in the house that would make her change her mind.

''You just think you have.'' When she didn't get up at once, Tyce shot her a shadow of his old grin and held out his hand. ''Where's your sense of adventure?''

Delaney narrowed her eyes at him in aggravation, but she got up from the couch. He ushered her across the lawn in the fading late-afternoon light and unlocked the back door. The inside of the house was enveloped in shadow, but Tyce did not seem to notice.

''Turn on the lights,'' Delaney said.

''I know where I'm going. Trust me.'' He reached out and took her hand, leading her close behind him through the dark house until they reached the front hall. Gray light filtered through the tall windows facing the river, falling in ribbons on the broad staircase.

''You're going to have to turn on the lights before I go up there,'' Delaney warned, peering into the upstairs darkness.

''We're not going up.'' The jangle of keys on his ring tinkled through the empty rooms like music. He found the key he wanted and inserted it into the lock of the ballroom door.

"Why didn't you give me that key earlier when I asked for it?" Delaney demanded indignantly.

"Didn't have it with me at the time."

"You're lying!" she snapped.

"Maybe. It really doesn't matter at this point, does it?" he replied, his hand on the porcelain doorknob.

"That's a cop-out, Tyce. I had every right to have the key, and you lied about it. It does matter to me."

Tyce stared at her a long minute, then said quietly, "This room is very special to me. I wasn't ready to share it with somebody who had no concern for Caroline. I'm still not, but I think you should see it before you destroy it."

He opened one side of the floor-to-ceiling double doors. Delaney followed him inside. With the flip of a switch on the wall, the room materialized like magic before Delaney's eyes, bathed in golden light.

"Oh, my God," she whispered, turning slowly as she took in the magnificent white ballroom. "Oh, my God."

Tyce leaned against one of the towering columns in the center of the room while she made her way from one end to the other, touching the smooth marble of the mantels, the perfectly carved wood that detailed the room. At one of the windows, she drew back the lace curtains, only to be disappointed. She had forgotten the ballroom was boarded up outside.

"Is this where Chloe stood to wait for Zach?" she asked softly.

"I don't know."

"Does it face the river?"

"Yes."

"Then it has to be this one. Look, Tyce, there are

rose petals here, on the floor. They've stained the white paint.''

Tyce bent down beside her, examining the dark stains in the paint. ''Odd that the paint would take the color,'' he muttered, ''but then I've never tried that kind of paint before. I mixed it from the original formula that was used when the house was built.''

''You're kidding. Did you do all of this?'' she asked in awe. ''Yourself? All of it?''

''Yes,'' he replied. ''Alphonse and I did all the manual labor except the frieze-work around the ceiling. I had to call in an expert to patch it in spots.''

This was not the work of a handyman or even an architect. The artist-creator in Delaney knew a kindred spirit when it saw one. The obvious research, the work, the vision behind this room was phenomenal. She looked at Tyce. He met her gaze, his eyes afire.

''It's not falling down, Delaney. Can you see that now? Caroline is still very much alive,'' he said, his voice deep with emotion. ''This plantation is a part of my life I can't give up. It would be like cutting out my heart.''

Tyce was not being melodramatic, he was stating a fact. Delaney felt a hard wrench of regret inside her, knowing she would be destroying something that was so much a part of him. But the wheels were in motion. She didn't know if there was a way to stop the inevitable if she won the legal battle. If she reneged on the sale, one way or another, the earnest money had to be repaid. Foolishly, she had already spent some of it, but that could be covered by money in her savings account. Then she would be broke for sure. Delaney sat down dejectedly on the window ledge near where he squatted on his heels.

"I don't know what to do," she said honestly. "I don't know what I can do until the legalities are settled. What if I win, Tyce? If I win and go back on my deal with the developers, can you buy Caroline from me? I can't afford to keep it, and I have things in my life I want to do, too. I was counting on this money."

"I'm not a corporation, but I can make you a fair offer," he said, a new eagerness permeating his voice. He took her hand in both of his. "Would you do that?"

"Yes, I think I would do it. Looks like I'm going to miss the closing date on the mall deal, anyway. You know how lawyers love to drag their feet."

"I hope the foot-dragging is over. I've had that closing date extended a week."

Delaney jerked around and stood up at the familiar voice from across the room.

"Mark!"

He was standing just inside the doorway to the ballroom, smiling at her in a way that made her feel like a naughty child doing something forbidden. She wondered how much of their conversation had been overheard. Tyce rose to face Mark as he strode across the room to them.

"Nice room," Mark commented offhandedly.

"I didn't expect you so soon. I thought you'd call from the airport."

"I thought I'd save you the trouble, surprise you. I see that I did."

Flustered, Delaney felt the heat creep up her neck and into her cheeks. Covering her discomfiture, she glanced at Tyce. "Mark, this is Tyce Brandon. As you know, he holds the second will. Tyce, Mark Patterson."

Mark shook hands with Tyce and smiled in his easy, practiced manner. "Tyce, we meet at last! Delaney speaks often of you. I certainly look forward to working out this little glitch to our mutual satisfaction.''

Delaney had forgotten just how suave and charming he could be when he had something to gain. He slipped his arm around her waist and pulled her close, giving her a kiss. She pulled quickly away from his delving mouth. His arm remained snugly around her, keeping her next to him.

Before she left New York, she would have taken his open display of affection in stride, but the look she saw in his face was disconcerting. He was making the noises of a challenged male in Tyce's presence, flaunting his right of possession, and Delaney didn't like it one bit, for he had no claim on her. She shifted away from him. His grip tightened to something akin to pain. He was playing for keeps, and he intended for her to know that.

"Tyce," Mark said, using his most polished manner, the affectation he reserved for clients he intended to woo and win at any cost, "we certainly have enough business to discuss, and I'd suggest going for a drink or two, but I didn't see any likely place on my drive out. And quite frankly, I'm exhausted from my flight." Mark looked down sweetly at Delaney and gave her a kiss on the forehead. "So, if you'll excuse me tonight, I'll give you a ring in the morning and we can get together and come to an agreement."

Tyce did not seem in the least charmed by Mark's offer. In fact, if anything, he looked angry. "I think you'll be surprised how quickly we can get through this business," he said, his blue eyes boring into Mark. Although his voice hid whatever he was feeling, Delaney did not care to interpret the smoldering look that Tyce gave them both.

"I'll be short and direct," Tyce said. "I have a valid

will. I want the house itself, not money, so I'm not in the market for a payoff. When the judgment comes down, then we can talk about the best options so that Delaney isn't the one who gets stiffed.''

Tyce didn't wait for Mark's rejoinder. Instead, he motioned toward the door. "If you two can find your way out, I'll lock up behind you."

"I'll call you in the morning," Mark said, undaunted. "Let's go, babe. Have I been missing you!"

It was not until Mark drew her along with him toward the door, away from Tyce, that Delaney realized how far her feelings had shifted since she had seen him last. She found Mark's pretentiousness disgusting. She had seen him work clients before, until he had them believing he could do no wrong.

But Mark's wrong was that he always made sure he came out on top, regardless of how the client fared in the end. And usually, it was too late before Mark's victim realized what was going on. Delaney was not going to let that happen to Tyce. She wanted to run back into the ballroom, but even if she could have slipped Mark's death grip on her waist, she did not want to face the negative reaction she would get from Tyce now.

Not knowing the house as well as Tyce, she reached to flip on the light switch in the front foyer. The rich scent of roses wafted to her on the still air, sending a shiver down her spine and drawing her eyes instinctively in the direction of the stairs. For a moment she hesitated, thinking she saw a flash of red at the top of the stairs.

"Let's go," Mark said impatiently, and the spell was broken.

Delaney continued to stare at the landing, but nothing else moved, and she decided her eyes were playing tricks. By the time they reached the *garçonnière,* her mind was on the business at hand. Mark closed the door behind them, gave a quick glance around the inside of the house, then leveled his eyes on her.

"Okay, Delaney, what's going on?" he demanded, all pretense of charm gone now that they were alone.

"We've got a problem," Delaney replied simply.

"Yes, I know. Two wills. I'm taking care of that. That's not the problem I'm talking about. What's going on between you and Brandon?"

"I don't know what you mean," Delaney hedged. Tyce had made his feelings for her clear last night, but she could not put her own emotions into perspective. What she did know, however, was that she no longer had any delusions about Mark or her feelings for him. How had she ever tolerated his arrogance, the dishonesty and deception that he used in his business dealings? There was no way Mark was going to get his hands on Caroline now, not if she could prevent it.

"Tyce has been very helpful getting the furniture appraised and that sort of thing. He's not going to bend about the will."

"No matter what I'm willing to pay? Then he's a fool."

"It's not about money. He wants the house. It was built by his ancestors and he wants to restore it. You saw what he's done in the ballroom. I think he could actually make this place beautiful again."

"I see something here I don't like," Mark said. "I knew you'd come down here and get soft. Of course, I hadn't bargained on Brandon being in the picture to brainwash you."

"I am not brainwashed."

"Sure looks like it. Looks to me like something is

going on between the two of you, and I don't like that, Delaney. I won't be two-timed.''

"Two-timed?" Delaney shot back. "How can you be two-timed?"

"We are getting married this summer. Remember? Or has Brandon made you forget that? I know some women get taken in by that unsophisticated, plowboy type of man, but I always thought you had better sense."

Fighting back her fury, refusing to let Mark get the upper hand, Delaney met Mark's gaze full on. "It only makes you look small to belittle somebody you know nothing about, Mark. As for getting married, if you'll recall, you were the one doing all the talking, and you weren't listening all the times I said no. I never told you I would marry you. You just assumed."

"Is that so?" Mark said haughtily. "Assumed? Well, babe, you might as well assume the same thing, because it's going to happen. And your hick is going to be without his plantation, as well, so get used to it."

Delaney chose to ignore the warning tone in his voice. She saw the futility of arguing with Mark, as always. He would hear only what he wanted to hear and believe only what he wanted to believe. Right now, she just wanted to get rid of him.

"Did you really get the closing date extended?"

"The closing date? Sure, that was no problem," Mark nodded. "Another week. This deal is important. You do understand that, don't you?"

"Oh, yes, more than ever, I understand its importance to you. But, if Tyce wins, there's nothing you can do about it."

"There's always something," Mark said shortly.

"Like what? He truly doesn't want money, just the house." Delaney mustered her nerve and broached what she knew was going to be an unpleasant option. "Mark, Tyce offered to buy the plantation from me. He can't pay as much as the developers, but he would be willing to drop his lawsuit, I'm sure, in exchange for a reasonable price. That way, everybody wins, just not as big as—"

"No!" Mark thundered, his fists clenched by his side. "No! Are you insane? We are going through with the original deal. We'll just find a way to convince Brandon to butt out."

Ire prickled along Delaney's neck at Mark's tone of voice. As if it were his inheritance, not hers. As if nothing mattered except the money to be made from it. As if Tyce's dreams were expendable.

"Suppose I've decided I made the wrong decision. After all, this was my family's home for generations, too. I will just pay back the earnest money and cancel the deal. Then I can sell it to Tyce. It's that simple."

"Simple, hell!" Mark shouted, his face contorted with anger. "It's not simple. There's a lot more to breaking this deal than earnest money."

"Like what?" Delaney demanded. She knew Mark too well. Something was wrong here. For the first time, the possibility materialized that she was just another client to him. Would love or whatever emotion he claimed to have felt for her go by the wayside if she interfered with his business dealings? A worrisome knot in the pit of her stomach warned her to expect trouble. "What else is there to this deal?"

"Nothing. Just don't back out."

"Mark Patterson, you're lying to me. What's in that sales agreement?"

"Just don't back out."

"Well, I'm going to back out. I'm going to call the

lawyer first thing in the morning and tell him to notify the buyer,'' Delaney snapped, glad to be rid of the indecision that had plagued her recently. Immediately she knew that she had made the right decision—and the wrong one.

''Then prepare yourself for bankruptcy, darling. I knew something like this might happen. You should have read the contract closer. If you back out now, you owe not only the earnest money, but lawyers' fees, as well as a penalty of twenty-five percent of the offered price.''

Delaney felt the blood drain from her face, maybe from her very heart as she rapidly did the math in her head. ''That's over a million dollars, Mark,'' she whispered.

Mark smiled in triumph. Delaney wanted to cry . . . scream . . . smash that smile off his face! She had trusted Mark when he told her the contract was just a standard boilerplate form, that he had checked it all over, and everything was in order. Trust based on a false assumption that he loved her. Nobody would do this to someone he loved.

''You . . . you . . . you lousy, no-good—''

''Thank you, you need not go further,'' he said smugly. ''I believe you've seen my methods before. Don't try to play Miss Goody Two-shoes all of a sudden. Now, if we can get down to the business of getting this backwoods yokel off our necks, we can get on with our life.''

''*Our* life! *We* don't have a life. Get the picture, Mark! I never want to see you again as long as I live!''

''Be that as it may, babe, you'll see me plenty until this deal is finalized. As soon as you get away from here and Brandon, you'll come to your senses. You and I were made for each other.''

"Get out! Get out of here!" Delaney yelled.

Mark grinned hatefully. ''Nope, I'm tired. I think I'll just go on to bed. Care to join me?''

"You're not staying here."

''I'm not going anywhere else tonight. What are you going to do, throw me out physically? Or get that yokel to do it for you?'' Mark gave a jeering laugh. ''I doubt it. Besides, I'm too tired to drive back to Baton Rouge. I might meet with an accident on the road, and you wouldn't want that on your conscience, would you?''

Delaney didn't bother to inform him that right now, it wouldn't matter to her in the least what happened to him. Nor that she imagined Tyce would have no trouble pitching him out the door. However, Mark wasn't Tyce's problem. He was hers. But he was mistaken if he expected her to sleep under the same roof with him. Even the cold, dark mansion seemed far more inviting. She watched for a moment as he lugged his suitcase into her bedroom and started to make himself at home.

"Fine! Stay here, then. I'll find someplace else to sleep." She whirled and strode out of the room.

"Where the hell are you going?" Mark called, following behind her.

Delaney slammed the front door in his face as she went out into the cold night. Trembling with fury and on the verge of tears, she stopped on the back porch of the mansion, fumbling in her pocket for the key to the door. It opened a few inches on its own. Too grateful to be startled, she rushed inside—and into Tyce's arms.

Chapter Twelve

"What's wrong, Delaney?" Tyce held her back from him far enough to see her face in the pale shafts of moonlight falling through the uncovered windows. She was shaking and almost in tears. "Are you hurt?"

"No. I'm not hurt. Just . . . just . . ." Delaney stammered. A storm of fury glistened in her eyes and Tyce was relieved to see that she was not injured in any way, only extremely angry.

"All right, what's going on?" Tyce demanded, out of patience with her and her newly arrived boyfriend. "A little lover's spat already?"

"Oh, Tyce, please don't," she managed. "I don't know what to do!"

"First, why don't you go home and calm down a little." Tyce was not about to humor Delaney after what he had seen in the ballroom. She and this Mark must be on the verge of marriage, the way he acted. And Delaney didn't seem to put up much resistance. She might think Tyce was going to stand by and let her blow his world to smithereens, but she was dead wrong. He had business to take care of with his lawyer and didn't have time to play nursemaid. No, let Mark deal with her.

"I'm not going back there," she said, defiantly. "I told Mark to leave, and he wouldn't go. So I left. I'd rather sleep in the fields than under the same roof with him!"

"Wouldn't go? Like hell! I can get him out," Tyce said hotly.

"It's not worth a fight. He'll leave tomorrow."

"And you'll sleep here in the house? I don't think so."

An anxious look swept over her face. "I don't want you to get hurt over something this silly. Please, just let him be for now."

Tyce took her by the arms and looked deep into her eyes, trying to read her feelings, but all he saw was fear and agitation. What had Mark done to her? No matter how angry he was with Delaney, he would not stand by and let Mark abuse her.

"I'm not going to fight with him. But he's not staying here the night. You go to my house and wait for me. Go on."

She started to protest.

"I'm not in the mood for arguments," Tyce said bluntly. "I'll be there in a few minutes."

Delaney did not glance toward the *garçonnière* as she passed, Tyce noticed with a twinge of satisfaction. He stepped onto the porch of the *garçonnière* and pounded the door with a vengeance, wishing it were Mark Patterson's face. He hadn't liked Patterson from the first time he saw him, and now Delaney was distraught over something he had done. Tyce wanted the bastard gone. In fact, right now, he wanted both of them to go back to New York. He wished he had never met Delaney Bienville with her hell-bent determination to be rid of Caroline. He hit the door full force with his fist when Mark did not answer at once.

"Open up, Patterson, before I break the damn door in."

Mark opened the door, his brow furrowed in aggravation. "Take it easy, man, I was in the john. What do you want?"

Tyce shoved the door wide and stepped inside, forcing Mark backward. "I want you out of here, that's what I want. Now."

"Look, Tyce, I know you're upset about losing your chance at this plantation, but I want to work with you. We can find common ground if we—"

"No, hell, we can't. There is no common ground. Now, get out of here!"

"I'm not going anywhere. This is Delaney's property, and I have every right to stay. Where is Delaney? I want to talk to her."

Mark's belligerence only infuriated Tyce more. "No way. As for your right to be here, this property belongs to Delaney or to me. Either way, this dispute is between the two of us. You're not involved, get it, Patterson? You're the real estate agent. That's all. The sooner you realize that, the better off we'll all be."

"I'm going to talk to Delaney," Mark said indignantly. "We are engaged to be married. That gives me some rights in the matter, I'd say. Now, where is she?"

"Stay away from her. I don't know what you did to

her, but I'm going to find out, and I may come looking for you again. If she wants to talk to you, she'll call you. Now, get off the property.''

"I'm tired, and I'm going to bed. We'll discuss this first thing in the morning,'' Mark said with a confident sneer.

"You won't be here in the morning,'' Tyce assured him.

Mark gave a nasty smile and shook his head skeptically. "You mean you'd revert to common physical violence, Tyce? I thought you people might be more civilized by now.''

Tyce ignored the insult—for the moment. He brushed past Mark into Delaney's bedroom. Mark's suitcase lay open on the bed, the contents still neatly folded within. Calmly, Tyce closed the suitcase, fastened the latches, and hoisted it from the bed. Passing Mark once more, he took the suitcase and flung it as hard as he could out the open front door. It bounced twice on the gravel drive and landed against the tire of Mark's rented Lexus.

"What the hell . . . !'' Mark yelled. "That's a five-hundred-dollar suitcase, you damned hick.''

"No doubt,'' Tyce said, unruffled. "Now, do you want to leave here the same way your five-hundred-dollar suitcase did, or do you prefer walking out on your own like a smart Yankee would?''

Mark stood his ground for a moment, then gave Tyce a vicious scowl as he strode past. He turned around on the porch to face Tyce. "If you think this is the end of it, you're wrong, Brandon. I know people who will make you wish you'd never been born. I'm going to leave tonight because you're not worth the trouble of bruising my knuckles. But don't think you've won anything by it. I'll be back, and you'll be the one paying. Do you hear me?''

"Get the hell out of here," Tyce said. "I'm tired of fooling around with you." Mark's threats irritated him, but he would just as soon have the man go the easy way. However, if Mark continued to dawdle, Tyce had no qualms about dumping him on the highway personally.

Mark jerked his suitcase off the ground and tossed it into the backseat before sliding behind the wheel. The Lexus purred to life. Gravel crunched under the tires as the car gained speed down the drive and out of sight.

When Tyce got to his house, he found Delaney sitting in the dark kitchen.

"Thanks, Tyce," she said softly, looking out the window into the night, as if to be sure Mark was gone.

"No problem."

Tyce switched on the light over the sink to fill the room with a soft glow, staring at his reflection in the window while he regained his composure. Then he turned to Delaney. She looked tired and dazed. Tyce waited for her to decide when she was ready to talk.

After a few minutes, she related enough of her confrontation with Mark for Tyce to get the gist. The more she told him, the angrier he became. Now he wished he had pummeled Mark into the ground.

"So you're out a million dollars if you renege," Tyce pondered aloud. "I don't understand anybody signing a contract without knowing the terms. Maybe there's a loophole somewhere that a good lawyer could find."

"I never dreamed he'd do something like this to me," Delaney said dejectedly. "I should have known better. I've seen him deceive his clients more than once."

"A client is one thing, but somebody he intends to marry is a different matter—or should be. You might want to redefine your idea of true love in the future.''

"No joke," Delaney agreed quietly. "Mark's a greedy man. He worships money."

Tyce gave a slight shrug. "But how much money can he make on this deal? Commission is what, a few hundred thousand? That's a lot of money, but not enough to do what he did, as far as I'm concerned."

"You have a different code of honor, Tyce. Mark's code is to come out on top, no matter who he suckers. I knew that, but I didn't know this particular deal was so important to him. Like you said, it's a lot of money, but Mark makes that kind of commission on most of his transactions."

"So what makes this one special?" Tyce asked, half to himself.

Delaney shook her head and whispered, "I don't know."

"Well, we're going to find out," Tyce told her firmly. "We need to know."

"Tyce, it's not your problem. I appreciate what you're saying, but I was the one who trusted Mark and didn't read the contract. My stupidity got me into this, and I'll have to deal with it."

"No, you're wrong. The problem affects both of us. You're going to be out a million dollars because I'm not giving up this plantation. You don't seem to be able to accept that. I will have Caroline, one way or another. I have nurtured this dream all my life. I'm sure as hell not going to let it die now because some hotshot realtor pulled a crooked deal on a gullible lover. But maybe you'll be married to the guy and he'll pay off your part of the debt, if he really loves you. Just the same, I have to know where his interest lies in this deal."

Delaney registered the impact of his words with a

wounded look as she stared down at the pattern her fingertip was tracing on the table. He saw her lower lip tremble before she bit back the sob and swallowed it down to no more than a tiny sound in her throat. Immediately, Tyce wished he had not hurt her.

God, why couldn't he let this woman go? She was on the verge of destroying him, and he was kicking himself because he had hurt her feelings with the truth. But he could see the fear in her eyes. She was up against more than she could fight alone, yet Tyce knew from experience with her that Delaney would never rely on somebody else for anything. Even if she needed help, she'd never ask.

He gave a defeated sigh. He couldn't let her drown without lifting a hand. The least he could do was offer her the security of his house until morning. Tyce didn't trust Mark Patterson to leave her alone if she went back to the *garçonnière*. The least he could do was convince her to stay with him the night.

In spite of his better judgment, he wanted to do more, to take her in his arms, to tell her how much he needed her, to admit to her and to himself that he loved her. But he hesitated. Now wasn't the time. He was too angry with her, and her emotions were fragile, her psyche bruised by Mark's betrayal. She needed time to sort out her feelings before being assaulted from another direction. Added pressure might drive her away, and he didn't want to risk her safety, so he crossed the room to stand before her.

Lifting her face to his, he promised, "I'm going to try to get you out of this, Delaney. No matter what happens, I don't want to see you hurt by Caroline again. Try to trust me."

Through unshed tears, she gave him a slight smile.

"I'll try, but I'm not very good at it, you know."

"I don't want you going back to the *garçonnière* tonight. I'll sleep on the couch. You take my bed."

Delaney started to protest, then thought better of it. "Thank you. I'm sorry to be so much trouble."

"You are a pack of trouble, I have to admit." He leaned down to give her a reassuring peck on the forehead. "But I'm adjusting. You go to sleep. We'll work everything out tomorrow."

At nine o'clock the next morning, Tyce sat with his back against the driver's door, right foot propped on the dashboard of his truck, patiently holding the cell phone to his ear, waiting for the secretary to put his lawyer, Wes Hartman, on the line. He was in his truck because he didn't want Delaney to overhear his conversation. Beyond the bedroom door, she had been quiet enough to be sleeping, but Tyce didn't want to chance her getting up in the middle of his call.

"Wes Hartman."

The familiar voice on the other end of the line brought Tyce's attention back to the business at hand.

"Good morning, Wes. Tyce Brandon. Any word yet?"

"Actually, there is. Ironic you should call just now. I was on the other line with an old law school chum of mine whose son is an aide for Judge Babineaux. Seems somebody from the enemy camp made noises that they were willing to donate quite a few bucks to the judge's campaign fund next election if he'd go their way. Babineaux's people are trying to find out the source of the bribe, but it came to the aide filtered through several channels, so I doubt they'll come up with anything concrete enough to press any charges."

"That's interesting," Tyce said. "The real estate broker who made this deal just got to town last night. Pollyanna he's not. Could be he stirred the pot."

"Well, he stirred it the wrong way. Maybe he heard all Louisiana officials are crooked and lying in wait for a bribe, but he picked the wrong one in old Babineaux. He's straight as an arrow and, besides that, he hates anybody from outside Louisiana trying to tell him what to do. The very idea of a bribe in this case set him off. I'm sure he was inclined in your favor, anyway, so this will help us and hurt them. Unfortunately, Babineaux's out of town until late next week, so the ruling won't come down until then, but I think I can safely say we'll win."

A bolt of elation shot through Tyce, tingling every muscle in his body with adrenaline. If Wes's hunch was right, Caroline was, in effect, his. The thought brought him upright in the truck, grinning like a man who had just hit a grand slam to win the game. As he listened to Wes, his gaze drifted to Caroline, refusing to see the neglect the plantation house had suffered but envisioning her as he always did, majestic and proud, just as she had stood in her glory days.

Then Wes mentioned Delaney. Suddenly, victory wasn't so sweet, as Tyce pondered her dilemma. The judge's decision would ruin Delaney. There had to be a way to get around Mark and his contract. And if not, then Tyce would help Delaney pay off the debt, if necessary. Now that he knew Caroline was his, he was willing to be generous in spite of what she had almost done. Nothing could daunt him. He was on top of the world, and there was nothing he couldn't overcome one way or another!

"Tell you what, Wes. Do me a favor. Get a private detective to look into this deal between Mark Patterson and the developer who wants this land. I suspect there's another negotiation going on between those two that hinges on possession of Caroline. I want to know what it is. This guy sounds like he's willing to spend a hell of a lot more than his real estate commission to see this thing through. If you get anything, fax it to me at my number at Caroline. Your secretary has it.''

''Sure, I can do that.''

As an afterthought, Tyce asked, ''Wes, suppose I drop the lawsuit against the Bienville estate before the ruling. Delaney would get the plantation, right?''

In the bewildered silence that followed, Tyce could have heard a pin drop across the distance. Finally, Wes found his voice. ''You've got to be kidding,'' he croaked. ''After all this? After you know you're going to win? Sober up, Tyce, and call me back later with that question.''

''I am sober, Wes. And the question was just hypothetical, so don't get excited. Let me know if you get anything on Patterson. Good-bye.''

Tyce clicked off his cell phone, laid it aside, and stared out the windshield at the dilapidated old mansion: his lifetime dream, his at last. Excitement welled up inside to the point he thought he might burst. There was so much to be done, and he had lost time having to deal with all the legalities. But now he could go on with his plans. He could do all the things that needed to be done. He could bring Caroline back to life. His mind raced ahead to the work that was left. Another good two years, but he didn't mind. He and Delaney could—

Tyce brought himself up short. Could what? Why did his vision automatically include her? Closing his eyes, he tried to force himself back to the time before she arrived to disrupt his life completely, when his dream was solitary, with nothing to sidetrack him. That time seemed far removed. Every thought of his future seemed to be infused with Delaney's presence. Try as he would to deny it, she colored the very fiber of his existence now. What if Caroline would never be complete without Delaney? And, more disturbing, what if Caroline alone was no longer enough for Tyce?

The thought was so frustrating that Tyce slammed his hand against the steering wheel. What the hell was he going to do? He was suddenly struck with the probability that she would go back to New York, leave him, desert Caroline, strip the joy from his dream, and leave only a difficult project that demanded completion.

Anger at the unpredictability of fate welled up inside him, crying for release. As a teenager, he used to go skidding through the sugarcane fields, cutting donuts and laying ruts when he felt this way. Back then, the thrill alone had been enough to settle him down. But he was long past being a teenager, and it was going to take something a lot more permanent than a muddy field to satisfy him this time. Adolescence did have its advantages, Tyce thought ruefully, as he walked back toward the cottage, wondering how he was going to manage to convince Delaney to spend her life with him, bankrupt and living on a plantation she despised. The outlook was not promising in that respect.

Delaney was up, sitting at the table, looking out the kitchen window with a steaming cup of coffee from the pot he had made before going out to call his lawyer. She looked up when she heard him come in and self-consciously ran her fingers through her hair. She probably thought she looked terrible. Her hair was disheveled from sleep, her eyes puffy and stained dark underneath with a wash of mascara. But Tyce thought she was rather fetching with her guard down, sitting there with the T-shirt that he had given her to sleep in hanging loose over her jeans. She could grace his table this way every morning.

In fact, the idea was so appealing that he might be better off thinking about something else as his body responded to the temptation. Besides, he didn't like the hurt, vulnerable look about her this particular morning. He wanted to throttle Mark Patterson. He wanted the old Delaney back. He would settle for a smile.

Taking her face in his hands, he looked into her eyes. "Hey, everything's going to be all right. Okay?"

She nodded dubiously.

"Trust me," Tyce said, and her lips turned up at the corners with the hint of a smile, which satisfied him for the moment. "That's better. Hungry?"

"No."

"I could whip up some beignets," he offered.

She shook her head. "I couldn't eat. Thanks, though."

"This Mark is a wheeler-dealer," Tyce commented.

"He's a sharp, ambitious guy. I should have known." She looked like she might cry again.

"You're going to be all right, I promise. We'll find a way to get through this. I talked to my lawyer this morning. Somebody tried to bribe the judge yesterday. I wonder who?"

"Mark?"

"Maybe so. What I don't understand is why this piece of land is so important. There are plenty of other sites around here that would serve the purpose of a shopping mall better than this out-of-the-way place. The buyer's not going to lose anything if the sale falls through; he'll just go shopping someplace else. Mark is the one with a vested interest in this particular deal."

"That's true," Delaney agreed, "but all he gets is his commission."

"I'd be willing to bet he's bargaining on more than his commission. Whoever bribed Judge Babineaux offered a lot of money."

"I'm so sorry, Tyce," Delaney said, her voice heavy with emotion. "If I'd known about all this before, I'd never have tried to take Caroline away from you. I wish I'd never heard of the place. I don't know what to do anymore."

"Just hang tight. It will all work itself out," Tyce assured her, weighing the pros and cons of telling her what he had learned that morning about the judge's upcoming ruling. He didn't want to add to her burden, but she'd learn in time that she'd lost. Maybe then he could convince her to let him help her. Maybe he could convince her to stay. Or maybe she would run away from him forever, ashamed of what she had gotten into and too proud to accept his help. She'd be ruined, and that would be hard for her to take, as independent as she was.

He pictured her struggling for years to pull herself out of debt or going bankrupt and having to start all over again. He couldn't stand the idea, and he held the power to change her fate. Caroline or Delaney. Tyce glanced out the window, then his eyes met Delaney's. If things boiled down to that one decision . . . *Dear God*, he prayed, *don't let it come to that*.

"Try not to worry, Delaney," Tyce said, attempting to delay the inevitable. "My lawyer told me this morning that there won't be a ruling on Caroline this week. We can't hurry fate, so why don't we just ignore it for a few days? We've got plenty of work to do. The furniture has to be moved. I'd have to do that, anyway, to work on the place. Let's get that accomplished, put the furniture in storage, clear out the attic. It'll keep both our minds occupied.''

Delaney smiled, though tears shone in her eyes. ''You're right. We should work on that together. We can salvage the furniture at least. I can't seem to think straight this morning. I just feel confused.''

''Hey, no problem. You're still a little shaken after last night. That's to be expected. We'll take care of everything.'' Tyce soothed her with words, when what he wanted was to kiss away her fears, lay her down, and love her until she forgot all about Mark.

As if she could read his mind, she pulled away from him. Taking her empty coffee cup to the sink, she washed it out and picked up a towel to dry it. ''I'm going home and change clothes. Thanks for taking me in. I don't know what I would have done.''

''I'll walk over with you,'' Tyce said, disappointed. Her shrinking back from him hurt. In spite of their differences, he had fallen in love with Delaney and would be a long time getting over her. Obviously, she was not interested, however, and unless he could change that rapidly, he was going to be a lonely man, even with Caroline to sustain him.

''You don't have to. I'm fine, really.''

''I know. I want to get Chloe's diary from the house.'' He gave that as an excuse, but he actually intended to shadow her every move until he was sure there would be no further threat from Mark. Tyce was not going to allow her to be hurt. He'd see this thing through with her, then she could make her own decision about her future. If he just kept his distance emotionally, hard as that would be, maybe she'd trust him more. He would not press her into a relationship she did not want. The decision to commit to him had to be hers and hers alone.

"But I haven't finished the diary. I wanted to try to decipher the rest."

"I'll give it back. It sounds crazy, but I thought we might try to figure out where she hid those rubies. They're supposed to be worth a fortune, and Chloe used the rubies to bait the Bienville men for years. Nobody ever found them, but knowing Chloe's mischievous little mind, I'd bet she put plenty of hints in that diary. Then you could decide what you wanted to do without having to worry about Mark."

"Oh, I know what I'd do," Delaney said emphatically. "I'd give you this plantation and take the next flight to New York."

Tyce flinched at her answer: half right, half wrong.

After a moment of thought, Delaney said, "She does go into detail about the wild-goose chases she gave her relatives, but surely you don't think we can find them when nobody else did."

"I don't know," Tyce grinned, "maybe the next time your old auntie appears, you could ask her. Chloe might have told her. After all, Donet was her favorite niece."

"Yeah, right, Tyce. Quit with that ghost business today. I'm not in the mood for jokes."

"Who's joking?" Tyce ducked as Delaney flung the damp dishcloth at his head. "I'll get you a coat."

When they entered the *garçonnière,* the phone was ringing. Before Tyce could intervene, Delaney answered it. Her blanched face told him who was on the other end. He took the phone from her, listened long enough to hear a few angry words, then said, "Don't call here again, Mark. I'll have you arrested for harassment."

Tyce slammed the receiver down. Immediately, it began to ring again.

"Don't answer it," Tyce ordered. After three rings, the answering machine in the other room picked up.

Delaney's mother's voice, frantic with worry, came to them after a few seconds. Quickly, Delaney picked up the receiver. "I'm sorry, Mother," she began. "No, I'm all right. Really. I stayed someplace else last night. What did he tell you?"

To avoid eavesdropping, Tyce walked into the bedroom. The Message Waiting light on the answering machine was blinking repeatedly. Tyce pressed the button to listen to the messages. One message last night was from Delaney's mother, after Mark had called and upset her. She sounded terribly worried as she begged Delaney to call her at once. The other seven were from Mark, one giving Delaney the room number of a Baton Rouge hotel where she could reach him. At first, cajoling and apologetic, the tone of Mark's last few messages was menacing.

"Poor Mother. Mark had her scared to death that I was being forcibly detained," Delaney said from the doorway. "He is such a low-life."

"That he is. I don't trust him. He's been calling all morning, leaving messages."

Delaney started to push the button on the answering machine, but Tyce caught her hand to stop her.

"You don't have to listen to them. They're all about the same."

The worried look in Delaney's eyes told him she understood.

"I want you to stay with me."

She looked uncertain.

"All right, so you don't trust me, either. You can stay with my mom. She loves company."

"I couldn't do that, Tyce. She doesn't even know me. And I'm not afraid of you, if that's what you think. It's just that I've already wrecked your life enough. I don't want to make it any worse by imposing on you again."

Tyce gave a short laugh and caught Delaney by the shoulders, gently rubbing his hands up and down her arms. "You haven't wrecked my life yet. If anything, you're making me consider the possibility that there is something more to living than the past. So, if you're not afraid of me, pack your things while I get the diary. Who knows, those rubies might be our saving grace."

"Why are you so good to me when I may be on the verge of destroying your dreams? You'll hate me when Caroline is gone."

"I'll never hate you, Delaney, no matter what happens," Tyce said truthfully, wishing he could find the words to make her understand exactly how he did feel. "Trust me."

He was on the verge of taking a chance on telling her how much he loved her when the phone rang again, jolting both of them. They looked at one another as the ringing was replaced by the click of the answering machine. When the message was done, Mark's voice came through. Tyce muttered a curse, then reached over and turned the machine off.

"Let him talk," he said angrily. "Get your clothes together and let's go home."

Chapter Thirteen

Delaney watched Tyce through the open window, talking to Alphonse, who had pulled up a few minutes earlier in his old Blazer, set far off the ground on huge tires. The morning was bright with sunshine and the chirping laughter of birds filled the trees. Tyce had raised most of the windows when he got up, and a breeze hinting of the warmth soon to come sweetened the cottage air.

With a foot propped on the Blazer's bumper and arms resting across his knee, Tyce looked serious as he spoke. No doubt, he was telling Alphonse about Mark, because Alphonse glanced toward the *garçonnière*, then at Tyce's cottage. Delaney drew back a few feet, embarrassed to be caught watching. But she didn't move far enough to lose sight of Tyce. She just wanted to look at him for a while, as if to make up for the time she had lost already.

Last night when he took her in, she had felt like a drowning swimmer pulled from the water as she went under for the third time. Now she knew the kind of man that Tyce was. As angry with her as he was and had reason to be, he had brought her into his home and protected her. He seemed to actually care what happened to her, even though she had unwittingly dumped her troubles on him.

From the beginning, her feelings for Tyce had been different from those she had developed for Mark or any other man to whom she had been attracted. Now she was beginning to realize why: Tyce was the first truly decent, honorable man she had ever known. In fact, he was the best thing that had ever happened to her, and she had let him slip through her fingers—no, driven him away—in an attempt to preserve a life that seemed foreign to her now. Why hadn't she known love when it hit her in the face?

Since being at Caroline, she had sensed her soul awakening, had felt her heart pound when Tyce kissed her, had opened her eyes one morning to welcome a new day. Delaney had come alive at Caroline, and Tyce was the reason. In a week the ruling would come regarding the plantation's ownership—a decision that would change their lives forever, one way or another. All she wished now was that when it was over, she still had Tyce, but that did not seem possible.

Tyce straightened, took his foot off the bumper, and seemed to be concluding his conversation with Alphonse. They made no move toward the house but shook hands instead. Strange how men always shake hands coming and going, Delaney thought, watching the friends part, but women only shake hands in the impersonal world of business.

For herself, however, she felt as if she had done nothing more than shake hands with the world for years; not out of camaraderie like Tyce and Alphonse, but in an attempt to keep everything at bay, to avoid emotional involvement, to avoid embracing life. The aloofness, the coolness toward others that she had developed as a shield against her own feelings had ultimately betrayed her.

She sighed to think how much she must have lost over time: friendships never formed, kindnesses never bestowed, love never exchanged. There was a lot of making up to do. As Alphonse got into his truck, Delaney turned away from the window, stopping before the stove. Cooking was something she needed to learn. Tyce could teach her. She would learn a lot of things, if he would be her mentor. If only she could win back his love and trust before the final decision was made about Caroline.

"Are you ready to get to work?" Tyce called as he came into the house through the front door. "We've got a lot to do."

Delaney smiled as she turned to him. Could he read minds? *You just don't know how much,* she told him silently, just in case. Then aloud, she said, "I'm ready. Where do we start?"

She joined him, and they left the house together. "I called a storage company," Tyce told her. "They'll be out Thursday to get the furniture. Alphonse is coming with his cousins that day to bring down the heavy pieces. I don't want the liability of having the movers go upstairs on the weak floors."

"You don't mind if Alphonse and his cousins fall through?" Delaney teased.

"Wouldn't hurt Alphonse as long as he lands on his head. Besides, he knows the flooring about as well as I do." Tyce drew her under his arm in a friendly embrace as they walked across the lawn. "Are you feeling better this morning?"

"Yes, much better, thank you," Delaney said, smiling up at him, delighted with his touch and the warmth of his body next to hers. Why had she ever turned this man's affection away? What a fool, she thought to herself. Never again.

"I thought you and I could move the lightweight furniture and boxes downstairs today. Then tomorrow I need to start dismantling the scaffolding from upstairs and lay some heavy plywood on the floors in the attic so we can get the trunks out."

"A man with a plan," Delaney commented.

"Yep. More than one, in fact," Tyce said, pulling her a fraction closer to his side.

"And what are the others?"

Tyce merely grinned down at her. "Wouldn't you like to know? But you'll have to figure it out on your own." He released her, reached in his pocket, and withdrew his key ring, opening the door and allowing her through before him.

The inside of the mansion was quiet and peaceful, with shafts of sunlight brightening even the far corners. For a moment, Delaney could imagine the house full of light and laughter and love, ringing with the voices of frolicking children. Little towheaded, blue-eyed children. It was one of the few times in her adult life she had thought of having kids, and the thought shocked her momentarily. Sooner or later, she would have to face her predicament again, but she was going to put it off until the inevitable was forced on her.

"Let's clear out the front parlor for the heavy furniture and put the smaller things in the dining room and back rooms," Tyce suggested.

All day, they worked together, moving small occasional tables, chairs, boxes of dishes and knickknacks, quilts, and blankets to the back rooms. Tyce told her that a lot of the contents of the old house had been packed up over the years as her aunt Donet gradually closed off more and more of the house. When she finally moved into the *garçonnière,* she took the best of the furnishings with her and the mansion became an extravagant storeroom for the rest. Tyce kept her entertained with anecdotes about her aunt and other members of the family as they worked.

"Tell me more about my aunt Donet." Delaney was intrigued by her great-aunt. At first, she could not imagine why Aunt Donet would bequeath her home to a man who was not even related to her. But as Delaney came to know Tyce better, she was beginning to understand why that might happen.

"Well," Tyce said, thinking a moment before he went on, "there was the time she decided she wanted to ride a horse—at seventy-five years old."

"You're kidding?"

"Nope, I'm serious. I was on break from college and was helping her out by doing some repairs on the *garçonnière.* There was an old plow horse that had belonged to one of the sharecroppers. When the old man died, the nag was put out to pasture behind the old barn. Miss Donet felt sorry for the old fellow, imagined he was lonesome, so she got in the habit of taking him carrots and apples. One day, she was petting him and she decided she wanted to ride him. I tried to talk her out of it, but she was a very determined woman. She hitched her skirts up between her legs and fastened them at the waist.

" 'I used to ride behind Lee,' she announced. 'I'm sure I can do it. He's a gentleman of a horse and will do fine. Now, boost me up or I shall get a mounting block.'

" 'All right,' I finally agreed, thinking I would lead the horse around the pasture for her once or twice and that would be it. Truly he did seem to be a docile old beast and hardly moved at all in the pasture unless he was made to."

"I can't believe you put her on a horse at that age!"

"Trust me, she would have gotten on him somehow by herself if I hadn't. I figured she was safer with me leading him than out there by herself."

"Okay, you put her on the horse and led her around the pasture," Delaney prompted.

"I started to lead her around the pasture," Tyce said with a disbelieving shake of his head. "But the old nag was a plow horse all his life, not a riding horse. He didn't know what to think about somebody on his back, even a little bird of a woman like Miss Donet had become. He bolted. Jerked the reins right out of my hands."

"Oh, no! Poor Aunt Donet. Was she hurt?"

"Thank God, the pasture was small and well maintained. The old nag didn't break his leg in a hole, and he wasn't mean, just startled. But I'm sure I made a fool of myself, flailing across that pasture after those two old creatures. The horse and I tired about the same time, which doesn't say much for our stamina. I grabbed the reins, ready to throttle the beast and send him to the glue factory. Miss Donet was making these little gasping sounds. I thought she was having a heart attack. I tied the horse to the fence and grabbed for her to get her down before she collapsed. Well, she collapsed all right. Collapsed into my arms giggling her head off like a schoolgirl. When she finally caught her breath, she beamed up at me and said, 'My goodness, that was exhilarating. I didn't do badly for my first time, did I?' '' Tyce laughed as he finished his story. ''I considered shooting both of them and putting them out of their misery on the spot!''

''I wish I had known Aunt Donet,'' Delaney said, wiping tears of amusement from her eyes.

''I wish you had, too. She was a gracious, charming lady,'' Tyce said. He looked up in the direction of the locked ballroom and she heard him say softly, ''I really miss her. The afternoon after I finished the ballroom for her, I took her to show her. She dressed up as if it were a special occasion, and I guess to her, it was. She and my uncle Lee were supposed to be married in there. That's probably why she wanted the ballroom restored first. We danced. . . .'' Tyce hesitated, his eyes narrowing as he went back to that day. ''She acted . . . oddly that day, as if she were in another place, another time. Her mind had started to wander, or at least I thought so. She had been talking about Chloe a lot lately, and I wrote it off to senility. Of course, now, I have to question that diagnosis.''

''Maybe she was make-believing you were Lee come back to her for a dance. You look just like the pictures of him, you know.'' Like an epiphany, Delaney's aunt Donet's reasoning became crystal clear. To her, this man was her Lee, come back to her just as he had left years before, a young, vital man with a dream. And she was intent on making that dream come true for him. Delaney was sorry to the bottom of her soul for the part she had played in destroying her aunt's plan.

Tyce lifted his eyebrows in consideration. "Maybe she did, at that. I hadn't thought about it that way. If that's the case, I'm happy we had the afternoon together."

Tyce placed the last box from upstairs on the floor next to the others, then squatted beside it to secure the flaps with packing tape.

"Tyce, if I ask you a question, will you tell me the truth?"

"Uh-oh, true confession time." He turned back to finish taping the box.

"Don't tease. I really want to know."

"Okay, shoot."

"It's about my aunt," Delaney began, but found her question hard to form.

Tyce gave a nod and waited for her to go on.

"Auntie . . . that old woman who visited me . . . Were you kidding when you said she was my aunt Donet?"

"What you really want to know is whether I believe in ghosts, right?" Tyce sat back on his haunches to look up at her.

"Well, do you?"

"The picture you showed me was of your aunt Donet. Now, what or whom you saw and talked to, I can't say, because I never saw anything myself."

"You're avoiding my question."

"Damn right. I don't intend to come right out and admit to believing in ghosts and haunts. People have been committed for less than that."

"You said you saw Chloe."

"I said I dreamed I saw Chloe."

"I think you think you really saw her and don't want to believe it."

Tyce shrugged. "And unless I see her again when I know I'm awake, I'm sticking to that story."

"I think Auntie was my great-aunt come back to me," Delaney said with conviction. "And I hope so. At least I got to know her a little bit."

"That's good, if you want to think about it that way," Tyce said, rising and dusting his hands off. "We've done enough for today. I'm beat. Come on, I'll heat up some gumbo for us."

"Sounds good."

Delaney was exhausted and starved. By the time they had eaten and they each had showered, it was late, and they were both ready to drop into bed. Tyce made up the couch again, and Delaney went to sleep in his bedroom, but tonight she missed him dreadfully.

On Tuesday, while Tyce worked in the mansion taking down scaffolding, Delaney finished packing up her great-aunt's belongings from the *garçonnière*. There were several more messages on the machine, but she didn't listen to them, knowing they were probably from Mark. She had no intention of communicating with him until the judge's ruling came. Then she would know where she stood and what her options were.

Delaney left the boxes of clothing and linens stacked neatly in one of the guest bedrooms, then packed up the statuary and books from the parlor. All those would go into storage for now, along with the furniture. She emptied the refrigerator and took her meager groceries to Tyce's kitchen, which, in contrast, was amply stocked for any occasion. She'd never be as organized as he was, but maybe if he had grown to love her, he would have overlooked her domestic faults.

Finally, she packed her own clothes and toiletries. Tyce was adamant that she was going to stay with him as long as Mark was in Louisiana. She had been commuting back and forth to get what she needed, but since the *garçonnière* was being emptied the next day along with the house, her things had to be packed up and moved over today.

When the only boxes remaining contained her aunt's possessions, Delaney sat down on a chair and looked around the cluttered parlor. What a difference from the lovely, neat room that had greeted her that first day at Caroline. It was symbolic of what had happened to her life in the same period of time, Delaney thought wryly. From order and control to complete chaos. Now nothing could entice her back to that time before Tyce. Whatever risks lay ahead, she would rather face them if there was a chance of staying with Tyce.

"Hello, dearie."

Delaney's heart thumped against her ribs as she turned toward the sound of Auntie's voice. The idea of speaking to this old woman who, in defiance of all logic, might be a ghost, was overwhelming. She stood in a corner of the room, dressed in a lovely ivory lace dress, her snowy hair covered by a shadowy veil, her hands encased in delicate gloves. She appeared to be dressed for a special occasion.

"The place looks quite forlorn, doesn't it?" she said softly. *"I suppose it was inevitable."*

"I'm sorry," Delaney said truthfully. "I didn't know . . . I never meant to cause so much heartache."

"I know, child. I know. Life will go on, I assure you."

Delaney hung her head for a moment, then looked back at the woman, afraid to voice her next question. Auntie spoke before she could. *"I have come to say good-bye, my dear. I have been called away by someone I haven't seen in quite a long while."*

"Where are you going?" Delaney asked in surprise.

"Far away, I'm told. But it will be a most welcome reunion, one I have longed for these many years. I would counsel you to follow your heart, child. Don't allow pride or fear or weakness to keep you from the one you truly love. The loneliness of losing him would be far worse than anything you might endure with him by your side. Tyce loves you, dear. And you love him. Don't let misunderstandings keep you from telling him so."

"Are you sure he cares for me, Auntie?" Delaney asked. "I have already driven him away with my foolishness. He is very angry. I can sense it in him, even though he is outwardly friendly to me."

"It would take far more than foolishness to kill that young man's love for you. Don't make the mistake that I made as a girl. Don't lose him as I lost Lee." The old lady's eyes glimmered brightly, as if with tears. Then, to Delaney's astonishment, her entire form began to shimmer with a silvery light. She was beginning to fade before Delaney's eyes!

"Aunt Donet? You are my aunt Donet!" Delaney called, rising to go toward the dissipating figure. "Aunt Donet, wait! Please don't go yet!"

"I have been called, child. Lee awaits me, impatiently, as always. This time, I shall not disappoint him. Good-bye, my precious niece. I wish you a lifetime of happiness."

"Aunt Donet!" By the time Delaney reached the corner, there was nothing there but a cool draft of air in the still room. Delaney felt the back of her neck prickle. Now that the apparition had vanished, she did not feel so brave in the room alone. The sense of comfort that

Auntie always brought with her was gone now, but her words rang in Delaney's ears.

"Thank you, Aunt." She called softly, blowing a gentle kiss after the ghost. "I will do all that I can to keep him."

With a last look behind her, Delaney left the *garçonnière,* locking the door securely behind her. Running along the graveled drive between the two houses, she hurried to Tyce's cottage. He was not there, and Delaney knew he must be hungry by now. She would make sandwiches and take them over to the big house and eat lunch with Tyce. He would be interested in Auntie's visit.

As she was putting the bread away, the phone rang. Without thinking, she picked up on the kitchen extension. "Hello."

"I know you got my messages, Delaney. Why the hell haven't you called me back?"

"Mark! How did you get this number?"

"I've got my ways, baby, and you know it. Now, why don't you come to your senses and quit playing this little game of hard-to-get with me?"

"There was nothing between us, Mark. Why won't you accept that? We went out a few times; that's it. And after what you did to me, I'm shocked that you have the gall to contact me again."

There was a long silence on the other end. Delaney was on the verge of hanging up the phone when Mark spoke again. "What did I do? I wrote a little clause into a sales contract to make sure the deal went through. So what? It was for your own good, so some yokel like Brandon wouldn't talk you into doing something stupid. We had a good thing, babe. Remember? Meet me and let's talk. This guy's got you so confused you don't know what you're doing."

"I know what I'm doing. We didn't have anything, Mark."

"Oh, so what do you have with Tyce Brandon? Love? You love this hick? You've gone off the deep end. Fine. Screw your brains out with him, for all it matters. But you're not getting out of this deal. Do you hear me? And if you think you're safe there with him, think again. I can get to you any time I want to. I'm keeping an eye on you, remember that."

"What do you mean?" Delaney demanded.

"Just what I said. I'm watching you, and you're not skipping out on this sale. I'll see to that."

"Stay away from me, Mark. Just stay away." Delaney slammed the phone down, her heart pounding. Her first reaction was to run to Tyce and tell him, but on second thought, she decided to keep Mark's call to herself. He was probably just bluffing when he said he was watching them. She'd seen no sign of anybody around, and it would only make Tyce mad again to bring up Mark's name. She took the sandwiches and left for the main house, but she couldn't help glancing around nervously.

They ate lunch in comparative silence. Tyce was tired, and Delaney was unnerved from her conversation with Mark. Not until she was on the way back to the cottage to unpack her things did she realize she forgot to tell Tyce about Auntie's visit. Whether to tell him all that was said was still under debate. Delaney pondered the wisdom of blurting out her feelings to him, only to be rejected. Still, she had to admit she didn't want to spend her life like her ancestors had, and sooner or later, she was going to have to take a chance. Maybe tonight.

After Tyce quit working late that afternoon, he showered, and they ate a light meal. Then they spent the evening poring over Chloe's diary together, trying to decipher enough of it to locate the rubies. Some of the pages were in terrible shape, and figuring out Chloe's delicate handwriting was difficult. With their heads bowed close together over the desk, Delaney soon found she was paying more attention to Tyce than to the diary.

His very nearness put her senses on edge. He smelled clean and earthily masculine. Delaney breathed in the scent of the soap he had used, the subtle aftershave that braced his close-shaven jaw, the freshness of his cotton T-shirt against warm skin, and underneath it all, that basic, pheromonal perfume given off by a virile male animal in its prime.

Delaney sensed the power within him like never before. She was hungry for his touch, but he had made no advances tonight. Studying his strong profile as he concentrated on the diary, she moved a fraction of an inch closer so that her arm touched his, sending fiery messages along the nerves of her skin. He was maddeningly unaware of her. If he felt her touch, he didn't respond. Delaney couldn't stand it. Where was the passion he had shown before in New Orleans, even as early as the excursion to Alphonse's, when they had danced into the night? Delaney wanted that back. She wanted him to love her.

Delaney closed the diary under his nose. With a puzzled look, he turned to her. She reached over and kissed him. Thank God, he didn't pull away. With her hand behind his head, she pulled him closer, wanting more. His lips covered hers with tender warmth, and she closed her eyes in relief. But he never went past kissing. Tonight, he was in complete control of his emotions.

Punishment for her past rebuffs? Or simply a destroyed sense of interest in her? What would it take to arouse him, to bring back the desire that had once been in his eyes? She ran her hand under his shirt, down the hard ridges of muscle along his back, but he eased her hands away.

Then, cupping her face with his own hands, he clucked disapprovingly. "Naughty girl. It's past your bedtime," he admonished with a wicked grin.

Tyce stood and scooped her easily from the couch. Her heart quickened in anticipation. He had been teasing her, but now he was taking her to bed, and she had no intention of discouraging him. Laying her gently on the covers, Tyce braced himself over her with a hand on either side of her shoulders. She reached up to wrap her hands around his neck and pull him down to her lips. He came readily, kissed her deeply and well, then disengaged himself from her arms and said, "Good night, Delaney."

Before she could react, he had left the bedroom and closed the door behind him. Delaney lay there openmouthed, stunned, and disappointed until it became obvious that he was not going to return. Finally, she undressed and crawled underneath the covers for another night. What was that old saying? Payback is hell.

Pondering Tyce's new attitude, Delaney decided she probably deserved his reticence, but, nonetheless, was beginning to resent this Southern gentleman's code of honor he seemed to live by. Auntie's words from that morning came back to haunt her. She was on the verge of losing Tyce if she didn't do something drastic—and soon. Unless she wanted to end up living her life like her ancestors had, she was going to have to revert to Northern brashness and take charge of the situation.

Unfortunately, the opportunity did not present itself the next morning, for Alphonse and his flock of cousins, wives, and children arrived early. The roar of automobile motors followed by laughter, yells, and commotion wakened Delaney from a sound sleep. To her surprise, the sun was up and so was Tyce, fully dressed and already headed toward the mansion with Alphonse and the men. The women and children began unloading baskets and boxes from the vehicles and setting up tables under the spreading oak trees on the lawn.

Whatever happened to that Southern sluggishness she was growing used to? These people were like ants in a disturbed hill, scurrying back and forth, chattering happily all the while. No matter what was going on, Delaney didn't intend to be left out. She made a hasty process of her morning ablutions and was dressed within a few minutes.

A half-dozen voices greeted her as she entered the hubbub. A couple of the faces looked familiar and were probably at Alphonse's café the night Tyce took her there. The rest of the women and girls were apparently just friendly souls, and for once, Delaney appreciated their openness. She was immediately engulfed in the merriment and put to work peeling still-hot baked yams.

"We'll put Tyce's stove to use later, *chére*," said Mercedes, a tall, large-boned woman with a broad, friendly face and fine, clear eyes spilling with laughter. "Remember last year, Rena, Fourth of July, when Miss Donet brought out all those pies?"

A young woman working on the other side of the makeshift table nodded her head slightly. "She was some nice, Miss Donet."

"You've done this before?" Delaney asked.

"Sure," Mercedes said. "We came a lot when Tyce was working on the ballroom. My Timbo and the rest of the men helped Alphonse and Tyce with the heavy work. We'd always make gumbo or jambalaya or have a fish fry. Guess this might be the last time.''

Delaney bent her head over her work, sick with regret that she was the reason there would be no more picnics at Caroline. Somehow, she was going to make up this dreadful loss to Tyce. Somehow.

In midafternoon, the moving truck came to load the furniture and relocate it to a storage facility in Baton Rouge. Tyce watched the process closely, making sure each piece of furniture was padded and securely braced in the truck to avoid damage to the valuable antiques. He and Alphonse followed the truck when it left, for Tyce wanted to be satisfied the furniture was stored properly as well.

While they were gone, the women laid out the feast of gumbo and rice, home-baked breads, crisp green salad, buttery mashed yams with a pecan and brown sugar topping, and a huge dish of bread pudding for dessert. They fed the children and sent them off to play before the men returned. Then, when the men arrived, the adults piled their plates with food, found a place to sit on the ground or on folding chairs under the canopy of early-budding trees, and laughed and joked as they ate.

Just when Delaney thought everyone was packing up to leave, the men brought out their musical instruments and pulled several chairs close together. Tyce and Alphonse built a huge bonfire to one side to ward off the chill settling in for the night. As darkness fell, the strains of fiddle, guitar, and squeeze box resounded across the fields. Soon, the only light other than the glow of the bonfire came from the full moon above and the head-lights of a couple of the trucks that had been pulled around to shine on the revelers.

After a few dances, Delaney found a place to sit within the warm outer circle of the fire and shared Tyce with the women whose husbands were playing in the band. She wasn't jealous of him, but found herself selfishly wishing to have all his attention for herself.

An hour or so later, the adults surrendered the spotlight to the children, who mimicked their elders with glee, two-stepping and whirling around as the grownups clapped in time and encouraged their antics. Tyce dropped down beside Delaney. He had not said much all evening, and she assumed he was thinking about the empty mansion. At least, that was what had been on her mind all night.

"I'm sorry, Tyce," she said, laying her hand on his arm.

"About what?" he asked, looking around at her.

"About losing Caroline. I am so sorry for what I did to you."

"The house looks pretty forlorn without the furniture, doesn't it?"

What had she expected him to say? she wondered, when he changed the subject. That he didn't mind losing his lifelong dream, that he forgave her? No, that would take a long time. She just wanted him to say he was all right, that he would go on with his life in another direction once all this was over. That he could still care for her after all she had done to him. But he didn't say any such thing. He watched the tiny dancers and clapped along with the rest, but he did nothing to salve Delaney's guilt.

Around ten o'clock, Alphonse and the band took a rest. The women had already shooed the children along to the trucks and cars and put the youngest ones to bed among blankets on the seats. The older children gathered around the leaping flames of the fire, toasting marsh-mallows and telling scary stories of ghosts and the loup-garou, which Delaney learned was a Cajun form of werewolf. Glad to have their men alone for a few minutes, the younger women took them in hand and sauntered off in a group toward the levee for a walk in the moonlight.

Alphonse and one of his cousins was sampling a bot-tle of homemade wine, and Tyce had disappeared into the mansion as soon as the music stopped. Delaney was about to excuse herself for the night, for she was not only tired but in low spirits as well. She had a sinking feeling that not only had she lost her heritage by her foolish deal with Mark but that she had lost something far more important: Tyce. He simply did not act the same way toward her, and she was at a loss how to fix what she had broken.

As she passed, Alphonse hailed her, then caught up to her in two bounds of his long legs. "Not deserting us, are you, *'tee chére*?"

Delaney smiled. "I can't seem to keep up with your family. They have much more energy than I do."

"*Mais* yeah, they do go on. But you ought not go yet. There's a lot of night left." Alphonse winked at her. "Besides, who's Tyce gonna dance with if you gone?"

"I don't think he's in much of a mood to dance with me. He seems pretty down over losing Caroline."

"*M'chére*, don' you worry 'bout that none. You listen to me one t'ing. Tyce ain't gon' lose what means most to him, not Tyce. You wait and see. But that's neither here nor there. I tell you how to perk him up for now. You still got that dress that was Chloe's? That red one?"

"Yes, Tyce told me to keep it."

"*Mais*, yeah, I bet he did. He tole me wasn't nothing ever as *jolie* as you was in that dress. Tell you what do. You go put on that dress. Come to the ballroom, and I play 'Lady in Red' just fo' you and Tyce. Guar-on-tee, that'll get his attention."

Delaney wasn't so sure anything was going to change Tyce's mind about her, but she liked Alphonse's idea, anyway. She wanted an excuse to be in Tyce's arms again, and it seemed only fitting that there should be one last dance in the ballroom before all Tyce's work was destroyed. Too, it gave her hope that Tyce had talked about her to Alphonse. Maybe in time, things would be right again.

"All right. I'll be there in about five minutes."

A few minutes later, Delaney stopped in the open double doorway of the white ballroom. The lights were on, but the room was quiet. Alphonse was nowhere to be seen. The red silk rustled slightly around her legs as she ventured farther inside. She gained the center of the room before she saw Tyce standing at one end, leaning with braced arms against one of the marble mantels, his head bowed as if in prayer—or heartbreak.

Was he saying good-bye to his lovely creation, this ballroom, this small part of Caroline that he had brought back to life and would have to let die forever? Feeling like an intruder into his private world, Delaney hesitated. Then the soft strains of Alphonse's fiddle from somewhere outside the room caused Tyce to look up.

The expression on his face was a mixture of bewilderment and shock. His face drained of color momentarily as he stared at her. Then, when he recognized her, he shook his head slightly and grinned.

"You startled me for a moment. I thought you were somebody else."

"Chloe?" Delaney asked. She hadn't thought about the ghost when she agreed to put on the red dress, but he had said he dreamed of Chloe wearing the red gown in this very ballroom, and Delaney still suspected he believed it was more than a dream. "I'm sorry, I didn't mean to upset you."

"Who's upset? I'd much rather see you than Chloe. Is this one of Alphonse's schemes?" Tyce asked, coming across the room toward her. "Trying to make me think I'm seeing ghosts?"

"No, that wasn't what he intended . . ." Delaney started, then realized she didn't really know what Alphonse had in mind by talking her into this. Maybe he had just been playing a joke on Tyce. If so, Delaney was going to give old Alphonse a good piece of her mind.

"What did he intend, then?" Tyce said, close enough now that she could see the lights of the chandeliers dancing in his crystal blue eyes.

"I . . . he . . . to get you into a happier mood, I think," she stammered, wishing she had not played along with Alphonse now. She could still hear the fiddle, and from the tilt of Tyce's head, she knew he was listening, too.

"This room is so beautiful," she said softly, glancing around at the pristine room with its stately center columns and ornate carved moldings. "It was meant to be here forever. If I'd only known what I was destroying."

"I told you, we're not going to think about any of that until next week. Right?"

She nodded and turned to him, her eyes filling with tears. "I've messed everything up. I've killed Caroline, destroyed the things that were important to you."

"Hush, Delaney. Caroline's not gone yet. One never knows what the future holds." He pulled her close, his hand pressing the side of her face gently against his chest. "We're wasting Alphonse's good music."

He kissed the top of her head, and she closed her eyes as he took her in his arms and slowly began to dance. If only for the moment, her wish was granted. She was once more in Tyce's arms, where she wanted to be more than anything else in the world.

In her ear, she heard the soft melody of his voice as he sang the words to the song he liked so much. Tonight she knew why it was special to him: It was a tribute to Chloe and always had been in his mind. As if the pop song had been written a hundred years ago just for Chloe Bienville and Zach Brandon as they danced their last dance together.

She felt herself melting in his strong arms as his deep voice permeated her very being. She wanted to tell him how much she loved him, to beg him to forgive her and love her forever, but the words would not come. The spell of the song could not be broken, and though she gave herself to him heart and soul then and there, she found no words to tell him so.

The gleaming white floor muted and reflected the brilliant scarlet of Chloe's dress as they whirled around the room. Tyce held her tightly against him, his breath gentle on her cheek.

Delaney's own breath had left her already. Her head felt light, her feet no longer knew the ground beneath them. They could have been in another time, a couple in forbidden love, safe in one another's arms with no fear of the future that lay ahead of them. Tyce's arm tightened around her. Delaney laid her head against his shoulder and listened, wishing that he meant the words of love he sang so easily.

As the song ended, Delaney clung to Tyce, never wanting to let him go. And she wanted to believe, oh how she wanted to believe!

Chapter
Fourteen

Early the next morning, Tyce began moving the scaffolding from the upstairs hall. He couldn't get Delaney off his mind. Every time he closed his eyes, he was met with the image of her in that fetching red dress that fit like a satin glove and turned her smooth skin to porcelain and gave her cheeks a rosy glow that could have been mistaken for a blush of passion.

Dancing with her the night before had nearly torn him apart with longing. It had been a constant fight to control his emotions, not do anything to frighten her off again. Tyce wanted her to come steadily toward him until he could win her trust and love, no matter how patient he had to be, no matter how many cold showers he had to take as she slept in the next room, so close to him, yet so untouchable.

He knew he had grown too dependent on Delaney, but there was nothing he could do about it. In spite of his anger over Caroline, he was in love with Delaney. The problem was that he had no idea how to make her love and trust him. The barrier she had built around her emotions over the years seemed impenetrable in the short time he had left with her.

Midmorning, he went home for lunch. Delaney told him that his lawyer had just called and wanted him to return the call as soon as possible. After they ate, Tyce took his cell phone back to the house, dialing as he went. When Wes came on the phone, Tyce sat down on the back porch steps to listen.

"I've got bad news about your friend, Patterson," Wes said, going on to explain that the private detective had uncovered ties to a New Jersey gambling syndicate. "Patterson's a gambler in more ways than one. He's in deep debt to these people. Like about to go under. He personally guaranteed this particular piece of land as a means of covering some of his debts to the mob. The development company has already sunk a lot of money into this operation one way or another. Your plantation has docking facilities for a riverboat and is going to be prime real estate when the New Orleans bypass is completed.

"My investigator got interested and looked a little deeper. From what he found out, looks like this crew doesn't plan to build a mall. With the gambling vote coming up, and sure to pass with the governor's support, these people are planning a full-scale gambling operation out there: riverboat, hotels, the works. It's located in a parish with a friendly sheriff, if you get my drift. Just what the mob needs to set up a big-time operation with minimum resistance.

"Mark Patterson is in up to his neck. There are definitely some strong mob ties here, Tyce. Patterson has his balls in a crack, and if the judge's ruling next week goes our way, the shit's going to hit the fan in New Jersey. I'd watch my step, if I were you."

"Thanks for the information, Wes."

Tyce turned the phone off and laid it down, a worried frown creasing his forehead. A numbness crept through him. Mark had more than his commission at stake, all right. He had bargained with his life and was about to lose. The situation had gone past money. Mark was a man running scared, and that made him dangerous. If the mob was connected to this deal, then nobody came out unscathed unless Delaney could sell the land.

How far would Mark go to fulfill his end of the bargain with the syndicate? Tyce didn't like the answer that came to mind. He didn't like his options any better. Either relinquish his own claim to the plantation and let Delaney make the deal, or deal with Mark and the syndicate once he had full title to Caroline. The former destroyed his lifetime dream; the latter put both Delaney and himself in jeopardy.

There was not much left to consider. Tyce knew the choice he had to make. He'd write a formal letter to Wes Hartman tonight to drop his contention of Delaney's will. That would free Delaney to sell the plantation and get Mark off both their backs.

Once Caroline was gone, staying in Louisiana would be like a slow death. Tyce shuddered as a cold chill racked his body. The wind picked up outside, slamming the door against the wall behind him and sending leaves fluttering across the porch floor. The sound startled Tyce, made him feel that somebody was in the house. The wind moaned through the hallway, as if mourning for the old house now that his decision was made. It gave him the creeps, especially since the dream about Chloe still haunted him, and Delaney's appearance last night in Chloe's dress hadn't helped. At first glance, he had been sure Chloe was paying him another visit to voice her displeasure that he had not accomplished what she mandated.

"Chloe, are you here?" he called softly, going into the deathly still mansion. The only answer he got was the wind crying through the open door. Shaking off the eerie feeling, he closed the door and went back to work on the scaffolding.

By the time he quit for the day, his back ached, his shoulder muscles cramped, and he had developed several blisters on his hands in spite of wearing gloves, but he made no complaints, for he could go home to Delaney. She doctored his hands with ointment, rubbed liniment into his sore shoulders and back, and opened another can of soup, which, besides sandwiches, was about all she knew how to do in the kitchen. Tyce vowed he would teach the girl to cook if they ever married.

After a shower and a change of clothes, he wrote his letter and put it on the fax machine. Punching in the lawyer's number, he waited for the familiar transmittal tones. The line was busy, but the machine would keep trying until it connected. Wes Hartman had faxed the information on Mark earlier in the day. Tyce hoped Delaney hadn't seen it, since it didn't seem to have been bothered since it came in. He put the papers in his desk drawer, out of sight. There was no need to tell Delaney what he had learned. It would only worry her more, and there was nothing either of them could do now but go through with the deal and start life over.

At last, able to relax on the sofa, he was contentedly

aware of Delaney moving about the house, doing one thing or another. He listened to the small sounds of her activity. The quiet domesticity was comforting and peaceful.

"Come here," he said, catching Delaney's hand as she walked by on her way to the kitchen. He pulled her into his lap and gave her a brief kiss. She leaned against his chest and drew her legs up onto the couch. Tyce ran his hand up the smooth, bare length of leg underneath the oversized shirt that she wore. He did not press on past midthigh, though his heart raced at the very thought of what he would feel if he did venture deeper into that warmth.

"Who's being naughty tonight?" she admonished with a pout, putting her arms around his neck.

"I can be very good," he countered, bringing her face close enough to kiss again.

Delaney pushed his hair back, combing through it with her fingers. Her soft, dark eyes studied his face intently as she lay back in his arms, "I don't doubt that."

Along with the thrill her words gave him, Tyce loved the sound of her voice: low, with just a touch of huskiness that made it very sexy. Actually, he loved everything about her, except her occasional stubbornness. Yet, as much as he longed to make love to her, he held back. She had to decide for herself, a decision not to be made lightly, one way or another. But, if she didn't hurry, he was going to have to get up soon and take another damned cold shower, because he couldn't sit there with his hand halfway to heaven and not react.

He shifted slightly. The fullness of Delaney's hips pressing against him as he moved sent new waves of need through his thighs and the pit of his stomach. He almost groaned from the exquisite torment of the feelings she aroused.

Lifting her face, he kissed her softly on the lips. She offered no resistance as he tightened his hold on her, pulling her against his chest, deepening the kiss. He wanted to love away her worries, to make her a part of him so that nothing could hurt her again without coming through him first. Most of all, he wanted to keep her close to him. He wanted time with her, for he was afraid he would lose her if he could not change her mind soon.

Her heart beat hard against his through the loose shirt she wore as his lips caressed the softness of her neck. The tension in her body began to melt under his touch. Their bodies molded together as Tyce knew they were meant to. She pulled herself tighter against him, the way he wanted it to be forever. His lips caressed her face, planting kisses on her eyelids, her chin, finally her mouth. He felt the subtle change in her as surely as if she had put it into words.

"I love you, Delaney. Stay with me. Please." The words came out uninvited. He thought he would regret them, that she would draw away from him again, then was surprised to find a sense of relief that he had spoken what was in his heart. It was the truth, and something he had never intended to happen. He could no longer fathom life without her at his side. "We won't stay in the South if that bothers you. We can live someplace else."

She sat up slightly and looked steadily into his eyes. "Where could we live? You're a Southern boy, born and bred. Where else are you going to be happy?"

"I'll be happy wherever you are. Except New York. I don't want you living in New York anymore," Tyce said, his mind on Mark and how he might retaliate, even after he won. "Why don't we go to London?"

"London? Why London?" Delaney asked with a curious frown.

"I know there is work for me there. It's always nice to have enough money to eat."

Delaney's frown deepened. "I don't understand. What work will you do in London?"

"I was approached a few months ago to spearhead the design of a large art center in the planning stages. One of the lord mayor's pet projects. I declined then, thinking I would be too busy with Caroline. I can probably still get the assignment."

"Oh, Tyce, do you really want me? I feel so responsible for all this. I can't imagine how you can love me." There was a trace of fear in Delaney's eyes. Tyce knew he couldn't expect her to forget years of insecurity in a few days' time. But, seeing the opening she was giving him, he was not going to back off now.

"I do love you. And I need you. Come with me, share my life. I want you to marry me."

Delaney's eyes shimmered in the faint light spilling from the kitchen. She wrapped her arms around Tyce and hugged him tightly. "I love you, too. I truly do. I was so afraid you couldn't love me after what I did."

Tyce closed his eyes, relishing her embrace, so freely given for the first time.

"So, will you?" he repeated. "Marry me?"

"Oh, Tyce. Yes! I will."

For Tyce, her answer merged a hundred years of separation into one soul shared by all the Brandons and Bienvilles who had been denied. She snuggled contentedly in his arms for a moment, as if she were meant to be there.

Delaney lifted her face to his. "Will you come back to your own bed tonight? With me?"

"If that's what you want."

"Please," she whispered.

Never one to need a second invitation, Tyce lifted Delaney in his arms and carried her into the bedroom where he could at last love her the way he had longed to do for days now. He soon realized however, that he was not to be in charge. She was. Slowly and deliberately, she unbuttoned the loose shirt until it hung open on her body. As Tyce watched, fascinated by her beguiling seductiveness, Delaney eased the material off her shoulders and let the shirt fall around her ankles.

Tyce hardly dared breathe for fear that he was dreaming and might awaken. Her naked body was the work of a master sculptor, molded from warm, yielding flesh. She moved toward the bed as his gaze roved her perfect body. Anxious to touch her, he reached out.

Delaney's hands covered his, as they slowly, lingeringly caressed her. She pushed him gently onto the bed, following him to pull the T-shirt over his head as he lay back. An intense craving for her exploded through Tyce's body. His hands slid down her, seeking, finding, seeking again. Delaney moaned. Tyce rose up to bring her down to him, to take her and make her his, but she eluded his grasp, easing herself down alongside his body until she could unzip his jeans and take them off. As she finished undressing him, her exploring touch—quick, gentle, fleeting—sent paralyzing spasms of sensation through him. He was at her mercy, powerless to object as she drove him mad with desire.

When he could bear the sweet agony no longer, Tyce pulled her across his body, smothering her with kiss after kiss. She wrapped her arms around his neck and returned his passion without reserve. Her skin slid like silk against his chest and legs as they made love amid the damp, tangled sheets. When they were both satiated, she sighed contentedly and snuggled against him. Running his hand lightly over her shoulder and down her arm, he rested it in the curve of her waist. She laid her hand on top of his and left it there.

"I do love you so much, Tyce," she said, as she drifted off to sleep.

And he loved her, more than he had ever loved anything in his life.

How long he had slept, Tyce couldn't say, but he awoke with a feeling that something was wrong. Careful not to awaken Delaney, he got up from the bed, slipped on his jeans and shoes, and went to the front door, looking instinctively toward the plantation house. The back door of the mansion was ajar, and Tyce knew he hadn't left it that way the night before. He couldn't shake the uneasy feeling that ate at him as he walked across the lawn to the big house. Everything inside was quiet and empty. He walked slowly toward the front hall. That was when he heard a sound from upstairs. He stopped, listening intently for it to be repeated. It came again. The creaking of the weakened boards of the attic.

The stairs were dark, forcing him to go slowly to the second landing. He crossed carefully to the attic stairs and went up. Now and then, the creaking sounds filtered down to him. The attic door was open and the dim light from within revealed the top few stairs. Easing into the attic, he noticed that the light was on. Nothing seemed out of place as he glanced around. Several trunks that they had decided not to store still sat across the room. His tense muscles relaxed slightly. Possibly, he or Delaney or even one of Alphonse's cousins had left the light on earlier. He moved carefully across the floor to the light cord, staying away from the rotten spots in the floor. As he reached for the cord, a movement caught his eye.

The woman in red that he had dreamed about weeks ago stood in the shadows of the sloping attic. She beckoned frantically, moving toward him. Startled, he stepped back too quickly and felt a board give slightly under his weight. Adrenaline shot through his muscles, tensing his body, as he caught his balance and found a solid beam.

The ghostly woman's stricken face frightened Tyce as much as did the fact that he could see through her, and this time he was fully awake. It had to be Chloe Bienville—or what was left of her. Rooted to the spot, he couldn't run nor could he find words to speak. It didn't help to recall that Chloe tended to like Brandon men. She was wild-eyed and furious just now, and Tyce was the only target in the room. Or so he thought. Then Chloe gestured wildly and wailed, *"Look behind you!"*

Tyce whirled in time to see Mark fling a gas can at him. Tyce ducked and the can flew past to land on its side with a heavy thud against the opposite wall, its contents gurgling from the spout. Mark stood on a section of thick plywood that Tyce had laid over the boards months ago to hold the heavy trunks. The secure footing gave him the advantage, but Tyce wasn't going to stand by and see Caroline burned to the ground by a madman. He knew the flooring well enough to get to Mark.

"Stay away from me," Mark yelled, as Tyce approached. He hurled a second gas can at Tyce. From the closer range, the full can caught Tyce on the shoulder, throwing him off balance momentarily. Before Tyce could recover, Mark put his shoulder into one of the massive trunks between them, and shoved it onto the rotten floor. Tyce felt the floor sag. A board gave way with a loud crack. His left foot went through. Grabbing for the nearest support, he caught the trunk. With a splintering groan, the entire floor collapsed.

Tyce felt the terrifying sensation of free fall for a moment. Then he hit the scaffolding below. Agonizing pain ripped into his side, then exploded through his head before the world went black.

Chapter Fifteen

Delaney awoke with a start. For a moment, she was disoriented; then she recalled the night before, and her hand went automatically to Tyce's side of the bed. It was empty.

Looking toward the window, she saw sunshine. She settled back onto the soft pillows, a smile of contentment on her lips as she recalled their tender night of love. He had asked her to marry him, and she knew in her heart he meant it. How he could love her after all the trouble she had caused him, she didn't know, but one thing was certain; she loved him. Given a lifetime with him, she would make up for the loss of Caroline somehow.

Where was he, anyway? Sitting up in bed, she called out for him. When he didn't answer, she got up and pulled on a robe and opened a window to let in the gentle breeze. The sun was up; birds called from nearby trees. The morning was peaceful and beautiful. Yes, she admitted, she did like Caroline. She would miss it when it was gone. But not nearly so much as Tyce would, she thought sadly. The guilt she felt for her unsuspecting part in this tragedy was overwhelming, but Tyce seemed willing to forgive her, and that was what mattered.

Tyce's truck sat in its usual spot. Delaney looked toward the big house and frowned. The door was open. Tyce never left the doors open unless he was working inside. There was nothing left to do but dismantle the rest of the scaffolding and bring down the three trunks Delaney had not wanted to store. Glancing into the kitchen, she noticed that no coffee had been made, which was usually the first thing Tyce did in the morning. She went back to the bedroom and dressed in jeans, a lightweight knit shirt, and loafers. Maybe he would like breakfast. She'd go over and ask him.

"Tyce!" she called from the doorway of the mansion. There was nothing but silence when the echo of her voice died. Puzzled, she started to close the door and go looking for him someplace else. Then she heard a sound from upstairs. A grinding, metallic sound. Anxiety churned the pit of her stomach as she started upward.

"Tyce?" she cried, taking the stairs two at a time until she reached the upper landing. Then she saw him. "Tyce? Oh, no!"

He was lying in the middle of the upstairs hall in a pool of blood. Several heavy lengths of the scaffolding had collapsed on top of him. Overhead was a gaping hole in the ceiling. She moved toward him, accidentally brushing one of the scaffolding supports. It shifted, threatening to bring the rest of the massive structure down to crush Tyce.

Panicked, Delaney forced herself to think straight. She had to get help!

"I'll be back. I'll be right back," she called to Tyce, even though there was no indication that he was still alive.

Delaney ran downstairs and back to Tyce's cottage for his cell phone. She dialed 911 as she ran back to the house.

A grating ring. Then another. After what seemed like hours, somebody answered: "911 operator. What is your emergency?"

Delaney stopped on the middle landing. "Please!" she begged, hearing the hysteria in her own voice. "Please send help. He's hurt badly."

"What's happened? Where are you? Calm down, ma'am," the man on the other end said.

"I'm at the Caroline plantation. Do you know it? Outside New Bienville. Do you know where it is?"

"Yes, I know it. What's happened?"

"He fell. He fell through the ceiling. And . . . and . . . the scaffolding fell on him. He's hurt. He's hurt! Please send somebody. The scaffolding's still slipping." She rushed back to the upstairs hall.

"Yes, ma'am. I understand. I'm sending rescue. Calm down so you can help me. Take a breath and calm down. Now, where is he? Can you get to him? Is the victim an adult or child?"

"Adult. I'm in the room. But I'm afraid to go near. I touched the scaffolding and it moved. It's about to fall. . . ."

"Listen to me. Don't go over there. Just stay where you're safe and talk to me. I'm sending the rescue unit now. Don't go near the scaffolding. Are you listening? Ma'am, are you there?"

"Yes. I'm here. He needs help!" Delaney was sobbing. Tyce was pinned beneath the heavy scaffolding, and she could not see his face. One arm was stretched out across the floor, and blood had clotted along a long gash on his bare back.

"I understand. Help is on the way. Is he conscious now? Can he talk to you? See if you can get a response."

"Tyce! Tyce, can you hear me? Are you awake?" Delaney spoke louder. "Tyce! Answer me!"

No answer.

"Tyce," she called louder, "say something."

There was only silence.

"He's not responding!" she told the dispatcher.

"Help is on the way," the man said, his voice sounding more concerned than before. "You should hear the siren any minute. They're turning off the main road now. Do you hear them?"

"Yes."

"Can they get in the house?"

"Yes."

"All right. Everything will be fine. Keep trying to get a response from him."

Delaney squatted as close to the scaffolding as she dared. Around her were the remnants of one of the trunks from the attic. It had split like a melon a few feet from Tyce's head.

"Tyce," she called, "Tyce, please answer me!

"He's not answering!" she cried. "What can I do?"

"The paramedics should be there. Are they there?" he asked.

Downstairs, Delaney heard the voices and noise as the men came in.

"Up here," she called, rushing to the staircase to

beckon them. "Hurry! He's caught under the scaffolding. It's slipping."

Four firemen came bounding up the stairs.

"Do you know who he is? What's his name?" one of them asked immediately.

Delaney told him. Two paramedics came up the stairs, hauling equipment with them.

"The victim's name's Tyce Brandon. He fell through there," one of the firemen said.

"Tyce Brandon? I know his sister." One of the paramedics dropped to his knees as close to Tyce's body as he could get. "Tyce?" he called in a loud voice. "Tyce can you hear me? It's Robert Jackson. We're going to get you out. Don't worry, we'll have you out in a minute."

The hall was instantly filled with furious, controlled activity. Orders were given. Men reacted. Cooperated. Slowly, the scaffolding was lifted off of Tyce, piece by agonizing piece. All the while, the paramedic named Robert talked to him.

The next minutes went by with dizzying confusion as Delaney stood by in helpless terror, afraid that he was dying or dead. With experienced hands, the medics did their jobs quickly and efficiently.

"There's a lot of blood," one of them said.

Delaney's heart jolted.

"Bad gash on his forehead and back."

"I don't feel spinal injury, but let's get him on a board and get a collar on him anyway. Is he breathing okay?"

"Tyce. Can you hear me, Tyce? Can you hear me?" Robert said, bending close to Tyce as they gently eased him over onto a backboard. Robert turned aside to the other medic. "Halo that blood for spinal fluid, Pat."

Delaney moved closer, watching anxiously. Tyce's

face was covered with blood. Robert took a pad and carefully wiped it away from his eyes.

"Tyce, can you hear me?" Robert asked again, his voice more demanding. The other paramedic was sticking an IV needle in Tyce's right hand while Robert checked his face and head for injury. "Can you hear me?"

There was no response from Tyce's motionless body. *Please don't let him die,* Delaney prayed silently.

"Is Air-Med coming?" Robert asked. "We need to get him out of here."

"On their way. Should be here any minute," Pat answered. "No evidence of spinal fluid loss."

One of the men placed an oxygen mask over Tyce's face as Robert finished immobilizing him, then unfolded a blanket and tucked it around his body. "How's his blood pressure?" Robert asked.

Pat glanced up. "Dropping slowly. I hear the chopper. Strap him down and let's go."

Robert turned to Delaney. "Are you a relative?"

"No," Delaney replied shakily.

"We need to notify his next of kin."

"His mother," Delaney offered. "She lives in New Bienville. I'll call her. I'll have to find her number. Where are you taking him? I want to come."

"Baton Rouge General."

Two men lifted the backboard and gingerly carried it down the stairs, where a stretcher waited, attended by an Air-Med doctor. The medics lifted the stretcher to the waiting helicopter. The blades picked up speed, beating the air like frantic birds' wings as the craft lifted into the sky and thundered away.

For a stunned moment, Delaney watched it disappear

into the distance. His mother! She had to call his mother. And get to the hospital herself.

Directory assistance gave her Mrs. Brandon's number. After four rings, a woman answered the phone.

"Mrs. Brandon?" Delaney asked.

"Yes."

"Mrs. Brandon, this is Delaney Bienville. Tyce has had an accident."

"What? What happened to him?" The woman's voice filled with panic. "Where is he?"

"He fell . . . from a distance . . ." Delaney explained, finding her own composure slowly returning. "They are taking him to Baton Rouge General. Do you know where that is?"

"Yes, I know. I'm on my way."

It only then occurred to Delaney that she had no idea where the hospital was.

"Wait!" Delaney cried, but the woman had hung up.

Frantically, she turned. The rescue unit was packing up the last of its equipment.

"Wait!" Delaney called to them. "Where is Baton Rouge General?"

They gave her explicit directions. "Miss!" One of them called to her as he climbed into the truck. "If he didn't have his wallet on him, you might want to bring it along. Might need it for insurance."

"Thanks, I will." Delaney went back inside Tyce's cottage to find the wallet. It was in the drawer of his desk, where it always stayed when he didn't have it with him. Delaney picked it up and noticed the papers underneath.

The letterhead was that of Tyce's lawyer. She would not have thought twice about it nor considered reading Tyce's private papers, except that her eyes picked out

Mark's name and the words "Judge Babineaux's ruling." Hesitantly, she picked up the paper. Her heart stopped as she read of Mark's dealing with gambling syndicates and the staggering amount of debt he owed to them. Never in her wildest dreams had she thought he was that foolish. No wonder he was adamant about her selling the plantation. If he didn't come through, he'd pay with more than money. And if she didn't come through, Delaney knew she might fare the same at Mark's hands.

Then she saw the last line of the letter. Judge Babineaux's ruling. The letter was dated yesterday, and it mentioned that Wes Hartman had already notified Tyce of the anticipated outcome—an almost inevitable ruling in Tyce's favor. Tyce had known he won and said nothing! *Why?* He had asked her to marry him. Why hadn't he told her about the decision?

She had to get to the hospital, her mind screamed, yet she stood there immobile, staring at the paper in her hand. Something else caught her eye. The blinking error light on the fax machine at the back of the desk. A piece of paper had jammed in the feeder before it was sent. Delaney automatically retrieved it, and the blinking light went out. The words jumped out at her. Her knees weakened as she read Tyce's letter to Wes Hartman.

Dear Wes:

   Considering what you learned about Mark Patterson, his connection with the New Jersey gambling syndicate and his involvement in the purchase of Caroline, I think it would be in everyone's best interest for me to drop my lawsuit against Donet Bienville's estate. Continuing this suit, assuming your information is correct concerning the upcoming ruling, might endanger Delaney Bienville and bring unforeseen repercussions later for both of us.

Therefore, I'm instructing you through this written notice to drop the lawsuit contesting the will immediately.

Thanks for all your work.

Tyce

Delaney pressed her hand against her mouth to keep from sobbing outright. He had intended to sacrifice Caroline for her well-being. Tyce loved her enough to do this, and now he might die before she saw him again. Somehow, she and Tyce would find a way out of the mess she had made, but they were not going to use Caroline to do it. The plantation meant too much to him—and to her, she realized. She tore the letter into tiny pieces and dropped them into the wastebasket beneath the desk, feeling a deep sense of relief at making the decision her heart told her was right. Taking the car keys from the desk where she had laid them earlier, she slipped them into her jeans pocket, then picked up Tyce's wallet.

"Going somewhere, Delaney?" Mark's voice sent a chilling wave of fear down Delaney's spine.

Turning, she found Mark close behind her. "What are you doing here?" she demanded, hiding her fear behind bravado that she didn't feel.

"Waiting until the crowd left."

"I have to go. Tyce has been hurt, and I'm on my way to the hospital." She tried to push past Mark, but he caught her roughly by the upper arm and snatched her back.

"He's not dead then," Mark muttered, and Delaney turned cold inside. Mark knew. Mark must have been there when Tyce fell.

"Did you push him?" Delaney demanded, futilely clawing at Mark's fingers. "You tried to kill him?"

"Yeah, well, I didn't plan it that way, but since he showed up when he did, I thought it might be easier all around. As it is, I'll have to take care of everything myself. You might as well help me."

"I don't know what you're talking about, but I'm not helping you do anything!"

"You're wrong, babe. We started this deal together, and we're going to finish it together." Mark dragged her out the door of the cottage, though she fought him with all her might. "You told me he didn't care about anything but the house, and he said the same thing. Well, we'll just see that he doesn't have the house to worry about anymore. And you, you two-timing little bitch, I'll have to decide what to do with you to keep your mouth shut." Mark fumbled in his coat pocket with his free hand, and to Delaney's dismay, withdrew a handgun, which he held menacingly beside her face. "If you don't do what I say, I'll kill you right now, do you understand?"

No longer did Delaney doubt the extent of Mark's ruthlessness. She considered screaming for help, but she didn't. It could trigger him to kill her, and besides, there was no one within hearing distance of the plantation. Trying to gather her wits and look for a chance to escape, Delaney stumbled along beside him until they reached the mansion. Mark forced her inside and up the stairs, past where Tyce's blood had soaked into the wood floor, up into the attic. The hole gaped where Tyce had fallen through, and Mark motioned for her to go ahead of him around the edge. Carefully, she tested for footing before each step. Mark remained in the doorway.

"Stay there," Mark commanded, when she was in the center of the attic. He sidled along the wall until he reached the thick plywood floor where the trunks rested. To Delaney's horror, he pulled out a gas can from behind one of the trunks.

"I brought these up here last night to burn the place, but your hick friend showed up. I had no choice once he saw me. He would have done me a big favor by just dying."

Delaney felt sick at his words.

"Mark, please don't do this. You're only bringing more trouble on yourself in the end."

"No way! Once this deal is finalized, I'm home free. I'll have all the money I could ever want, between the three mil for this place and my cut from the developers. I'll be set, Delaney. Don't you understand? I have to make this deal. I have to." Mark's voice cracked slightly as he stared at her with frightening intensity, his eyes wild, yet almost pleading. "Don't you understand?"

Seeing the desperation in his face, Delaney sought to defuse the situation. "I know you're in trouble, Mark. I know about the gambling debts and all that. But if you burn this house, you'll be in prison for arson."

"Nobody's going to know. You aren't going to tell on me, are you, babe?" Mark said, his ruthless confidence returning.

"Why would I do that?" Delaney hedged. "But they have ways of finding out. Arson experts can determine what caused the fire and trace it back to you. You don't want that, Mark. You don't need to burn the house. Tyce has already agreed to drop the lawsuit. You can make the deal, okay? I'll sign the papers.'' Right now, Delaney would have told him anything to get him to put the gas can down and leave the house.

"Forget it. I'm going to do it my way, make sure there's nothing left," Mark said, looking around nervously. "Let's go, I get the creeps up here. Both of my other cans spilled last night, but this one should be enough to start a nice little blaze downstairs. Then this old place will go up like kindling. Come on." He motioned toward the door with the gun.

Slowly, Delaney made her way across the weak floor near the gaping hole where Tyce had fallen. When she was within reach, Mark stuck the gun in his pocket, grabbed her by the arm, and said smugly, "Brandon played you for a fool, you know. He was two-timing you all along."

"What are you talking about?" Delaney said impatiently, trying at every step to extricate her arm from Mark's relentless grasp. They were almost to the bottom of the stairs.

"He was meeting a woman in the attic. She's the one who warned him I was there. I never saw her until he came in. She must have been hiding."

Delaney was perplexed. Another woman? By now she knew Tyce well enough to know that there was not another woman in his life. But, then, who did Mark see? Delaney's eyebrows shot up as a wild thought came to mind. "Was she wearing red?"

"Red?" Mark repeated. "Come to think of it, she was. An old-fashioned-looking party dress. You know her?"

"Yes. I do. Her name is Chloe, and I hope she's still here."

"Why? You think she can help you out of this?"

"I don't know, but she might be able to," Delaney said with an admonishing frown to Mark. "She won't like what you intend to do to her house at all."

"Her house? What are you talking about?" Mark said, his eyes darting into the shadowy corners of the big house.

"She's a ghost, Mark. She haunts this house. She won't like you trying to burn it."

Mark gave her arm a fierce jerk. "Shut up. You're trying to make a fool out of me. Well, it won't work."

Mark dragged her along beside him. He opened the doors to the ballroom. "We'll do this room first. That way I know it's gone for sure."

Chapter
Sixteen

Morning was long in coming, waking a chore. Tyce's
eyelids felt weighted closed as if defying him to open
them. The very air seemed heavy, hard to breathe, and
filled with a loud pulsating throb that sounded like some
kind of engine. The noise split his head into a thousand
fragments of pain, vibrated completely through him. His
whole body ached like he had been hit head-on by a
Mack truck. He tried again to open his eyes, then gave
up the effort, floating in the thundering darkness for a
few more minutes.

Hell, he thought ruefully, he might be a little out of
practice, but good sex wasn't supposed to devastate a
man like this. Making passionate love to Delaney was
the last thing he remembered from the night before.

Maybe Chloe had taken revenge on him for making love first, marrying later.

"Delaney," he muttered, then realized his mouth wasn't working right, either. His throat was dry as parchment, and his lips felt cracked and chapped. He reached for Delaney, found nothing but air. Panic swept through him. Something was wrong.

Struggling to wake up fully, he tried to turn over but met resistance. Pain knifed through his midsection, laying him flat on the bed again with a moan, but it brought his eyes wide open. He had no idea where he was, but judging from what he could discern within his limited range of vision, he certainly wasn't at Caroline any longer. He was strapped down in a tiny room with close walls and dim artificial lighting surrounded by machinery, tubes, and monitors. The whole room was vibrating with noise that never abated. When he attempted to lift his right arm, he found its movement restricted by an IV.

Realization hit hard. He was in a hospital of some sort. Something had happened. Something that had left him hurting like hell every time he drew a breath. He sensed more than heard somebody in the room with him.

"Delaney," he whispered, hoping against hope that she was there. Trying desperately to raise up, he called again: "Delaney?"

"It's all right, Tyce. Keep still; you're going to be okay. I'm Dr. Richardson." The doctor held him until he quieted. "You're on your way to a hospital."

Tyce could barely hear the voice over the noise. Blurred vision kept him from making out the man's features.

"I'm glad to see you awake, but you need to lie still. Can you hear me?"

Tyce nodded weakly, trying to get his bearings, to recall what happened, to remember where Delaney was. "Where am I?" he managed to mouth.

"Air-Med chopper. On the way to Baton Rouge General. We're taking good care of you. Just hang on and don't try to move."

The doctor didn't have to worry about that anymore. Tyce had already decided he didn't want to do anything that required movement. It bothered him that he could not think straight. An aggravating oxygen tube ran under his nose. His head was pounding, and his lungs felt as if they were on fire with every breath. Everything seemed distant to Tyce, unreal, but the longer he was awake, the more uneasy he grew with this unexpected lapse of memory. He had to know where Delaney was, to be sure she was safe. A foreboding shadow enveloped his mind. Something he had to remember. Something he had to warn Delaney about. Something . . . God, his head hurt. If the throbbing would just stop for a minute. And that damned noise! And the irritating smell of engines and fuel . . . Delaney . . . Caroline . . . gasoline! He remembered the gasoline! Mark!

"Oh, God," he moaned, as a flash of memory revived the vision of Mark standing in the gloom of the attic.

"Are you all right, Tyce?" The voice seemed to hover just above his face.

"Where's Delaney?" he mouthed soundlessly. "Need to see Delaney."

Mark intended to burn Caroline, if he had not already succeeded. There was no way Tyce could stop him now, but if Delaney was there and tried to interfere . . . The heart monitor caught Tyce's attention when it jumped erratically.

Immediately, the doctor and the med-tech on board were in action, adjusting the tubes that fed fluid into Tyce's body. From the instant response, Tyce knew he must be in pretty serious condition. For the first time, the idea occurred to him that whatever had happened to him might have happened to Delaney as well. Tyce's vital signs spiked on the monitor screens. Frantically, the men groped at him as he tried to get up. He had to know what was going on. He had to find Delaney before he blacked out again.

"Delaney!" he called out, almost out of his mind with pain and worry.

"Be still, Tyce. Come on, man, be still." Dr. Richardson tightened the straps that held Tyce down.

The med-tech tested a hypodermic needle, then inserted it into the IV.

"No!" Tyce begged. "Don't give me anything." Struggling upward against the straps and the man's hands and his own agony, he cried, "Don't! Where's Delaney? Is she hurt? I have to know!"

"She was at the house when we left. She was going to call your mother, then follow us to the hospital. She'll be there waiting."

Tyce hadn't cried in years, not since his dad died, but he felt the tears streaming down his cheeks at his helplessness. Something told him Delaney wouldn't be waiting for him, that she was in grave danger. The sedative was taking effect, trying to lull him into forgetting. He caught the doctor's sleeve and pulled him closer. "Call the police. Send them to Caroline. Call the police, please! He'll burn Caroline. Mark . . . burn . . . Caroline. Delaney . . ."

Whether he was heard or understood, Tyce didn't know, but he couldn't overcome the stupor that was closing in on him. Fighting furiously against the darkness and the unrelenting straps securing him, Tyce arched upward as a convulsion of pain gripped his chest like a vise, cutting off his breath. The doctor turned him loose. Suddenly, he was falling . . . falling . . . falling.

"He's flat-lining!" the med-tech cried.

"Where are we?" Dr. Richardson yelled to the pilot. "Get us down stat! Call in a code to ER. I'm jumping the cart!"

Through the black haze, Tyce could barely hear the distant roar of the chopper. Then Mark's laughter floated down to him in the darkness and he hit bottom.

Tyce felt a sudden jolt, but there was no pain. He concentrated on the brilliant whiteness ahead of him. *This is so much better than before*, he thought as he drifted toward the light. Something nagged at him, in spite of his attempts to put all his thoughts aside. He yearned for the serenity that the light promised. If only that one final worry would leave him alone. Besides, he couldn't even recall what bothered him, just an aggravating anxiety that should have been left behind with everything else.

Somewhere in the distance, within the blinding light, he heard the strains of music. A waltz. The music drew him into its core, taking over his being, whirling him around with its lovely *one*-two-three-*one*-two-three. He felt gentle hands upon him and opened his eyes. The face into which he gazed seemed very familiar. He struggled to recall who this beauty was. Her hair was dark and long, swept up on her head, with curls cascading down her back. She smelled of the roses that had been fixed into the shining curls. Her shimmering red dress rustled gently as they moved around the floor, and she smiled up at him with ageless eyes.

Only then did Tyce recognize her and realize where he was. The white ballroom at Caroline. And he was dancing with the woman who had come to him in a dream weeks before. Chloe Bienville—or her ghost, at least. The one who had insisted that he marry Delaney. Like an electric shock, memory crackled through him: *Delaney. Mark. Fire!*

He tried to pull away from the woman, but she held him firmly. *"Dance with me, Zach,"* she whispered.

"Turn me loose. I'm not Zach."

"I know," she murmured. *"But let me pretend for another moment. You are very much like him, and now I may never see him again."* Her voice was so plaintive that Tyce gave in and continued to glide across the floor with her to the music flowing from unseen musicians, but he couldn't get his mind off Delaney. He attempted to free himself once more, but she clung to him and would not let him go.

"I have to help Delaney!" He tried to pry her hand off his arm. "Please, I have to reach her!"

She caught his attention with her glowing eyes. *"It's too late to help her. Stay awhile longer with me."*

"No!" Tyce pleaded. "I have to go."

"Listen to me."

Tyce saw that he had no choice. She was not going to let him go until he heard her out. Her grip was not painful nor exceedingly tight, but it was beyond his strength to escape. "Tell me fast," he ordered Chloe, "then help me find Delaney."

"How can I tell a lifetime of grief fast, Tyce? Don't you see? You have an eternity to listen to me. And I have eternity to tell you, now that I have lost my Zach

altogether and you have lost your Delaney.''

The sudden sinking feeling inside him told Tyce that something was terribly amiss. He was not dreaming, exactly. This was far too vivid for a dream. Eternity? Was he . . . ? No, surely not. *Flat-lining. Cardiac arrest.* The words floated back to him, held by a thread of latent memory.

Dead. He had died on the way to the hospital! Beyond hope. Beyond helping Delaney. Every fiber of his being screamed in protest. It couldn't be! His life with Delaney was supposed to be ahead of him.

"I don't believe you. I'm dreaming," he argued. "It's only another dream like the other time when I saw you."

"It wasn't a dream the first time, Tyce," Chloe said patiently. *"I came to you because you were my last hope. Don't you see? The only way I could get to Zach was to bring the Brandons and Bienvilles together as it was intended from the first. Zach and I were supposed to be married. We were supposed to spend our lives together at Caroline.''*

Tyce gave an impatient wave of his hand. "I know all that. I've known it all my life. I don't have time to rehash your whole history."

"Sadly, you don't have anything else to do, young man, as I've tried to make you understand. You are here, with me, until the time for you to go on. I myself have been in this state of unrest for nearly seventy years now. And now I shall be here for eternity. What makes you think you'll be passing over to the other side any sooner? There are no Brandon men left. There is no way to undo the curse that my father put upon us. We are doomed, you and I, to suffer together now.''

"What in hell are you talking about?" Tyce demanded. "Make sense, woman!"

"Do not speak to me coarsely, sir!" Chloe fired back, her eyes burning brightly. *"And you would do well to mend your blasphemous language, considering the state you are in. There are those listening who do not take kindly to sacrilege."*

"Fine, I'll try to watch my mouth," Tyce snapped. A waver of uneasiness shot through him, and he glanced warily around the room for the wrathful God depicted by the Baptist preachers of his childhood. He lowered his voice significantly. "Just tell me what you're talking about. Why are we doomed to limbo, as you suggest?"

"Because the only way to release my spirit to go to Zach was for a Bienville and a Brandon to marry and reclaim Caroline for the both of them, as it was supposed to be with Zach and me. But you are the last Brandon, and Delaney is the last Bienville. There is no chance left for me. Nor, probably, for you, either, as you left Delaney behind."

"You're crazy," Tyce insisted, fighting the panic that welled up inside him. "This is just another dream. We are going to be married! She agreed to marry me."

"I know you tried, Tyce love. You did your best, and I can't fault you for that, but then this other event happened. It's too late now, I'm afraid," Chloe said sadly, then opened her arms to him. *"Shall we dance again? I close my eyes and see my beloved. . . ."*

The hard truth landed on Tyce like a ton of lead dropped on his chest, stifling his breathing. He wasn't dreaming this time. He had to accept Chloe for the ghost that she was. What he was experiencing was far more permanent than a dream. But Delaney wasn't dead—not yet, anyway.

"No! We can't dance. Don't you understand? That madman is going to burn Caroline. Burn it to the ground.

And he'll hurt Delaney, if he finds her. He might kill her. Don't you see that?"

Chloe's eyes glowed with soft empathy. *"I am truly sorry. I know what it is to worry about someone you love, but under the circumstances, I don't know how you could help her at all. As for Caroline, once the house is gone, you and I will be disattached. Wandering spirits, without a home."*

Drifting aimlessly around the pristine room, Chloe ran her fingers lovingly along the walls, the mantels, stopping before the window that faced the river. To Tyce's surprise, the boards were gone, giving a clear view of acres of meandering gardens stretching away toward the river. He shook his head, trying to clear it. Those gardens hadn't been in front of Caroline for over a century.

Chloe turned back to him, her sorrowful eyes brimming with tears. *"I did love it here at Caroline. At night, I would dream of sharing it with Zach instead of my father, whom I had learned to hate. Even after my death, I could make myself more content simply because I was allowed to remain here. Now, without it to anchor me, I shall feel like a ship tossed to and fro on a stormy, endless sea. And where will you go? Since you died violently, you must wander like me, until you find peace. Oh Tyce, why couldn't things have worked out for us?"*

Chloe's words only reinforced the uncomfortable feeling that Tyce was not going to like this new situation at all. He had always been grounded by Caroline, too. The idea of roving the spirit world was beyond anything he wanted to comprehend. Besides that, being disembodied was growing annoying. He was accustomed to flesh and blood and bone. To being able to take charge of a problem and deal with it. He didn't care much for this spiritual existence in which he had no power, no strength, no substance. He wanted to be whole again—and he wanted Delaney!

"There's got to be some way out of this, Chloe," Tyce suggested. "Some way I can make things right. I'll do anything. Anything to save Delaney. I swear it."

"Swearing is unbecoming in a gentleman," Chloe admonished. *"It's too late, I'm afraid. What could you do?"*

"I don't know. You know these things!" Tyce said in exasperation. "You appeared to me, to warn me about Mark. How did you do that? Tell me. Let me warn Delaney."

"Yes, I did. And, I might point out, my interference only served to get you killed."

Strangely, the idea that he was dead did not bother him nearly as much as his inability to help Delaney when she needed him most. He closed his eyes in misery. "This can't be," he moaned. "I love her so much. I have to help her."

Time was running out. Surely, Delaney was still close by, and Mark was in the house somewhere with his gasoline. Tyce knew that as well as he knew he was not among the living any longer.

"Do you want me to beg?" Tyce dropped to one knee before Chloe, his voice breaking with emotion. "Because I will, if that's what it takes. I have to get to Delaney. If it means that Caroline burns, and that I am banished forever to the netherworld—if I have to sell my soul to the devil himself, I will do it. But help me now, Chloe. I beg of you, help me save Delaney."

"Do you truly love her, Tyce?"

"Yes, I love her. I've never loved anybody as much as I love her. Or anything," he added softly.

"Not even Caroline?"

"No. Not even Caroline."

"I will try to help you."

The sense of relief was immediate and intense. "Thank you," he whispered, as Chloe approached him.

"I'm going to try to intervene in your behalf to send you back," Chloe's eyes suddenly flared bright red as she stared toward the double doors leading from the ballroom.

With a start, Tyce realized that the room had gone dark. The boards he had nailed over the windows were there once more. Something was happening that he did not understand. "What is it? What's wrong?" he hissed to Chloe, watching her agitation increase.

"You have to go. I'll do all I can for Delaney. You have to go now, or you may never be able to go back."

"No!" Tyce shrank back from her wild countenance. "You promised to help me!"

Suddenly, the doors to the ballroom slammed open. Tyce saw Mark drag Delaney inside, giving her a shove toward the middle of the room. From under his belt, he snatched out a gun and pointed it at her.

Tyce lunged toward Mark, but Chloe caught his arm. *"You can't!"* she ordered.

Mark managed to get the cap off the gas can with one hand by holding the can between his knees. Then he caught it up by the handle and started splashing gas along the floor. The strong fumes permeated the room as the gas dissolved great spots of paint from the beautiful floor.

"Please stop, Mark. Please!" Delaney begged. "I'll do whatever you want. Just don't destroy the house."

Mark shook his head wildly. "As long as this house stands, he'll fight to keep it. It's got to go."

"I don't care!" Tyce yelled at him. "I'm dead, you

son of a bitch! The house doesn't matter anymore. Let Delaney go.''

"He can't hear you, Tyce. Go back while you can!" Chloe was moving across the room toward Mark. Tyce followed until she turned abruptly and held out her hand to stop him. *"If you come with me to the other side, you might never be able to return to life. If you want Delaney, you have to go back. Now!"*

The least spark could reduce the house to cinders in a matter of minutes. There might not be time for Delaney to get out. Tyce took another step toward her. If only he could distract Mark long enough for her to get away.

"Chloe!" Delaney called suddenly, as Chloe moved between her and Mark.

Mark's nervous laugh echoed through the still room. "You've lost it, Delaney. You're crazy. Calling a *ghost*?"

"Look out, Mark, she's coming!" Delaney warned. He held a lighter in his hand, poised to strike a flame and bring the house down. "She doesn't like this."

"Shut up!" Mark yelled, charging toward her.

"Don't antagonize him, Delaney!" Tyce warned. "He'll hurt you!" He was only a step behind Chloe.

"Crazy bitch, shut up!" Mark yelled at Delaney. The butt of his pistol came smashing down against her cheek.

"Chloe!" Delaney screamed, as she slumped to the floor and tried to crawl away from Mark's abuse.

Cursing violently, Mark came after her with the gun.

"Don't touch her!" Tyce roared, rushing headlong for Mark. The sound of his voice exploded through the room. Mark stopped in his tracks. Delaney stared for a moment, then her face crumbled in terror.

"Tyce!" she cried pitifully. "Oh, no, no, Tyce!"

"Tyce, stop!" Chloe shrieked, her eyes on fire as she whirled around. *"I bade you stay away!"*

A lightning bolt of energy hit Tyce when her eyes locked on him. An agonizing burst of pain erupted in his chest, shooting out in all directions into his arms, legs, fingers, toes, into his brain, into his soul. But all he could think of was Delaney. He had to get to Delaney!

He tried to dodge Chloe's anger, but he couldn't. Rushing at him in a fury, she shoved him abruptly off the plane of death and he plummeted downward. God, he was tired of falling! And this white-hot agony tingled every nerve in his body. And Delaney was going to die. . . .

Chapter Seventeen

Tyce was there for a brief moment, then he was gone. Holding her aching jaw, Delaney peered in the dimness to see him again. All she could see now was a vague image of Chloe, sweeping toward Mark with a vengeance. But Tyce had been there long enough for Delaney to understand that he was with Chloe and not with her any longer . . . that he was dead. And that he had done everything within his power to stop Mark from hitting her again.

"Stay away!" Mark snarled at Chloe, grabbing for Delaney's arm. "Stay away, or I'll kill her!"

Delaney felt Mark's cruel grip on her arm, then it was as if her arm were ripped away from him. Delaney was thrown well out of Mark's reach by a searing force that had to have come from Chloe or Tyce. Frantically, Mark flicked the wheel on the lighter in his hand. Once. Twice. His unsteady hands couldn't work the mechanism. He snapped the lighter again. The flame caught as Chloe slowly enveloped him in a red mist.

Mark screamed and began to writhe furiously. At first, Delaney thought he was on fire, but he wasn't, not in a flesh-and-blood sense. He was caught in Chloe's grasp, her human form metamorphosed into a shimmering, ever-changing scarlet mist that wrapped itself around Mark and would not let go.

The lighter dropped from his hand, along with the gun. The last flicker of flame from the lighter ignited the puddle of gas near Mark's feet. Fire shot across the white floor.

"Help me, Delaney! Help me! Call her off," Mark begged. He twisted this way and that, desperately attempting to escape Chloe's torment. "I'm burning up, I'm on fire. Help me, for mercy's sake. Delaney!"

Delaney stood mesmerized by Mark's face, contorted in agony, his high-pitched shrieks of terror rending the air of the empty mansion. As if in slow motion, he fought the red fury that held him fast, his arms flailing around him, meeting no resistance, yet unable to free himself. His eyes bulged as if he were choking, and his cries took on a strangled edge. Chloe was taking her revenge.

A bright and frantic flickering caught Delaney's eye, jerking her out of her trance. The fire was spreading rapidly! Delaney snatched off her coat, beating at the greedy flames that were devouring the magnificent room—all that was left of Tyce's dream. But the fire streaked along the trails Mark had laid with gasoline far faster than she could put it out. Tears streamed down her face as she fought on against the odds. Mark's piercing cries still rang out, but they seemed to be growing dimmer. Thickening smoke choked her, stung her eyes until she could barely see. Suddenly, flame leaped up around her. If she didn't get out, she was going to be burned alive.

With a last sob of despair, she stumbled from the room, collapsing to her knees just outside the ballroom door, overcome by smoke, her head still swimming where Mark had struck her. She had no willpower to get up, to save herself. The fleeting vision of Tyce came forcefully back to her. He was gone! Now she understood how Chloe had felt all these years without Zach. Sorrow swept over her, and she crumpled to the floor, weeping.

The heat of the inferno in the ballroom reached her. Then, a blast of frigid air swept past as Mark ran screaming from the ballroom, through the hall, toward the back of the mansion. A red haze trailed him for a short distance, then drifted toward the floor. Delaney pushed herself up to her knees and crawled hesitantly across the hall until she reached the crimson mist that had settled into the shape of a woman. Looking into her face, Delaney knew without doubt that this was all that was left of Chloe.

"Chloe?" Delaney whispered to the prostrate wisp of a form, the face young and smooth, eyes closed, lips parted slightly as if in repose.

Chloe's eyes flickered open, still smoldering in their depths. For a moment, Delaney was frightened; then Chloe reached out for her and she felt the chill touch of the ghost on her face.

"Come with me, Chloe. We have to get out!"

"No. I shall stay with Caroline until the end. But you must go."

"How can I leave you like this?"

"I belong to Caroline, my dear child. I will stay. But you must leave before the fire overcomes you. Tyce is waiting for you."

Her words brought fresh tears to Delaney's eyes. "No, he's dead. I saw him with you," Delaney sobbed. "I've lost him."

"He was caught momentarily between the two worlds, but he was called back," Chloe said weakly. *"He waits for you, hovering on the brink between life and death, waiting to see which way you go. He will follow you, either way."*

"Oh, Chloe! Thank you. I have to go to him. But isn't there something I can do for you?" The flames were licking at the ceiling of the white ballroom, inching toward the door.

"Nothing, Delaney. My waiting is over. I will lose my Zach forever once Caroline is gone. Leave me and go to Tyce, sweet child, before he gives up on you. He loves you more than you know. He was willing to sacrifice everything for you, even his life. Now you can give that back to him."

With a lingering look at the paling ghost, Delaney fled the burning mansion. Having no idea where Mark might be, she hazarded the open space between the mansion and her car, groping to recover the keys from her pocket. Once inside, she locked the car doors and fumbled with the ignition, cursing when the car did not start immediately. After what seemed to be forever, the car engine sparked and fired. Within moments, the tires touched the end of the gravel road and the car swung onto the main highway, headed toward Baton Rouge.

The wailing sirens bearing down upon her barely registered. She glanced into her rearview mirror to see the flashing lights of fire engines and at least two sheriff's cars turning down the road to Caroline. It was too late for the fire trucks, no doubt, but she hoped the deputies found Mark, wherever he was, and put him away for a long time.

Flying along the highway, she tried to avoid thinking about Tyce being dead. She was taking the word of a ghost that he was still alive. But the terrifying question plagued her: *What if Tyce is really dead?*

In the hospital parking lot, Delaney pulled into the first space she saw and ran the rest of the way to the hospital. At the information desk, Delaney was told that Tyce was in Intensive Care, and the receptionist gave her directions to get there. She punched the elevator button repeatedly until the doors opened. Pushing her way past the exiting passengers, she gritted her teeth until the last person was out of the way, then stabbed the button for the Intensive Care floor.

Two women sat in the waiting room. Delaney had never met Tyce's mother, but she recognized his sister from her strong resemblance to Tyce. Delaney approached the women.

"Mrs. Brandon?"

The older woman looked up. Her eyes were bloodshot, but she was not crying now. "Yes?"

"I'm Delaney Bienville. How is Tyce?"

"He's alive . . . barely. . . . He went into cardiac arrest on the way to the hospital. He's out of surgery but still in a coma."

Delaney sank into the nearest chair. "Is he going to be all right?"

Maddie answered quietly, "They're not being overly

encouraging. There was a lot of internal damage and head injuries. Hopefully, there's no brain damage, but they can't be sure yet. He had broken ribs and his left leg is pretty bad, the doctor said. Torn ligaments and that sort of thing.''

Mrs. Brandon looked away before her tears fell. She sat in silence for a few minutes, then turned to Delaney. ''I wish that plantation had burned to the ground during the war.''

The bitterness in the woman's voice startled Delaney, making her feel guilty and responsible for what had happened. Before she could find a response, Maddie spoke up.

''This is not the time, Mom.''

Mrs. Brandon buried her face in her hands and began to weep quietly.

''Have you been able to see him?'' Delaney asked, worried that he would not know she was there. Chloe's warning that he might think she was dead and give up ran like a broken record through her mind.

''Mom went in for a minute. He hasn't regained consciousness,'' Maddie said, fighting back her own tears. ''One of us can go in for about five minutes every half hour.''

''When is the next visitation?''

''About now,'' Maddie said, checking her watch.

''I know I'm not family, and I don't have any right to ask this, but could I please go in to see him this time? I can't explain it to you, but it might make some difference if I can speak to him.''

''He can't hear you. He's in a coma,'' Mrs. Brandon said abruptly, her eyes swollen from crying. ''I'd rather you didn't go in. I think he needs his family now.''

"Mother!" Maddie cried. "That's not fair. I know how he feels about Delaney. He told me." She turned back to Delaney. "Are you sure you're all right? You look so pale."

Delaney smiled gratefully at this selfless and compassionate young woman. "I'll tell you the whole story someday," Delaney said, then added softly, "And if it will help, you can tell your mother that Caroline is burning down, as she wished it would. It won't be there to obsess Tyce anymore."

The color drained from Maddie's face. "Oh, no! Just when he was finally getting Caroline. It'll break his heart."

"Getting Caroline?" Mrs. Brandon cried, then lowered her voice when the other people in the room stared. "What are you talking about?"

"Tyce told me the judge was probably going to rule in his favor," Maddie said.

"No, don't tell me that," Mrs. Brandon moaned, turning aside to cover her eyes with her hand. "I can't believe—"

A nurse came to the door of the waiting room. "Mrs. Brandon, one of you can go in to see your son now. Only for a moment."

Mrs. Brandon rose to face the nurse. "How is he?"

"No change. I'm sorry," the nurse replied. "Who would like to come in?"

Delaney waited, her heart pounding. She couldn't force her way into his room, but how long would he wait for her?

She was on the verge of begging his mother when Maddie spoke up. "It's my turn to go in. I want you to take my place, Delaney." Before Mrs. Brandon could voice the disapproval evident on her face, Maddie laid her hand on her mother's arm. "Please, Mom. I want her to go. Tyce needs to know she's here. But don't tell him Caroline is gone."

"No, I won't," Delaney promised, squeezing Maddie's hand gratefully.

Mrs. Brandon's face did not soften toward Delaney, but she held her silence. Thanking God for Maddie, Delaney followed the nurse down the hall to Tyce's room.

"Only five minutes," the nurse reminded her.

Delaney's breath caught in her throat as she approached. She admonished herself to stay in control, even though all she wanted to do was cry at the sight of him. He was hooked up to several monitors and had an IV in his arm. There was an oxygen tube under his nose. His face was dark with bruises below the bandages that swathed his head. She took his hand carefully and leaned over him. The coldness of his skin was frightening as her lips touched his bruised cheek.

"Tyce, can you hear me?" she said quietly. "I'm here. I'm not hurt. Do you understand? I'm okay."

The total lack of response worried her. What if he had gone too far into Chloe's world? What if he couldn't make it back into his body again? But he was breathing, the monitors marked his steady heartbeat. He was in there somewhere. She had to reach him.

"Tyce, please listen to me. Chloe wanted you to come back. She wanted us to be together. You have to wake up."

He lay like death itself. Frustrated tears seared Delaney's eyes. "Tyce!" she cried in anguish. "You can't leave me! What will I do without you? Come back to me!"

The nurse came to the door. "You'll have to leave now."

"Please, just another minute. Please!"

"I'm sorry," the nurse said firmly, holding the door open for her.

Tears ran down Delaney's cheeks as she leaned over to kiss Tyce. She squeezed his hand hard. "I love you so much. So much!"

"Love you."

At first, she thought she imagined the almost inaudible words because she wanted to hear them so badly. Then she felt his hand move ever so slightly in hers.

"Tyce!" she cried, wiping the tears with her free hand. She looked hopefully at the nurse. "I think he spoke to me."

The nurse came into the room, looking closely at the monitors. "Something happened," she agreed. "See if you can get him to respond to you again."

"Tyce, can you hear me? Can you wake up?"

Delaney's heart leaped as he mumbled something in reply.

The nurse smiled at her and nodded. "I heard him."

"What did you say, Tyce?" Delaney asked gently.

Tyce opened his eyes slowly. "Don't leave me," he murmured.

Delaney looked questioningly at the nurse. "May I stay?"

"Only another minute or so. He needs to remain very quiet."

"Won't," Tyce breathed.

"I didn't understand you," the nurse said, bending over closer.

"Won't be quiet," Tyce repeated slowly, his voice hoarse and nasal, "unless she stays."

The nurse laughed softly. "Are you trying to black-mail me, Mr. Brandon?"

"Yes," he said.

"Well, it won't work. The only way you'll be able to lie around and hold her hand is to get better so we can move you into a regular room. I'll have no hanky-panky in my intensive care ward, do you understand?"

Tyce gave her a half-smile and closed his eyes wearily. "We'll see," he whispered, as he drifted off to sleep again.

Chapter Eighteen

Chloe lay motionless on the floor, drained of all energy and hope. There was no reason to move. The only way the fire could hurt her was in her heart, and that was already broken. When Caroline was reduced to ashes, she would have no home. Zach would not know how to find her, even if he were still searching for her after all this time. She wondered about that. Maybe he had gone over to his final peace long ago. From years of dealing with her father and brothers, she had a good command of male traits. Emotion rarely motivated men; reality did. Zach might have decided early on that it was useless hanging on to what might have been. Perhaps he had recognized the inevitable and gone on without her.

She would have cried at the thought, but she had done all her crying when she was young. After she learned the extent of her father's cruelty, she was too stubborn to let him see her cry. And now she was too exhausted for useless tears.

One consolation was that she no longer felt Tyce's presence. She prayed that he had made his way safely back to life and that he would stay there until Delaney got to him. He was stubborn, too, and would likely come looking for the girl if she didn't hurry. But all that was out of her hands now, Chloe thought sorrowfully. Her last chance to make amends for the damage her father had caused. Even if Delaney and Tyce married, Caroline would be gone. The final piece of the puzzle would still be missing.

"Oh, Zach, I tried so hard," she whispered. *"I'm sorry."*

A blast of thunder shook the very walls of Caroline, rattling the panes in the windows, jolting Chloe. Too late for rain, she thought wearily, still unwilling to move. Too late for everything. Then she realized that she was resting in the center of a pool of water in the hallway just outside the ballroom. Jerking her head up, she was surprised to see a steady stream of water flowing through the double doors. Lifting herself with great effort, she drifted that way. Water was flowing down the walls of the room from the ceiling, soaking everything in its path, dousing the raging flames as it came.

"What in the world?" Chloe said to herself, as she stared in amazement at the weeping walls of Caroline.

"All the tears of our lifetime, Chloe."

The words were no more than a whisper in the air, but Chloe knew the voice. Slowly, she turned. Zach stood behind her, his arms outstretched. For a moment, Chloe was paralyzed with disbelief.

"Lucky for me, the piping in the walls was in bad

repair. I was able to shake them loose and release the water from the roof cisterns. Come to me, Chloe, my love.''

''*Oh, my love. My Zach!*'' Chloe flew into his embrace and he enveloped her into his being. Outside, the wail of sirens pierced the air.

''*Let's go someplace peaceful while these modern contraptions take care of this little crisis.*'' Zach lifted her easily into his arms and moved lightly through the wall and out of the mansion.

Where he was taking her, she did not question. She would gladly follow him to the end of eternity.

Chapter Nineteen

A month and a half later, Tyce stood at the open window of his old bedroom, bracing on his right leg to relieve some of the pressure from his injured left knee. Looking out the window at the deserted street in front of his mother's house, he welcomed the first rays of the morning sun as they struck his face with warmth. The newly green trees swayed gently, and a pair of birds called to one another from the uppermost branches.

Waiting by the window for Delaney, Tyce thought with an amused twitch of his lips. That was supposed to be Chloe's thing, not his. But the waiting was almost over; only a few more hours. Tyce breathed in the sweet, morning air. *A perfect day for a wedding,* he thought happily, *especially when it's mine.*

Over the past weeks, Tyce had spent a lot of his time

undergoing physical therapy at the hospital and exercising at home to recover mobility in his knee. He could walk without crutches now, though he limped noticeably when he grew tired. His ribs hurt if he moved wrong, but the doctor told him that was to be expected, due to the severity of the blow to his chest and the extensive surgery he had undergone for internal injuries.

He had fallen through the attic floor less than six weeks ago, yet it seemed more like another lifetime. And maybe it was. Everything had changed since then. Caroline no longer existed. Tyce himself had looked death in the face and made his way back somehow. He had developed a firm appreciation of life that he had not had before.

Losing Caroline was not the worst thing that could have happened. Losing Delaney would have been worse. But knowing that the venerable old mansion was gone forever was depressing. Over the past weeks, he had tried to come to terms with the unexpected turn his life had taken, forcing himself to be pragmatic about it, but letting go of his lifelong dream was no easy matter.

He found he could cope better by keeping his mind off Caroline altogether. After learning that fire had badly damaged the mansion and virtually destroyed the ballroom, Tyce avoided any discussion of Caroline or what had happened. He didn't have the heart to think of starting over again. His family seemed relieved not to have to talk about the plantation. Before Tyce was able to drive, Alphonse had offered to drive him out to the ruins, but he had declined. He had no wish to see Caroline's blackened skeleton. Maybe someday far in the future he would be able to say a final farewell to a part of his soul that was lost forever, but not now.

Throughout the past weeks, the bright spot on his horizon, the day his new life would really begin, had been his upcoming wedding day. And now it was here, at last. This day would be a symbol of closure to the past. Tyce could start over again on a different road, with Delaney at his side.

Through the toughest hours in the hospital, the frightening times when he wasn't sure if he was going to make it, Delaney had been there, along with his family, their presence a constant beacon in the agonizing darkness. Delaney's love for him was obvious to everyone, and the nurses teased him constantly to propose to her.

"I think I already have," he told the nurse who was in the room when he first regained consciousness. Her name was Judy and she was his favorite of all the intensive care personnel because of her dry wit and straightforward manner.

"What did she say?" Judy wanted to know.

"I'm not sure," Tyce had to admit, for anything that had happened for most of the day before he fell until he woke up holding Delaney's hand was a confusing blur in his mind.

"Then you have to ask her again."

As he grew stronger, Judy kept after him. She wanted him to propose to Delaney before leaving the intensive care ward, so she could be a part of the celebration. Her enthusiasm was contagious, and with Judy's help, when Delaney came into the room on the morning that he was to be transferred to a regular room, Tyce sat propped up in bed with a bouquet of red roses from the lobby florist and a token engagement ring that Judy borrowed from her brother's jewelry store. Judy had shaved his bruised and sore jaw with utmost care and brought him an LSU baseball cap to help cover the bandages on his head. He knew he looked a sorry mess, anyway, but he appreciated her kindness.

"You'll have to be a bridesmaid if she says yes," Tyce warned Judy.

"Love to," she smiled in return. "Just let me know when."

So now Maddie was to be the maid of honor and Judy was a bridesmaid. Alphonse was Tyce's best man, of course, and Maddie's boyfriend Steve the other groomsman. Tyce knew all the details of the wedding ceremony—except where it was going to be.

Delaney couldn't seem to make up her mind. First she said Tyce's family church. Then she changed her mind and wanted the wedding at Gran's house in New Orleans. Three days ago, she had announced that she had a better place in mind, where they could have the reception outside. Delaney refused to tell him where they were to be married, and there was a definite conspiracy going on between the women in his life to keep him from finding out. Although he teased them about their vacillation, the location was not important to Tyce, only the ceremony.

Anxious to get on with the day, Tyce turned from the window and went downstairs, not expecting to find anyone else awake at this early hour. He was surprised to hear the muted sounds of the cast-iron skillet that told him his mother was in there, with breakfast started on the stove.

Tyce stopped in the hallway just outside the door to the kitchen, drinking in the sounds of his mother's home, so familiar and comforting, yet now seeming to be a part of another life that he had lived before. The next time he visited his mother, he would bring a wife with him, and his role as his mother's son would take on a different slant. There was no regret at the changing of his role, but still he lingered to savor the poignant feeling a moment longer.

Delaney's mother's voice startled him. He had not realized she was in the kitchen, too. Mrs. Bienville had turned out to be charming. Tyce liked her at once and she, him. She had a lovely face, an older version of Delaney's, and was vibrant and active. Her eyesight was failing, but she seemed to be at peace with her fate.

Mrs. Brandon would not hear of Delaney and her mother staying in a hotel and insisted that they all stay at her house. It was a bit crowded at times, with only the two bathrooms, but Tyce liked having those he loved close around him.

"So you don't have bad memories of Caroline?" Mrs. Brandon asked. Tyce waited for the answer with interest, knowing how Delaney had resented the plantation for taking her father away from her during her childhood.

"Bad memories?" Mrs. Bienville sounded surprised. "Oh no. As I told Delaney when she called after Tyce's accident, so upset, pouring out all her grief, thinking she had somehow betrayed me by falling in love with a Southerner, those were some of the best days of my life. I loved Joseph so much, and the place was beautiful back then. Thirty years ago, Caroline was thriving and vital. His aunt Donet and his mother lived in the big house, and Joseph lived in the *garçonnière*. When we married, they remodeled the *garçonnière* for us while we were on our honeymoon."

Tyce heard the excitement and enthusiasm in Mrs. Bienville's voice. "Joseph was so very handsome and I was petted and pampered like a princess. Why, I sat many a hot afternoon on the front gallery upstairs and watched the ships go down the river. I dreamed of living my life just that way, at peace in my solitude, while the rest of the hectic world sped by."

"Why did you leave then, *chére*? We always assumed you were homesick and wanted to go back North."

"No, no. It was never my idea. Joseph was a brilliant man, an astute geologist, in great demand with the oil companies, but he couldn't endure the discipline of a high-pressure career. He began to drink. He had always resented his mother's interference in his life, and when he lost a job, she would really berate him about it. Before long, he began to rebel against me, too, construing the least thing that I said as criticism."

Tyce listened in silence. He knew that Delaney had never realized her father's condition until recently. Maybe if she had known, she would have felt differently about Caroline.

"Joseph wanted to move away, and I agreed, only because I thought things would be better between us. Delaney was four years old, and I wanted a secure, happy home for our child. Unfortunately, that was not to be. The last company Joe worked for gave him an assignment traveling around the world in search of new oil fields. He was gone from home longer and longer on overseas missions.

"He hardly knew Delaney at all. Then he grew ill from the harsh life he was leading and from the drinking. After he developed cirrhosis of the liver, he spent a lot of time at the Tulane Medical Center. He preferred doctors he had known all his life to New York specialists. It wouldn't have mattered where he went for treatment; he was the one who had to change his lifestyle, and he never succeeded at that."

A brief lull allowed Tyce to hear the sizzling of bacon in the skillet and the gurgle of the coffeemaker. When

Mrs. Bienville continued, Tyce could sense that she was fighting back tears.

"The disease can affect the brain in its later stages, and he gradually lost his mind and forgot all about us most of the time. I came down when he was beyond help in the hospital to put him into a mental hospital where he could be taken care of. Aunt Donet was not physically able to tend to him, although she would have preferred to keep him at home."

"I remember when he was committed," Mrs. Brandon said. "It was hard on Donet, but everybody knew it was for the best. He didn't live too long after that, did he?"

"He died less than a year later, after a bout with a liver infection. Delaney was young and easily wounded. She took her father's absence hard, and she saw his sickness and death as a betrayal. She really never got over it, I think. I couldn't get her to talk about it, and I even suggested therapy, but it's taken her a long time to accept help. She has changed so much since she met Tyce. I think he will help her more than anything else could."

Tyce's mother's voice sounded clear and strong, like it always did, all Tyce's life. "Well, *chére*, maybe now she can heal. Tyce will love her well, that I know."

"I know he will, too. He's all I could have wanted for her."

Although Tyce didn't mind basking in their praise, he felt guilty about eavesdropping any longer. As he started into the kitchen, his mother chuckled and said to Mrs. Bienville, "And can you still see yourself sitting on the veranda, sipping a mint julep while the world passes by?"

Mrs. Bienville's eyes were alight as Tyce came into the room. "Indeed, I can, if the children allow it—"

She saw Tyce and broke off her sentence abruptly. Now he wished he had stayed in the other room another minute.

"Tyce, we didn't hear you," his mother said in surprise. "How long have you been up?"

"Not long. What were you ladies talking about? What veranda is it you want to sit on?"

"Oh, nothing," Tyce's mother said with a flick of her hand to dismiss the subject. "We were just going on. You know how old women are. We like to relive the past now and then. Nothing that would interest a young man." She and Mrs. Bienville exchanged a quick conspiratorial look that was not lost on Tyce.

"I don't know about that," Tyce said, eyeing them closely.

"What you want for breakfast, *cher*?" his mother asked, changing the subject.

"Whatever you've got fixed."

"It's sure to be a long day for you. I'll fix you a good breakfast to keep you going."

Tyce ate the biscuits, eggs, grits, and bacon that his mother put before him, along with a tall glass of juice and a mug of hot coffee. The women turned the conversation to the wedding preparations for that night. He still did not know where the ceremony would take place, and he had stopped trying to find out. His mind was well past the vows, anyway, to the time when everybody would leave and he and his new bride would be alone. Little else mattered to him.

"I guess I need to pick up my tux this morning," Tyce said.

"Alphonse and Steven will be here after lunch to take care of you. They'll bring your clothes."

"Fine, but I have to—"

"You don't have nothing you got to do, *cher*. It's all taken care of. You just have to be dressed and ready to go by four."

Alphonse arrived around two that afternoon, and Steve came in a little later. By four, Tyce was dressed in a black tailcoat for the formal evening wedding. At one point, he had tried to convince the women to have a simple ceremony in the church chapel, but that suggestion went over like a ton of bricks. Instead, they had planned a formal ordeal, complete with some rituals that he might have to wing, not having paid close enough attention in the rehearsal.

The rehearsal had been held on the evening that Delaney returned from New York, and he had not noticed much other than her. He did remember every word she said to him that afternoon, however, and how her eyes sparkled when she looked at him, and how very beautiful she was. But, as far as which candle he had to light and what to do with it—well, he was going to have to improvise on that one. And he knew his part of the vows, especially the "I do" and "Kiss the bride" lines. The really important things.

He ran a finger underneath the tight cravat, trying to loosen it a fraction, and wished the night was already over. He was not looking forward to sharing Delaney with a hundred guests. Alphonse came up behind him.

"All right, man, let's go." Just before Tyce got into the car, Alphonse stopped him, holding a long red silk scarf in his hands. "One more detail, friend," he said. "Your bride-to-be insists on you wearing this."

"What?" Tyce eyed the scarf skeptically.

"A blindfold. I done tole you it was a surprise where I'm bringin' you. Now put this on before we get ourselves late."

Steve grinned as he stood by, holding the door open. "It's a losing battle, Tyce."

"Give me a break, okay? I'm not wearing that."

"Yes, you are," Alphonse insisted. "Else you not going to your own wedding. Now, you gon' leave that sweet girl standing at the altar?"

"Great," Tyce muttered, then let Alphonse tie on the blindfold. "You're damn lucky I'm a good-natured man, you know that, Alphonse?"

"Yeah, you good-natured, all right, when you outnumbered like this," Alphonse said agreeably, securing the blindfold so that Tyce could see nothing at all, not even a sliver of light. Then Steve guided the bridegroom into the car. Alphonse clapped Tyce lightly on the shoulder before closing the door and assured him, "It's gon' be worth it, I can tell you that. Let's go get you married, *mon ami.*"

"How the hell am I supposed to know who I'm marrying?" Tyce complained, as he felt the truck stopping after a few minutes of twisting and turning down God only knew which streets and roads. After the first few turns, Tyce had given up on trying to figure out where they were going. "You might slip a ringer in on me in place of Delaney."

"Might," Alphonse agreed. "You just have to wait and see."

"Can I take this damn thing off now?" Tyce muttered, reaching for the blindfold.

From the backseat, Steve's hand caught his. "Not yet. Just hang tight for another few minutes."

Tyce didn't bother to utter his thoughts. After all, it was supposed to be a happy day, and he had expected Delaney to trust him blindly on more than one occasion. She must have a good reason for all the mystery. One thing Tyce knew, however, was that he was not getting married in New Orleans. They had not driven nearly far enough for that. He allowed Alphonse and Steve to guide him into a building that smelled of fresh plaster and paint and roses. With a pang of melancholy, he recalled how Caroline had sometimes smelled faintly of roses. Chloe's signature, he knew now. Well, he was doing what she wanted, after all, just a little too late.

Alphonse placed Tyce in position and ordered, "Stay there." Lovely and peaceful music filled the room. A cool evening breeze brushed Tyce's face, smelling of new grass and budding spring flowers.

"Can I take this off?" Tyce whispered, indicating the blindfold. He knew from the quiet murmuring and rustle of clothing, that there were other people in the room with them and that he must be standing at the altar waiting for Delaney.

"Not yet," Alphonse whispered. "But soon, yeah."

When the music paused momentarily, then swelled again with the Bridal March, Tyce reached for the blindfold, determined to see what was going on. Alphonse beat him to it, slipping the knot loose and pulling the scarf easily off Tyce's face and out of the way.

"It can't be," Tyce said softly, staring around the room as if he saw a ghost. And in a way, he did—the ghost of Caroline—for it was within the walls of the plantation, in the flickering candlelight of the great ballroom chandeliers, that he now stood.

His eyes found Delaney, angelic in a flowing white wedding gown, standing at the other end of the long room, holding her breath, waiting for his reaction. When he shook his head in wonder and smiled at her through his tears, she began the slow march down the red carpet that ran the length of the white ballroom at Caroline. Somehow, she had made his dream come true, and in another few minutes, she would make his life complete.

Epilogue

At nine o'clock that night, the music started. The band was set up on the balcony just outside the ballroom, since it was warm enough to open the tall windows. Red roses were placed sparingly around the room. The mantels were graced with garlands created from red and white rosebuds and fragrant stephanotis. That was all the embellishment Delaney would allow, and she felt even that was too much, for the room was as flawless as it had been before the fire.

As a wedding gift, Alphonse had insisted on repairing the damaged room at his own expense. Everything was done to perfection, down to the tiniest detail. There was no longer any sign of the damage inflicted by the blaze Mark had started.

Mark was safely interred in a mental institution, pending psychiatric evaluation for his trial. Delaney had seen him only once since he was found cowering in the bathroom in the *garçonnière*, muttering wildly about a demon in the ballroom. When she had to appear in court to testify at his indictment on attempted murder and arson charges, she was shocked to see that his gaunt face was framed by hair as white as snow. It was caused by the fright of whatever had happened to him in the ballroom, the psychiatrist had told her when she asked about the phenomenon later. A rare occurrence, it had been known to happen in instances of extreme stress. Delaney quickly brushed Mark out of her mind on this happiest of days and turned her attention to Tyce as he led her onto the pristine white floor to begin the dancing.

At two o'clock the next morning, the band packed up and most of the guests left. Only family and close friends remained. By three, Delaney and Tyce were hugging her mother and his good night, as Maddie brought the car around to take the women home.

Then only Alphonse was left. Delaney had told Tyce all that Alphonse had done to restore Caroline. The look on Tyce's face told her that he wanted a few minutes alone with his friend to thank him. Delaney kissed Alphonse on the cheek, then excused herself and went back into the mansion.

In the ballroom, she picked up the remnants of roses and leaves that had been plucked or knocked from their stands, waiting for Tyce to come back inside. A thrill shuddered through her as she considered her new status: Mrs. Tyson Lee Brandon. She liked the way it sounded. Delaney Bienville Brandon. Yes, she liked it a lot. Memories of the past few hours brought a smile to her lips as she began to pull down the heavy windows, starting on the side by the *garçonnière*.

Delaney went to the next window and lowered it easily on its track. At the last window, the one Chloe had stood beside all those years, waiting for Zach, Delaney paused. Earlier, she had laid Chloe's diary on the windowsill as a memorial to Chloe. Only Tyce knew the meaning of the book lying there undisturbed all night. Delaney stooped to brush her hand across the cracked leather cover of the diary, then gazed around the quiet, empty ballroom.

Unexpectedly, she felt a stab of overwhelming loneliness and she wanted Tyce to come back. She turned to stare out the window, trying to find him in the darkness. Was this how Chloe had felt that morning when her love left her for the last time, this feeling that a part of her soul was missing?

"Hurry, Tyce," she whispered, searching in vain for a sign of movement on the quiet lawn. She considered going to find him but forced herself not to, for he would think she was silly to worry just because he was out of her sight for a few minutes. It was silly, but she didn't like this feeling, this unbidden empathy with Chloe's plight; this uncanny understanding of why Chloe would have waited forever for someone who never would return. Delaney tried to shake off the unsettling thoughts but found she could not. She wished Tyce would come back.

Behind her, she heard a barely audible sound. Before she could react, his words reached her. "Are you watching out the window for me, like Chloe?"

Delaney turned, her heart suddenly pounding in her throat with joy.

"I suppose I was," she said with a smile. "Although I believe I once swore I never would."

"I knew better, though," Tyce said, his impish grin now so familiar to her. "After all, you are—were—a Bienville. Would you honor me with one more dance in this lovely ballroom before the night comes to an end?''

"There's no music," Delaney reminded him.

Tyce's lips touched hers as he drew her to him. "We can make our own music," he said. "Now and forever, we'll make our own music right here."

He led her off into a floating waltz. She could detect the favor he gave his left leg, but otherwise his movements were strong and fluid.

Tyce held her tightly against him, his breath gentle on her cheek. She pulled back slightly so that she could see his face. She loved him so well, so deeply, that she felt a stab of pain whenever she recalled how very close she had come to losing him. The vision of him standing beside Chloe still haunted her.

Delaney laid her head against his shoulder, envisioning waking up beside him for the first time tomorrow. They had decided to forgo a honeymoon until later, when Tyce was completely recovered. Tonight, or what was left of it, they would spend in the *garçonnière*. The sway of Tyce's body lulled her peacefully. Even though she would love to get him in bed, she was reluctant to break the spell of this last dance.

Tyce's grip tightened around her waist as he stopped moving. She looked up to find his gaze riveted across the room. Following his stare, Delaney looked in that direction. They were no longer alone.

Two ghostly dancers had joined them in the white ballroom, their shapes dim but visible, flickering like candlelight. Dressed in the red ball gown that Delaney had found in the trunk upstairs, Chloe's glowing face was turned upward, enraptured by the man in whose arms she whirled, her slender neck graced by a stunning ruby necklace. The light caught the facets of the rubies, setting them ablaze as the dancers spun to their own music.

The man wore Confederate gray, a dress uniform complete with golden sash wrapped around his waist. A sword like the one in the trunk in the attic hung at his side. His hair was longer and darker than Tyce's, and his face was leaner, but there was no mistaking that he was a Brandon: Zach Brandon. Chloe had found her Zach at last.

Delaney and Tyce stood rooted, watching as their unearthly guests floated closer and closer until they could have reached out and touched them, had there been substance to them. When they were directly before Tyce and Delaney, the pair ended their dance and turned to face them. Zach's arm went protectively and lovingly around Chloe's tiny waist. He smiled, that irresistible Brandon smile that lit his sparkling blue eyes, and bowed gallantly to Delaney. She felt Tyce's arm instinctively draw her closer to him, but she had no fear of Zach Brandon.

"My congratulations on your marriage," he said, his mellow voice seeming to come from all sides of the room. *"And my deepest gratitude for freeing my beloved Chloe. We have lost a lifetime waiting for each other."*

Tyce's rib cage rose and fell against Delaney's side with increasing force. Delaney slipped her hand around his waist for comfort. She knew the depth of emotion he was feeling, for he had related to her what it had been like in that other dimension, as much as he could remember. For herself, however, she was glad to be able to say good-bye to Chloe and to know that she would be forever with the one she loved so dearly.

"I am happy for you," Delaney said softly, her eyes turning to Chloe. "I was afraid you had lost everything.

And my aunt Donet, is she at peace now?''

Chloe smiled tenderly. *"Yes, at peace. She has gone on ahead to meet Lee. My child, I was deeply moved by the concern you showed me when last I saw you. Your heart is exactly what Tyce needs. And as for you, young man,''* she gave Tyce a frown of teasing displeasure, *''I was at the end of my patience with you more than once. However, I did promise you the rubies if you did as I bade, and in the end, with however much dawdling, you did your part.''*

With that, Chloe moved into Zach's arms and they began their ethereal dance once more, floating out through the open window where Chloe had waited patiently for so many years. As she passed through to the other world, a shower of ruby red rose petals fell to the floor, scattering across the white surface like jewels from a broken necklace.

Tyce stooped to pick up a petal that landed at his feet, staring at it; then his gaze flew to the diary on the windowsill. Fanned by the gentle breeze that riffled the curtains on either side, the yellowed pages were slowly turning over, one by one.

''I forgot. Just before he left, Alphonse told me to look underneath the diary. He said I'd be surprised what he found secreted in the windowsill when he tore out the sashes.''

Delaney followed Tyce across the room.

''Tyce, look!'' Delaney cried, kneeling to smooth open the book. ''I never saw this page. Did you?''

Tyce came closer, inspecting the page. ''No, it's almost to the back. I thought the rest of the pages were blank after Chloe died.''

''So did I!''

But this page was not blank. On it, a very legible poem was written in Chloe's hand:

Rose Red Rubies

Precious rubies, red as the rose,
Where they are, nobody knows.

Waiting for me, so close at hand
Nearby this place where I stand,

Thy gift, my treasure, forever entwined
Silled within the heart of Caroline.

"What does it mean?" Delaney asked, rereading the poem.

"I think she was telling us where the rubies were hidden. Pick up the diary. Alphonse must have discovered them."

Delaney slowly lifted the white leather book. Underneath, instead of the small stand she had originally used to display the diary, was a carved rosewood box. Delaney sank to the floor at Tyce's feet, staring at the ornate box.

"Open it," she whispered.

"Cross your fingers." Tyce released the latch and raised the lid of the box. "Oh, man!" he breathed, then held the box down for Delaney to see inside.

On a bed of purple velvet lay the elusive Brandon rubies. Tyce lifted the necklace aloft. The brilliant gems caught every glimmer of light from the chandeliers and flashed fire back at them. Laying the box aside, he placed the heavy gold necklace around Delaney's neck and fastened the clasp. The jewels caught every glimmer of light from the chandeliers and flashed fire.

Tyce kissed her lips and said softly, "They're where they belong at last."

She went into his open arms and in the timelessness of the white ballroom, the two of them spun slowly across the floor. There was no present, no past, no future. She could have been Chloe or Aunt Donet, any of the other Bienville women who had loved Brandon men. She felt the strength of this man and his dreams. Their love would heal the wound that had been inflicted upon Caroline so many years ago.

Tyce stopped before the open window. A mockingbird's song fluted down from the rooftop. The rays of the rising sun streamed into the room. The morning air riffled the curtains and made tinkling music among the glass prisms of the chandelier.

"I love you for all eternity," he whispered, as his lips touched hers.

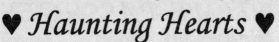

TIME PASSAGES